THE STREET

GILLIAN GODDEN

Boldwood

First published in Great Britain in 2024 by Boldwood Books Ltd.

Copyright © Gillian Godden, 2024

Cover Design by Colin Thomas

Cover Photography: Colin Thomas and Alamy

A CIP catalogue record for this book is available from the British Library.

Paperback ISBN 978-1-83561-460-0

Large Print ISBN 978-1-83561-459-4

Hardback ISBN 978-1-83561-458-7

Ebook ISBN 978-1-83561-461-7

Kindle ISBN 978-1-83561-462-4

Audio CD ISBN 978-1-83561-453-2

MP3 CD ISBN 978-1-83561-454-9

Digital audio download ISBN 978-1-83561-456-3

Boldwood Books Ltd
23 Bowerdean Street
London SW6 3TN
www.boldwoodbooks.com

I dedicate this book in loving memory to Avril. You will be sadly missed. Sorry you never got to read the end x

1

MOVING IN

'Oh God, I'm knackered. Someone put the kettle on.' Sitting down on a wooden dining chair, Maggie Silva looked around the kitchen. It looked pretty gloomy and needed a lick of paint but at least the walls were newly plastered and in time could be painted something nice and cheerful. But the nicotine-stained ceiling looked almost brown. Her heart sank; another moving day and another escape, but at least this was a great step up from where they had come from. Sevenoaks was one of the richest towns in Kent. The landscape was beautiful, the streets were clean, and you could breathe in all that lovely fresh air.

'What did you say about the bloody kettle missus?' After putting a cardboard box down on the table in front of her, Maggie's husband, Alex Silva, stood there with his hands on his hips and a frown on his face. 'You might have a kettle, Maggie, but there are no taps to fill it with. Look around the kitchen; haven't you noticed there's something missing?'

Maggie scanned the room. For a moment she couldn't see what he was talking about. They had travelled a long way, and she was tired, and there was still a lot to do. But looking around the kitchen and following her husband's lead, she let out a gasp. He was right, there was no kitchen sink!

Numbly, she walked to the corner of the kitchen which held the carcass of a double unit, but no kitchen sink, no draining board. Nothing.

'What do you think has happened?' Bewildered and confused, she stared at the blank space again and ran her hand along the wooden unit.

'I think we need to look around Maggie. The brewery gave us this pub in good faith. They must have checked everything was in order before giving the previous landlord his marching orders, but I've a feeling he's cleaned the place out and taken everything with him that he could scrap and sell. Bastard!'

They walked from the living quarters into the bar of the pub. Just as Alex had predicted, it had been stripped bare. 'There isn't a sink in here either and the glass washer is missing. Look at the gap, you can see the water pipes on the floor.' He pointed. 'And where is all the stock Maggie? They gave us an inventory. We were told it was fully stocked apart from the barrels of beer. Christ, everything has been taken. Get your phone out and take photos of this lot and then ring the brewery. I don't want them thinking we've stolen it. Christ, we're up to our neck in enough shit without this!'

'Do you want the beds in first Mr Silva?' Two removal men stood in the bar and looked around. Giving a low whistle, they met Alex's eyes. 'Looks like the locusts have been through here.'

Alex picked up a nearby dusty glass and turned towards a half-empty optic and poured himself a shot of whisky. 'I take it they didn't want this one. Do either of you want one?' He gulped back the drink.

'Sorry Mr Silva but I'm driving and we have a lot to do... If you don't mind, sir, as I said, do you want the beds bringing in first?'

'Yes, I suppose. If nothing else, we're going to need somewhere to rest our weary heads tonight. Come on, I'll give you a hand.' Alex walked out to the back yard where the removal van was parked and tried not to think about the mess they had been left.

The previous landlord had been hastily told to leave the pub after pocketing a lot of the takings. After being given notice, the terms were that he was to stay for a week until they were settled in and the brewery would refrain from bringing the police into the matter, if he left quietly. By the looks of it he'd totally ransacked the place and done a moonlight flit. Well, Alex mused to himself as he rolled up his shirt sleeves, he'd left quietly all right. Like a thief in the night.

'Dad, the boiler is flashing a number, and there isn't any hot water.'

Alex turned and raised his eyebrows at his son. 'What? Do you mean there's a sink and taps in the bathroom? Bloody hell, Dante, that's a nice surprise. I thought you were going to tell me you had to have a shit in a bucket.' Alex laughed. 'Come on son, let's have a look.'

Dante laughed. 'Don't say shit, Dad, Mum doesn't like it. You know what she's like.'

'Especially now we're in Sevenoaks. We're all going to have to watch our P's and Q's... Very lah-di-dah.'

Dante looked up at his father, a flash of concern crossing his face. 'We are going to stay here, aren't we Dad?'

Alex looked at his fourteen-year-old son and ran his hand through his black hair. For a young boy he'd already had a lot to cope with. His life had been turned upside down over the last few months and seeing the worried look on Dante's face, he felt the guilt wash over him. It was all his own doing that his family were living like this and Alex felt suddenly very guilty. 'There's nothing that a bit of time won't help, plus a lick of paint. As for the rest, that's for the brewery to sort out and then we will be publicans with jobs, a home and a family life – and a kitchen sink!'

A big grin crossed Dante's face. 'I thought the saying was everything *but* the kitchen sink!'

'Yeah, well, they hadn't met the previous landlord when they made that saying up, had they? Come on, first job, let's sort out the boiler, then let's get the beds up. Where's your mum got to?'

Just then Maggie joined them, holding her mobile phone in her hand.

'Well, that's sorted boys. I've just spoken to the brewery and someone is coming to sort out the damage. Although they didn't sound too surprised when I told them what had happened.' Maggie looked at the state of the mess around them and sighed. 'Where's Deana?'

Dante shrugged his shoulders as he watched his father turn different buttons on the boiler and watched the arrow on the pressure gauge rise. 'There you go son, give it an hour and we'll have hot water at least.'

Looking up at Maggie, Alex grinned. 'Deana's sat in the car sulking. It's her age, sixteen with attitude. Let her get on with it, she'll come in when she's hungry and thirsty.' Walking up to them both, Alex put his arms around their shoulders. 'Time for a group hug. We don't need to open up for a month, and that's more than enough time to get sorted. Fuck, if the worst comes to the worst, I will go and buy a sink myself and fit it. I'm not totally useless, you know,' Alex laughed, trying to bring some humour into the situation.

The banging and crashing of the removal men upstairs reminded them both that it was time to get sorted out. Then Deana popped her head around the door with her arms folded.

'God, this place is a dump. What's the point of moving in when we'll only be moving again soon?' she said sulkily.

'If you get your act together madam, we won't be moving again. I for one don't intend to.' Maggie glared defiantly at her husband. They both knew what she meant, but there was no point in talking about it, it was all they'd done for the last few months. Everyone had their skeletons in their cupboards; it just seemed they had more skeletons than most.

'Deana, you can make the beds, your dad can sort out the television and electrics and you, Dante, can help bring in some of those boxes. These removal men are paid by the hour – so move!'

Deana turned and stomped up the staircase, loudly banging her feet as she did. Maggie rolled her eyes to the ceiling and shook her head. Kids, who would have them?

Just then, Alex spotted two men in suits walking toward them. Instantly, his hackles were up and he was prepared for a fight. Looking around the kitchen area quickly, he spotted a carving knife in one of the boxes and reached for it. 'Who are you?' he asked suspiciously.

'Brewery. Your wife called us.' The two men looked at the mayhem surrounding them and instantly they started making notes. Alex felt the stress leave him and put the knife back down. 'Let me show you the rest, gentlemen. Believe me, it's not pretty.' Alex led the way while the two men from the brewery spoke in hushed whispers with their heads locked together.

Making herself scarce, Maggie went upstairs to help Deana and hastily pulled the duvets over the beds. 'That will do for now. All our clothing is in vacuum bags so for now, they can stay there. That's tomorrow's job. Thank God these floors are laminated. At least we don't have to wait until the whole place is carpeted, because I don't fancy moving those bloody wardrobes again.'

'Why is most of this stuff second hand? Couldn't they buy us new stuff, Mum?'

'The police budget only goes so far and when we start making a proper wage we can replace it, but for now it will do.'

'You mean they don't want to pay for new stuff when we're always on the move. I hated that military base, it felt like a prison camp.' She sighed.

'Hush now Deana, the removal men have big ears. Let's make the most of it, shall we? It's a chance, which is better than any of the other options. Your dad has stuck his neck out here. We're on the run from the gang lords, Deana, you know that. The police owe us nothing, other than a watchful eye in return for answers to their questions. We've opted out of witness protection to be able to walk in the sunlight again as ourselves. I don't know what fate has in store for us but, we all agreed this was the right thing to do, remember?' Maggie paused. They were all tired of looking over their shoulders in fear. Which was why Alex had given them all a choice. If they opted out of the witness programme, they'd be taking their chances, but they'd be able to live a normal life for as long as possible. If they stayed in the protection programme, they would still be hiding away at an ex-military barracks surrounded by detectives. There was no privacy. No days out like they were used to. Alex had always known he could be facing time in prison or death, bit his wife and children were serving his sentence alongside him, and he hated that. Anxiety and depression were creeping into their family. They didn't recognise each other any more. That was not freedom. It was hell!

'Nobody owes us anything, Deana. We've got to work for what we want and rebuild our lives. We can do this; it will take time but, we can do it.'

'I know Mum, but look at some of this stuff, it's scratched or broken. It's all from charity shops. When I think of how we lived and the things we had. We were rich, Mum...' Tears brimmed on Deana's lashes, and she brushed them away with her sleeve.

'They're just things, Deana! Are you really that shallow?' Maggie snapped. 'We've been provided with a home and a job. What we make of it is up to us, but it will be honestly earnt. You've already lived a life some people only dream of. Now you have a chance at another life. What little we have we should be grateful for and in time we will replace this lot with new stuff. It's better than we've been used to lately.'

'I know, it's just that...' Deana stopped speaking as one of the removal men popped his head through the door and asked Maggie which room she wanted the dressing table in. As she followed him out of the room, she turned to Deana and put her fingers to her lips to stop her saying any more.

After what seemed like an age, they heard Alex laughing and joking and waving off the brewery men. As Maggie went downstairs, she was surprised at Alex's high spirits and, more to the point, intrigued at what the brewery men had decided.

'They are going to replace the lot.' Alex took Maggie's hands in his and admired her. 'It seems like an age since I've looked at you properly, Maggie; I suppose life has just got in the way.' Her blonde hair was pulled back into a ponytail, and noticing a wisp of hair that had escaped and fallen down her face, he reached out and put it behind her ear. Although only in her late thirties, these days she looked older with dark rings under her eyes. Alex knew he had caused the worry lines on her face and yet she had been his rock throughout.

Her waist looked even slimmer than usual in her tight jeans and her blue vest top showed just enough cleavage to cause a stirring within him. 'I love you, Maggie Silva.' Pulling her towards him, he put his arms around her waist and kissed her on the lips. Instantly Maggie's arms went around his neck.

'You need a shave, my Portuguese prince.' She rubbed his dark stubble on his chin and looked lovingly at him. 'This could be a fresh start for us Alex. Fingers crossed all goes well, but I've got a good feeling about this place.'

Looking around, Alex shrugged. 'Well, you're the only person who does – look at it!' Alex looked at where they were standing, the space around them full of boxes and chaos. 'Sorry about all this, Maggie. You've had a lot to put up with lately and you just accept whatever is thrown at you.' Kissing her again, he squeezed her tightly around the waist.

'You're my skunk, Alex Silva. I'd follow your scent anywhere.' Maggie laughed.

One of the removal men made his presence known by coughing to attract their attention. 'We're off now, Mrs Silva. We just need you to sign this document and we're all done.' Waving his clipboard in the air with one hand, he walked up to them both. Quickly signing her name, Maggie reached into the back pocket of her jeans and handed them a twenty-pound note. 'Thanks boys, we appreciate your help.'

The removal man quickly snatched it out of her hand before she changed her mind. 'Thanks missus.' Then to Alex, he said, 'Good luck, Mr Silva,' before heading out of the door.

A broad grin crossed Alex's face. Clapping his hands together to brighten the mood, he turned to his wife again. 'Tell you what, I'll find a local chippy and get us some food. I wouldn't bother unpacking any more boxes than you need to tonight. Let's just settle in, eh, and see what the brewery has to say tomorrow? I'll also let the local police station know we've arrived...'

Maggie nodded. She felt determined to make this work, no matter what. 'That sounds like a plan. Now, go and get some chips and bring some bread and butter back. Tonight, I feel like feasting and ditching the diet.' She laughed and pinched Alex's cheek.

* * *

Over the next couple of days their lives were full of an army of workmen traipsing in and out. Much to Maggie's delight, the kitchen was being ripped out and new cabinets replaced the old ones. The long-awaited sink was fitted, which caused a huge smile to spread across Maggie's face. She promptly turned on one of the taps excitedly. 'Running water and a sink, Alex. Goodness me, you know how to turn a girl's head!'

'I hope that's not the only thing of mine that turns your head Maggie, but if it makes you happy, that's okay with me.' He laughed and gently patted her bottom.

Maggie looked around as their new home slowly began to take shape. 'This is a lovely little village Alex, and we are the new hosts of the village pub. The streets are clean, and the people around here seem to take pride in where they live. It's so different to London – this is suburbia at its finest.'

'Yeah, well, sometimes you can hide better in public than you can anywhere else. It doesn't matter where we go, there's a bounty on our heads and we have to live with it... or I do at least,' Alex said bitterly.

'Don't piss on my parade. We're in this together – all of us. We're a family. And I'm excited with the place. Me and the kids have had a walk around and people already know we're the new publicans. Word has spread. When they see me, they say good morning and that's enough for me.'

'It all sounds a bit Stepford Wives to me,' Alex said. 'But I don't need to warn you about being careful; you know the score and so do the kids.'

'Of course I do. And you'd better make the most of your Stepford Wives' scenario and blend in, because that's the only way to survive this!'

Alex held his hands up in submission. 'Whoa Maggie, I wasn't criticising. It's a lovely little place and we can earn a living here and build a life – hopefully. I was just saying...' Alex trailed off. For the first time in a long time, that old familiar smile had appeared on Maggie's face. She wanted this badly and he was happy to go along with it. How could he deny her, when she had stood by him so vehemently?

A fleeting thought passed through Alex's mind. His memories seemed like a distant dream. He had once been up there with the Portuguese and Spanish gangland bosses, respected and feared as their right-hand man and a boss in his own right. He's given out orders and money had never been an issue. He'd worn Armani suits, Rolex watches and had had an almost celebrity status. His children had gone to private schools.

Looking back, Alex had never realised how suffocating it had all been. Whatever you did, you did together. There were no outsiders, and sadly, Maggie hadn't been able to choose her own friends. The other gangland wives had become her friends and eventually, she had lost touch with her old acquaintances.

Most of the time he had been working so Maggie was left to her own devices with the kids. Which meant spending time with the other wives and their kids. Even when Maggie's parents visited, the wives turned up with homemade dishes of this and that and made a big thing of it and hosted a party or a big 'family' lunch. You were never alone, and you never left the family. Never. Unless you were dead, or they exiled you. Which, Alex mused, was what had happened to him.

Alex had never strayed from Maggie. With her, he had everything he wanted in a woman. They were partners, husband and wife. She never nagged or complained about his absences like he had heard other wives do. Just the thought of going home to her stirred his loins. That loving look in her eyes and the way she held him; he knew he would never find that anywhere else. He would die for her and would do anything to protect her, which was why they were now running this place.

Alex had once been the mafia's assassin, killing whoever they ordered him to. But his last murder had been personal – the man who had tried to rape his beloved Maggie, and the brother of Alex's old boss, Paul. Matteo had thought he could take what he liked, when he liked, including Maggie. Seeing her bruised and bleeding that day had set Alex's teeth on edge.

And now, Alex would have to pay with his own life. The others had all turned against him and his family, but especially Paul. He'd lost favour in the mafia so quickly, it made his head spin. He'd been a ticking time bomb and he'd feared for his family's safety. Alex had felt there was only one thing left to do and that was to give himself up to the police.

He was now known as a 'rat'. The lowest of the low, betraying the mafia's golden rule. Life had been hell and his family had put up with a lot, but now it was his turn to pay his family back. So, if suburbia and the Stepford Wives was what made them happy, then that was okay with him.

He knew they were coming for him, but if they wanted a shoot-out, they could bloody well have one. At least he would die with honour and not in hiding!

2

MEETING THE NEIGHBOURS

'Oh my God Alex, look at the place, you wouldn't recognise it.'
Maggie walked from room to room, surveying the massive changes
a little bit of tender loving care had made. 'Have you seen what
they've done to the kitchen?' Maggie couldn't contain herself; she
was buzzing with excitement. This picturesque village was the stuff
that dreams were made of, and it was a world away from the life
they'd been leading lately.

While they had opted out of the protection programme, the
police were still offering them limited protection because of
Alex's high profile as a witness. And the police still had to
approve of certain activities. They weren't allowed to use social
media and mobile phones were also a no-go area as they could
potentially be tracked and traced. That was the hard part, especially for the kids. All kids these days had a mobile phone, but
they both had to agree to certain conditions. Alex had also
warned them all that the pub landline would probably be
bugged, and the police would listen in on their calls, so they
needed to be careful what they said and to whom. The police
were also suspicious about whether Alex would beg forgiveness

from the gangland bosses, change his statement and return to his old ways.

It was a high-profile international case involving many known mafia bosses across the globe. Their worlds would be blown wide open. Although a chill ran down Maggie's spine when she thought of the other option; they'd had so many death threats, it sickened and saddened her at the same time. Living in fear all the time had caused all kinds of problems. Fun loving Dante had retreated into himself. Deana had lost a lot of weight and Alex seemed to have sunk into a depression and at one point had lost his libido, which was unusual for him, because he was always ready. Night or day. When she looked at herself in the mirror, she didn't recognise herself either. She saw an old woman looking back at her, a world away from the woman who'd had her hair done every day before going to the supermarket.

Life had been so good and then it had turned sour. Inwardly, she blamed herself. Alex had only done what any husband would have done. There were times when she wished she'd kept her mouth shut about what Matteo had tried to do. But would her attempted rape have been a one off, or would he have come back for more? Mentally, she already knew the answer to that, and it chilled her bones.

'I'm glad you're happy Maggie. Even Deana seems to have a smile on her face lately, considering she's usually a sulky teenager slamming every door she walks through!'

Maggie looked at her husband. He was a handsome man with his jet black, shoulder-length hair. His swarthy Portuguese looks and chiselled jaw made him quite striking. There were many times since they'd met that she'd felt she was punching above her weight, but he had brushed all of her insecurities aside and married her despite his family's disapproval. And by family, she meant the gang lords of Portugal and Spain. They had objected to him marrying out of their circle. She would never be good enough, because she wasn't one of them. They didn't like outsiders who didn't know the rules, but Alex had ignored all of that.

Maggie was from the East End of London; a publican's daughter from a back-street pub where people wiped their feet on the way out. She'd had a good childhood, and she had loved her parents, but there had been times when she'd cringed at the clientele. They had all been duckers and divers, using the pub as a marketplace. Fences came in selling gold chains, and whatever else had fallen into their corrupt hands. Everyone had turned a blind eye; it was the code in the East End where no one saw or heard anything. This lifestyle had been the norm; even when some mad man came in waving a gun about, it was all hushed up away from the police. Of course, there was the usual protection rackets that went on and her father had let the back-room illegal poker games, set up by the local gangsters, carry on. But then he hadn't really had a choice if he'd wanted a roof over his head. Life was tough, but that was the East End and people just accepted it. The good side, she thought to herself, was that your dear old granny could walk home from bingo with her winnings and no one would think of mugging her. It wasn't allowed. These local gangsters had their turf and they looked after their residents. They were like Robin Hood heroes.

When she'd met Alex, her life had spiralled out of control, but that was another story, she thought to herself. Things were different now, and in some ways, she felt she had come full circle, living in a pub again. It was the only thing she was qualified for and the only thing she had ever really known. But only time would tell if they made this new life a success.

'I love you Alex, my Latin lover, you know that don't you?' she said without thinking.

Blowing a kiss at her, he smiled. 'Believe me, I know you do. No one would show someone they didn't love so much loyalty.' They made themselves a cup of coffee and chinked their coffee cups together. 'To love and loyalty.'

Once Maggie had finished her coffee, she followed the sound of Deana's shouts from upstairs and left Alex alone.

Standing up, he put his hands in his jean pockets and looked around the place that was their new home. Wandering into the main bar, he let his hands trail along the newly refurbished oak bar, tables and chairs. Although the smell of the fresh paint was making him sneeze, Alex felt a fluttering of butterflies in his stomach. This was a big leap into the unknown for his family, but they were determined to make it work this time. But what did he know about pulling pints or cooking and serving food to customers? They needed staff to help them. Thankfully, they'd been given the number for an agency. It wasn't as simple as putting an advertisement in the window. Well, not for them, anyway. Each and every new team member would have to be vetted, he knew that.

He worried that maybe Maggie was getting ahead of herself and didn't want this new life to come crashing down around her. He'd let her down once too often and vowed to himself he wouldn't do it again. In two days' time, their name would be above the door as the official publicans. He had made his choice and stood his ground; there was no room for turning back now.

Letting out a huge sigh, he peered through the windows to the street beyond. To his surprise he saw two women coming towards the pub. Curiously, he put his head closer to the glass. He recognised one of them. He'd seen her out jogging. Jogging! The very thought of it made him laugh, as he'd watched her from his newly decorated lounge. He'd called her the pink lady and had laughed out loud when he saw that she reached the end of the street and turned the corner red faced. 'That bloody woman doesn't run anywhere apart from the bottom of the street and then she stands around the corner having a cigarette. For someone who runs every day, she doesn't half look purple in the face and gasp for breath a lot,' he had joked with Maggie and Deana.

'Maggie!' he called now. 'The witches of Eastwick are coming calling.'

Hearing Maggie's feet coming down the stairs, he carried on watching the two women from his spot at the window.

'The who? Who is it Alex and should I be concerned?' Frowning, Maggie walked over to the window where Alex was stood.

'Them two, there. It looks like those busybodies are coming calling. They've waited long enough to look polite, but here they come. I'll leave you to it Maggie. You wanted suburbia, and I guarantee they are nosey bastards. On your head be it.' He laughed and walked out of the room as the expected knocking on the door started.

Checking herself in the mirror, and cursing herself for not having time to change her paint-splashed top, Maggie opened the door and smiled. 'Hello, can I help you? I'm sorry I don't look my best, but there's been a lot to do!' Excusing herself as politely as possible, she looked on as an earthenware dish was pushed towards her.

'I'm Olivia and this is Emma. We live at number 73 and 75. We would have come sooner but we didn't want to intrude. We've cooked this lasagne to welcome you to the neighbourhood. Well, I have...' Olivia beamed. 'It's my special recipe. I thought it might come in handy while you're busy setting everything up.'

The other woman, Emma, thrust a bunch of flowers towards Maggie.

'And these are from me. Welcome to the neighbourhood.' They waited.

Taken aback, Maggie put the bunch of flowers under her arm and took the lasagne. 'Thank you, Olivia, Emma. I'm Maggie, Maggie Silva. I would ask you in, but we're in a bit of chaos at the moment,' she lied. 'But we will be open in a couple of days, so be sure to pop in for a drink on the house.'

'Silver? I do hope your husband isn't called Long John.' Olivia laughed.

'Not that spelling.' Maggie smiled. 'And believe me, that joke has been done many times. It's Silva, with an A. It's Portuguese.'

Slightly embarrassed, Olivia nodded. 'Well, that is different – sorry.' Maggie could tell Olivia was itching to see inside. 'You have two children, don't you? I've seen you with them down the local shop.'

'Yes, my kids are called Deana and Dante. I think I've seen you both around, too.' Mentally, Maggie thought about Alex's nickname for the pink lady and smiled.

'We can let you know where the local schools and colleges are. Avril, a little further up, is a teacher. Maybe she can put in a good word for you.' Tapping her nose as though keeping a secret, Olivia grinned. 'It's not what you know, Mrs Silva, it's who, especially around here.'

Giving her a knowing look, Maggie smiled. Inwardly, she wanted to laugh. These two were better than the Spanish Inquisition. 'That would be lovely. Every little helps. Anyway, I had better go and put this in the oven, and thank you for the flowers – both of you. I'll return the dish as soon as possible.' She smiled and closed the door. Hearing a cough behind her, Maggie looked up the stairs and saw Alex standing on the landing.

'Very well executed, Maggie love. They will be the first of many. Long John Silver my arse.' He burst out laughing and walked away, leaving Maggie holding the lasagne dish. Her heart sank. She had to be on her guard – they all did – they knew that. Each day felt like walking on eggshells. But she had come through it and for now Olivia and Emma had just enough gossip to spread around the neighbourhood. She hoped she hadn't given too much away.

* * *

'Ooh Mum that looks good.' Taking the lid off the earthenware dish, Deana sniffed at the freshly made lasagne. 'Crikey, we could feed the whole village on that. How many of us do those old biddies think live here?'

'Old biddies? Cheeky bugger! That Olivia looks younger than me. Still, it's a nice thought though, isn't it?'

'If you say so Mum; personally, I'm with Dad. They thought it was a passport into the Silva palace. They can wait and pay like the rest of them,' Deana laughed. Taking the dish out of Maggie's hands, she put it in the oven.

'My Deana, who made a housewife out of you?' Maggie laughed as she watched her usually uncooperative daughter.

Both women laughed and began setting the table.

'Wow, something smells good. Which takeaway was that?' A hungry Dante followed his nose into the kitchen.

'This is the Olivia and Emma takeaway, otherwise known as considerate neighbours introducing themselves. Along with those lovely flowers. See?' Maggie pointed to the vase she had filled and put on the long dining table.

Not impressed by the vase of flowers, Dante took a seat at the table and waited patiently. 'Is it ready yet?'

'Five minutes, let me just fill a jug full of sparkling water and put some lemon in and then we can start. Where's your dad?'

'Out back, looking at the beer garden. He has no idea what he's looking at, so he's talking about sorting out a gardener, or asking the brewery if they can provide one. I said we should do it ourselves and then claim it back on expenses.'

'Ooh, listen to the accountant,' Deana joked. 'He might not be as good looking as me but he has brains, I'll give him that!'

'Of course he has. He's a natural-born mathematician my

Dante, aren't you love?' Maggie grinned, then opened the oven door and let the smell of the lasagne waft out into the kitchen. 'Deana, get the salad bowl out of the fridge, and that crusty French bread; it will go with this nicely.'

Alex walked into the large kitchen. With its eight-seater dining table, the freshly painted white walls made it look even brighter under the spotlights and the warmth of the oven made it feel homely. 'What's this feast? Is this your present from the pink ladies?'

'You make them sound like the girls from *Grease*. I presume you're their dark-haired Danny Zuko from the T-Birds, eh?' Jokingly, Maggie waved her serving spoon at him as though to hit him, but burst out laughing.

He laughed. 'I think we need a celebration night.' Waving a bottle of red wine in the air and searching through the drawers for a corkscrew, he grinned. 'This place is just about finished. All we need is a restock of alcohol, a tidy up and your name above the door, Maggie. Then we can begin our new life. But tonight, let's just be a family and drink this red wine. Dante, even you can have half a small glass. Tonight is for us.' Reaching in the cupboard, Alex took out four wine glasses. As they sat around the table, Alex raised his glass. 'To the Silva family and new beginnings.' Each of them raised their glasses in return.

'To new beginnings!' they chorused.

* * *

The next day, Maggie walked down the street towards Emma's and Olivia's houses, clean earthenware dish in hand. As she approached the gate, Olivia's door seemed to open instantly, as though she had seen Maggie approaching from the window. She ran to greet her.

'Thank you so much Olivia, your lasagne was absolutely lovely.'

'You're so welcome Maggie.' Opening the door a little wider, Olivia invited her in for a coffee. Maggie sensed that this was for another interrogation and, given the long day she had in front of her, declined. 'Another time. We're busy finishing up the place. Now the workmen have gone, it all needs a good sweep and a tidy.' Maggie felt slightly embarrassed and a fraud. These people she was now rubbing shoulders with had earnt their suburban houses in Kent through hard work. Most of them would have been born and bred in the area and had never known anything else. Whereas the Silva family came from a very different background. 'I do hope you'll come to the opening of the pub tomorrow evening, though. The restaurant is opening at the weekend, but it would be nice if a few of the neighbours could pop in to say hello. Maybe you could spread the word. All drinks are two for one. A happy hour for a grand opening, you might say.' Maggie blushed.

'Oh, I most definitely will spread the word. Everyone is dying to meet you!'

Maggie waved goodbye and made her way back to the pub.

* * *

'Right my beautiful girls, there is a man downstairs and this calls for an official ceremony. I've dragged Dante out of that pit of his and he's coming too. Shift your arses!'

Curiously, Maggie and Deana, who were sitting in the lounge, looked up at Alex and started to stand up as he ushered them towards the staircase. 'Who is it, Alex? What's going on?'

'All will be revealed Mrs Silva.'

Tentatively, Maggie and Deana looked at each other and followed Alex down the stairs, closely followed by Dante. Nothing impressed him, so this must be good.

Once downstairs, Alex put a makeshift blindfold over Maggie's eyes, intriguing her even more and making her giggle. Guiding her by the hand, he led her to the front of the pub where Maggie could hear banging. Standing behind her, Alex took the blindfold off. 'Ta-da!' he shouted.

Maggie blinked and looked up at a workman stood on a ladder, hammer in hand. She could see that he was putting her name up on the front door as licensee of the pub. Letting out a huge gasp, Maggie turned and hugged Alex excitedly. 'Oh my God Alex, it's happening, it's really happening!' Tears streamed down her face as she held out her arms to Deana and Dante for a group hug.

'There you go Maggie, it's all yours. Margaret Silva: licensee.' Alex beamed.

A pang of guilt hit Maggie. 'Are you okay with this? It should be your name up there, or at least both our names.'

'We both know that's never going to happen. There's no way I would ever get a licence. You're the official breadwinner and that's okay with me. I like the idea of being a kept man. Crikey, you're a bloke's dream. Good-looking woman, owns a pub and a tigress beneath the duvet. What else does a man want?'

'It's ours Alex, we're together in this. Mentally, I see your name up there with mine. We're a family. The Blacksmith pub and restaurant will be known as the Silva pub and restaurant in no time, believe me. Everyone will say, let's pop down to Silva's for a drink.' She smiled and nestled herself under his arm as she looked up at her name plate in all of its blazing glory.

As they both looked up at the sign, they cast a glance towards each other. 'Any regrets, Alex?' she asked. 'Our name is there in black and white for the world to see.' Maggie's stomach churned as she ran her tongue across her lips to moisten them. They both knew this would happen, but to see their family name emblazoned above the door almost felt like putting a target on their heads all over again. 'Are you worried?'

'It's the path we've chosen, Maggie love, and if nothing else, we could use it on our headstones.' He laughed, trying to make light of the situation. They were both pensive, but he was the man of the house and had to take it on the chin – for the sake of the family. He could see she was happy and sad all at the same time.

Glaring at him, she shook her head. 'Don't say that Alex, it's not funny. But it's done now, so we might as well put an advert in the daily rag. The Silvas live here,' she shouted. 'Are you ready for this? We can't change our minds again. We're officially on our own.'

'We've always been on our own. Now we, no, you, Maggie,' Alex corrected himself, 'have to make the brewery pleased that you're working for them. This is a blank page for your future.'

'I'm excited but nervous at the same time, if you know what I mean.'

Alex squeezed her shoulder. 'I do love, but you're going to make this place a gold mine. Come on, you can pull me a pint.' Pulling her to his side, he kissed her.

While she hugged him, she cast an upward glance at the sign again. Had they made the right decision? Or had they been too hasty? Only time would tell.

3
_____

OPENING NIGHT

'Mum, do you really need that much bunting? Aeroplanes will think it's semaphore signalling!'

'You want to see what Deana is doing to the beer garden – that's even worse!' Totally exasperated by the number of flags Maggie was putting out to advertise the pub's grand opening, Alex beckoned Dante to follow him around the side of the pub, where the boy's jaw dropped.

'Oh my God, it's winter wonderland!'

Astonished, Alex and Dante looked on as Deana threaded Christmas lights around wooden poles in the beer garden.

Wobbling on her ladder with a string of wire and bulbs in her arms, she shouted, 'It would be nice if you two stopped moaning and helped!'

'Why?' Alex laughed. 'You look like you're doing okay on your own.'

Dante grinned as he looked up at his dad, who gave him a cheeky wink.

'Come on son, let's leave the ladies to it. Even if we try to help, we'll get it wrong.'

'You can write on the chalk board for me Dante,' shouted Maggie. 'Happy hour 7-8 p.m. Two drinks for the price of one.'

Frowning, Alex walked around the corner towards Maggie, who was fighting with more gaily coloured bunting around the windows of the pub. 'Has the brewery agreed to this Maggie? Won't everyone just piss off by 8 p.m.?'

'Yes, they have agreed to it; I'm not totally stupid, you know. And they won't piss off at 8 p.m. They will carry on drinking, just to get the gossip and get to know us. You'll see. Believe me, we're going to be rammed.'

'Maggie, it's a street, with a couple of other adjoining streets. It's not the West End.'

'True, but these local pubs have regulars who like to think of the place as their own watering hole. Plus, when the restaurant is open properly, it will save them cooking. Good wholesome food, nothing too adventurous for now. Let's see what the supply and demand is. Pubs like these are always full. People can drink and walk home without spending a fortune on cabs.'

Alex realised she had a point. Putting his arm around Dante's shoulders, he decided to leave them to it and headed back inside. 'You sort the chalk board out, while I put the kettle on.' Suddenly a thought came to him. 'I hear you're starting school next week; are you nervous?'

'A little,' Dante replied. 'There have been quite a few new schools lately, but we never put down roots to make friends.' Dante took off his black rimmed glasses and started to clean them with his T-shirt, avoiding his dad's stare.

'It won't be for much longer son,' Alex sighed. 'This time, things will be different.'

'Is that why you've made a point of keeping our surname?' Dante asked.

Alex let out a huge sigh. 'Yes, I'm fed up of losing my identity. If people want to find me, it doesn't matter what we call ourselves. It makes no difference in the world. But, if I am going to die, I will die in my own name.'

'What about us, Dad? Have you thought of that? What would we do without you?'

'You'd manage, but I don't intend to go anywhere. Now go and get that chalk board written for your mother, or she'll kill us both!'

But it was as though a knife had been twisted in Alex's guts, hearing his son's fears. All he could do was try and protect his family and hopefully this nightmare would be over soon.

Watching Dante leave, Alex turned to see two official men in suits coming through the door. 'Morning Alex.'

'Inspector, what can I do for you?' A nervous smile crossed Alex's face as he wondered why they were here. Holding his hands up in submission, he grinned. 'I've done nothing wrong. Keeping my head down as you said.' Alex watched nervously as they cast a furtive glance between themselves.

'Come on fellas, spit it out.' Alex waited with bated breath.

'It's your old house Alex.' Giving a small cough to clear his throat, one of the detectives spoke.

'My old house?' Confused, Alex looked from one to the other. He could feel his heart begin to beat faster. 'What about it?'

'Last night, two adults, man and wife and two kids, a boy and girl, around the same age as Deana and Dante, were shot dead. It was definitely professional, one bullet each to their heads. It was cold blooded with no scuffle. There wasn't even a break-in.'

Alex's heart sank, and he felt bile rise in his throat. A million questions ran through his head, but none seemed relevant. Some poor family was dead because of mistaken identity. Trying to compose himself, he let out a deep sigh. Sweat ran down his back, making his shirt stick to him. He inhaled again and looked up at the inspectors. Alex realised that next time, the assassin, whoever they were, would get the right family. His. Inwardly, he wanted to shout, 'What the fuck have I done?' but he held it in and tried to remain calm. He licked his lips and swallowed hard to moisten his throat. 'Why would anyone go back to my old house? We haven't lived there in an age. Is anything known about the killer, who they were?'

The police inspector let out a sigh. 'We don't know. There's not a scrap of evidence. No one saw them go in or out of the building. Are you sure you still want to do this, Alex?' The inspector waved his arm around the pub. 'This isn't the safest place to be, you know. We do our best, but sometimes our best isn't good enough.'

'Did you see Maggie as you walked in?' Alex paused as they both nodded their heads. 'She's happy and she's smiling. I haven't seen her like that in ages. I can't take that away from her now, you know that, don't you? I agreed to this, and I know you boys in blue pulled a lot of strings to get us this place. Maggie's place.' He smiled, although it was a very weak one. 'I've made my choice. Just don't tell her anything about the family, poor bastards. What can I say?' Alex ran his hands through his black hair. His mind felt tortured as he thought about what the inspectors were telling him.

'We won't say anything about this to Maggie,' the police inspector reassured him. 'We'll let her think this was just another social call. Let's just carry on as we agreed.'

Standing up, the other inspector nodded and held out his hand to shake Alex's. 'It's your funeral Alex, make the most of it.'

'I will and thank you.' Shaking hands with them both, he watched them leave then paced the room. His mind was in turmoil. His earlier life hadn't exactly been law abiding. He'd been a gangster for as long as he could remember, always ducking and diving with the wrong crowd. That was until he'd got in with the right crowd. Matteo wasn't just part of the gang, he was the boss's brother and that had given him the excuse to cause chaos wherever he went with someone else having to clean up his mess after him – usually Alex. It had been Paul Pereira's idea to put the two boys together. He felt they would make a good team, and to be fair they were. As kids, it had worked but as time moved on, Matteo had found the adult addictions of booze and drugs. Matteo also carried a gun like some cowboy, always waving it around, when in truth he was a coward and an even worse shot! Even Paul was tired of hearing about his younger brother's antics and many a time Alex had heard the two of them arguing in another room.

Alex had always given respect to the heads of the families and in return had gained respect from them. Matteo they simply tolerated, and he had grown to resent the respect Alex got from the other family members. This had grown into a bitter jealousy and every petty incident turned into an argument between the two men. And then Alex had met Maggie. Matteo had always liked Maggie, but she had never entertained or encouraged his flirtation. She would often make herself scarce when he was around, claiming he made her skin crawl. Thinking back now, Alex realised that Matteo knew everyone had an Achilles' heel and Maggie was his. Maybe Matteo had thought his antics would cause a little disruption and that Alex would be thrown out of the family circle? Puzzled, Alex wondered to himself whether Matteo's attempt to rape and hurt Maggie had been his way of finally getting his revenge on Alex. Letting out a sigh, he shook his head. He would never know the answer to that... not now. Because Matteo was dead.

John, one of Alex's comrades and an assassin like himself, had been the only one to stand in Alex's favour and disagree with the families that it was Alex who should be punished for protecting his wife. But Paul Pereira had already convinced the families that blood was thicker than water and that Alex had never asked for permission to take action against Matteo. Like they would have agreed! He laughed to himself. Alex had wanted justice, but the families had brushed it off. Now Alex was getting his justice and so was Maggie, but at what cost? Already a family had been sought out and murdered in cold blood and Alex cursed himself for being grateful that it hadn't been *his* family.

Rubbing his face with his hands, Alex felt tired. Tired of everything lately. For over a year they had been constantly on the run, living in boarding houses, hidden in military barracks, never knowing what one day or another would bring. Now it was just him and his family, like any other, fighting to make a living legally, and on their own. Sometimes, when he'd laid awake at night while Maggie slept beside him, he'd thought about it and to be honest, it scared him a little. The fear of the unknown. His mind was in turmoil. He had always been part of something and now it felt like he was alone and being thrown to the wolves to survive – alone.

Hearing laughter outside the pub, he walked to the entrance and saw Maggie and Deana laughing and joking about their decorations. Taking a breath and swallowing hard, he joined them.

Maggie looked down from her ladder with a concerned look on her face. 'What's wrong? What did those two want?'

'Social call,' Alex lied. 'I'm fine Maggie. Just a bit nervous about our first night, I guess. It's make-or-break night, isn't it?' Rubbing his hands together, he forced a wide grin.

Getting down from the ladder, Maggie put her arms around him and kissed him. 'If you're sure?'

'I'm fine,' Alex said, reassuring her.

Maggie looked at her husband. She could tell that the visit from the two inspectors had unsettled him, but she could also tell that he didn't want to talk about it, so she changed the subject. 'Well, I don't know about you two, but I'm famished. Phyllis and Pauline, the barmaids, will be here soon, so let's eat and then I can get ready.'

'We have a barmaid called Phyllis? Blimey, not exactly exotic is it,' Alex laughed. 'But you're the boss Maggie. Let's eat and then you can have four hours to put your make-up on.'

Kissing his cheek, Maggie stood back and surveyed the decorations. Satisfied, she walked inside, ahead of them both. 'And don't be rude about Phyllis, or to her,' she shouted behind her.

* * *

'I've been a barmaid for twenty-eight years, Mrs Silva, so you just leave things to me.' Phyllis pouted and ran her fingers along the bar to check it had been polished.

Alex sat at the back of the pub. All afternoon Maggie had had him walking up and down from the cellar carrying crates of orange juice and other mixers.

Spying Phyllis, he cast a glance towards Maggie. Phyllis was at least six foot two and just as wide and by his reckoning in her late fifties, her *very* late fifties, he decided to himself. Her bleach blonde hair gave her home perm more of a frizziness than a perm. Looking her up and down, Alex winced. He hoped the beer was good because the bar staff wasn't going to attract attention – that was for sure! When Pauline, the other barmaid, came rushing through the doors, Alex's heart sank even more. She wasn't quite five foot, which made him wonder to himself how she was going to reach the top shelves. It was obvious to him that she dyed her hair red to cover the grey, but the grey roots looked more pinkish to him than red. Clearly, he mused to himself, she needed to use a different colour. Her make-up was heavy and her red lipstick represented a cupid's bow.

'Mrs Silva, shall I start setting things up?' she asked.

'No Pauline, everything is in order for now. Would you like to make yourself and Phyllis a pot of tea or something before we open up?' Avoiding Alex's eyes, Maggie did her best to greet the new barmaids and make them feel at home. 'Alex, can I have a quick word? I think you might need to bring up some more crisps.' Maggie winked.

Taking this as his cue to leave, he stood up and followed Maggie. Once she had shut the door, she pulled him aside, wagging her finger in his face. 'Not one word,' she whispered, 'I can read your face like a book, Alex Silva, so none of your sarcastic comments. It's experience we need and those two both have it.'

Taking her finger wagging in good humour, Alex laughed. 'Personally, I think we should have opened on Halloween night. You have one with an arse the size of the Titanic and a surly attitude and the other one needs twenty-four hours before the cement of make-up sets on her face. Bloody hell Maggie, is that the best they could come up with? They'll scare the bloody customers; I know for a fact that Phyllis already scares the shit out of me! You might get a few complaints from the male drinkers, too. They aren't the usual kind of barmaid you'd hope for.'

'That's bloody sexist Alex,' she snapped. 'Promise me you'll keep your opinions to yourself.'

The cheeky grin dropped from Alex's face as he looked into Maggie's eyes. She was almost pleading with him and yet he couldn't understand why. She knew he was a joker, that was his way. He had always laughed his way through life. 'Maggie love, I'm sure they are nice women, and their recommendations come very highly. I'm only messing.' Leaning forward, he gave her a peck on the lips and saw the smile reappear on her face. 'Come on, let's open up!'

Dante, Deana and Alex were watching from the back of the bar to support Maggie in her long-awaited moment of glory. Excitedly, Maggie slid the bolt across the door and opened it, turning towards Phyllis and Pauline standing at the beer pumps. Maggie gave them the thumbs up. 'Ladies, at your battle stations.' Looking past them towards Alex, she gave him a cheeky wink, then she almost fell forward as the door flung open and hit her in the back, as the customers nearly trampled her underfoot as they walked in.

Time for opening night!

4

A ROARING SUCCESS

As the music blared out, the whole neighbourhood seemed to pour through the doors ordering their drinks. The quiet, freshly painted pub that had recently stood silent, now burst into new life, full of laughter and chatter. The ladies let their husbands stand at the bar, ordering their drinks, while they wandered around looking and admiring the new décor and carpeting.

Olivia was the first to wave Maggie over, smiling like a Cheshire cat in the knowledge that she knew Maggie.

'Oh Maggie, this place is beautiful. Let's have a drink together to celebrate your opening.'

'That sounds lovely Olivia. I'll go and get us both a white wine.'

Maggie walked to the back of the bar near the optics and picked up a wine bottle. 'Come on you kids, time to go upstairs and leave everyone to it. And you Alex can join in and meet the new neighbours. We need to fit in,' she whispered under her breath and walked away to re-join Olivia. Taking her lead, Alex followed her and greeted Olivia at the bar.

'Alex, Maggie, this is my husband, Mark,' Olivia gushed.

Alex and Maggie cast each other a furtive glance then stared back at Olivia and her husband. They both seemed slightly puzzled. Never in their wildest dreams would they have put Mark down as Olivia's husband. Mark was a huge bulk of a man. His head was shaved, and he had a long dark, gingery beard that almost touched his chest. He was wearing an open denim shirt showing his black vest underneath and a casual pair of jeans, whereas Olivia was quite petite, and her soft, ash blonde hair was styled to perfection. Alex and Maggie had both assumed Olivia's husband would be an office worker, with a suit.

'I'm a mechanic. You might have seen my mobile van. Quick Fix.' He held out his hand to shake Alex's, his smile wide and genuine.

Alex liked him instantly. He could sense Mark was one of those gentle giants, and everyone who came in or was stood at the bar waved and shouted Mark's name. Musing to himself, Alex realised that Mark was probably the key to the neighbourhood secrets and a couple of rums would hopefully loosen his tongue.

* * *

Phyllis and Pauline were run off their feet and Maggie watched them as they joked with the customers like old friends. She felt a bit guilty that she hadn't pulled a pint yet, but tonight she had to play hostess.

Emma and Olivia had beckoned her to their side of the bar and linked arms with her. 'Let me introduce you to some of the neighbours,' Olivia whispered. 'There's Percy, you see over there, the old man with the white hair.' Cocking her head and looking beyond the row of customers, Maggie spotted an old man stood at the far end of the bar with a roll-up cigarette in the corner of his mouth and nursing a pint of lager.

'I think I've seen him before. He was helping the builders when they were here... I do hope that cigarette isn't lit, we do have a beer garden for smoking. Maybe I should say something,' said Maggie.

'No, it's not lit. He won't smoke his own tobacco. He'll wait till Mark and the boys go out for a smoke and then sponge one off them. He's probably had that one since the queen's jubilee.' Emma laughed. 'He lives alone. No one goes in his house because he stinks so God knows what his house smells like.' Emma wrinkled her nose and smiled. 'In summer he shaves his head and sits outside his house on a dining chair in an old off-white vest. He's like the unofficial neighbourhood watch. If you ever need a parcel taken in, or your bins putting out, Percy will do it.'

Olivia nodded. 'Yes, but he does take the odd liberty Maggie. He'll knock on your door to see if you have two slices of bread to spare, and then he goes to one of the other houses to find out if they have any cheese. By the time he's been round the neighbour-hood he's got a whole sandwich, and it hasn't cost him anything. I don't think he realises there are shops up the road. He must be worth a fortune, because he never spends his pension!' They both laughed.

'So why do you give it to him?' Although Maggie could see the funny side that Percy stocked up his cupboards with the help of his neighbours, she couldn't understand why they put up with it.

'We're neighbours and that's what neighbours do, isn't it? Although he is a pain in the arse sometimes, especially with those bloody racing pigeons he has. They shit all over my garden fence!' Emma laughed.

It was the first time in a long time that Maggie had shared adult female companionship, and she was enjoying it. Another glass of wine was poured as they all laughed together. Glancing across the bar, Maggie could hear Mark's loud voice above the music, laughing and chatting with friends that had gathered in a half circle around him with Alex at his side like an old friend. Breathing a sigh of relief, Maggie felt contented. This was home, warts and all.

As predicted, Mark reached into his pocket and took out a packet of cigarettes. 'Come on, outside for a smoke. You might as well come too Percy; it will save you sneaking up on us later. Wench!' Mark shouted towards Phyllis, making his friends laugh. 'Line up another round of drinks, we're going outside to the beer garden!'

Glaring at him, Phyllis picked up a glass and started filling it with beer. 'I'll get you another round of drinks in, but who's going to take it outside? Wench indeed,' she muttered under her breath with a stern look on her face.

Mark pointed his finger towards Percy. 'He will, and pour him one before he orders one on my bill anyway. Come on Percy, earn your keep.' Winking at Phyllis, Mark led his group of friends, including Alex, outside.

Maggie looked up and caught Phyllis's eye, smiling. Phyllis was definitely going to be an asset and she knew how to control a crowd.

'Silver?' shouted Mark above the others, while exhaling his cigarette smoke into the cool night air. 'Is that foreign? It's unusual.' Frowning, he waited for an answer as the others turned to face Alex.

'It's Silva, not the jewellery kind. I'm not sure where it comes from. Both my parents were English,' Alex lied and quickly changed the subject. Fortunately, Alex could see that Mark was becoming slightly tipsy and he hoped that none of it would sink into his brain.

Alex listened happily as Mark took over the conversation again, regaling them with stories about how he used to be a bouncer on the nightclub doors, which didn't surprise him, given Mark's build. Obviously, all his friends had heard his stories before, and laughed along with Mark's boastings, as long as he kept sending Percy in to collect more drinks for them. Alex bought his round of drinks, but noticed the others seemed to have sticky pockets and couldn't get their money out. After a while, Mark reached into the back pocket of his trousers and took out a small plastic packet. 'Do you fancy a key, Alex?' Using the end of a yale key from the bunch he had in his pocket, he put it in the packet containing a white powder and winked.

'What is it Mark?' asked Alex nonchalantly. Alex had a fair idea what it was, but was taken aback slightly. He'd only known these men for a short time and they were already pulling out their drugs and offering them to him. Was this for real? Trying to keep his cool, he looked at Mark and listened whilst Mark grinned like a chimp and explained.

Mark put his finger to his lips and whispered, 'Cocaine. Good stuff too.' Mark happily sniffed the powder up each nostril, then passed Alex the packet.

Holding up his hand to stop him, Alex looked around. He knew he should say something, especially as Mark was doing drugs on licensed premises, even though it was outdoors in the beer garden. 'No thanks. I'm on medication so best not.'

Mark shrugged and passed the little packet around to his friends who were more than eager to join in. So, Alex thought to himself, these people thought, because they had a better postcode than some, they sang a better tune. 'Be careful to not let Maggie catch you doing that, Mark. She's open minded, but drugs on public licensed premises don't actually bode well together, do they?' Alex felt this was suitably gentle but inwardly, he wanted to push the packet, including the plastic, up Mark's nose.

'Oh, yeah.' Mark blushed and averted his eyes. 'Point taken Alex. Wasn't thinking.' Mark could see by the frown on Alex's face that he had overstepped the line. 'Are you an anti-drugs man?' Mark whispered curiously.

Through gritted teeth, Alex flashed a glance at him. 'I'm an anti-anything man when it's on my property. But I am not judgemental. People make their own fun in their own way.' He didn't say what he really felt, which was that he hated drugs. It was a mug's game and he had seen too many lives ruined by it. The dealers he had known and mixed with laughed about customers like Mark who thought they were important and worldly because they could buy an overpriced packet of rubbish, because that's what it usually was. Mark was so drunk, Alex noticed, that he probably wouldn't realise if it had an effect on him or not. Like his boastings, it just made him look the man in the 'know'. A deluded nobody, killing the boredom and trying to be a somebody. He'd obviously seen too many movies.

Alex wanted to ask where Mark got the drugs from but decided not to. There must be dealers in the area, he mused to himself, but then again, these days there were dealers everywhere.

Hearing a bell ring loudly, Alex and Mark looked up and heard Maggie's voice shout last orders. Quickly looking at his watch, Alex hadn't realised how long he had been out there listening to all the neighbourly stories. It had been enlightening, but it was time to call it a day.

'Don't suppose your Maggie is going to allow us a lock-in tonight, Alex?'

'Not on the first night; she'd have my guts for garters. Probably will anyway considering I haven't lifted a hand to help her tonight.' He laughed.

'Yeah, you're right. My Olivia will be moaning too. Come round to my house if you ever fancy a few beers and to get away from the women.'

Alex realised that Mark's friendship was genuine. He was an open book but let himself be taken advantage of by all of the spongers around him, as long as they listened to his stories and let him be the centre of attention. But he was clearly proud of his achievements and why not?

After saying their goodnights, Alex shook Mark's hand and walked back into the bar. Phyllis, Pauline and Maggie were busy clearing up after what seemed a successful night and so he joined in.

'You seem to have made a friend for life there Alex, and from what I gather, Mark seems to be popular in the neighbourhood. That's good because there's no better promotion for the pub than word of mouth. Just wait until the restaurant starts up.' Excitedly, Maggie climbed into bed beside him and snuggled up close, gently rubbing the black hairs on his firm and muscular chest. She could feel his instant arousal, which matched her own, thankful that he wasn't the worse for alcohol.

Turning on his side towards her, he flicked her pert nipple with his tongue, then trailed his tongue up her neck, to her lips. As their kiss turned to passion, his hands roamed over her body. He felt a need to hold her tonight.

Lying on her back, she moved to accommodate him further, welcoming him in between her thighs, gasping and moaning while their bodies moved in unison until Maggie's body trembled and quivered as she reached her peak and cried out in pleasure.

Throwing his head back and panting, Alex felt his own release.

Gasping for breath, they lay beside each other. It had been a long time since they'd made love in such relaxed surroundings. Opening his arms, Maggie laid her head on his chest, satisfied and content as her breathing returned to normal and they both drifted off to a peaceful sleep.

5

BENEATH THE SURFACE

Days passed into weeks, and it was as though the Silva family had never lived anywhere else. They had been welcomed into the community with open arms, with Mark's encouragement. Every moment he had, he seemed to introduce Alex to another one of his 'mates'.

The restaurant had become a big asset too, just as Maggie had predicted. It served steak and chips, burgers for the kids, and half of it she had changed into a carvery which seemed to be proving very popular.

'For God's sake, Maggie, how are you making a profit? Those vultures are piling their plates higher than Everest with everything in sight.'

Maggie rubbed her husband's chin and smiled. 'That's why, Alex, love, in the pub trade we give them smaller plates. That way they think they are having a lot, but it's not that much, really. York-shire puddings are just flour, water and eggs. You can make a lot and give two or three at a time; it fills the plate.'

'You're a sharp one, Maggie, I will grant you that. And that chef who cuts the meat couldn't cut it any thinner if he tried. No wonder I love you so much. I thought I was the con man in the family, but I can see I am going to have to watch my back.' He laughed and slapped her bottom. Taking another sip of his morning coffee, he looked up as the door opened, and Phyllis walked in. 'Morning, Phyl.' He beamed. 'Coffee's through the back.'

'Thanks, Alex, I'll pour Pauline one too. I've just seen her get off the bus.' Trailing her finger along the bar, she pulled a face. 'I see that cleaner is still on short measures. She sprays polish into the air, trying to make us think she's been busy. I'll bring a cloth out from the back with me and give it a spruce up for you, Maggie; that will give you time to get changed.'

Maggie gave Alex a knowing look. 'Besties are we now, eh?' She smiled.

'Yeah, she's all right really, even though she looks down her nose at everyone. She used to run her own pub until her husband died, then she gave it up. Did you know that Pauline's sister is a teaching assistant at Dante's school?'

'My, you have been busy, Alex. Is there anything you don't know? You're like the oracle.' Maggie couldn't help but laugh. Alex seemed to have questioned everyone and ingratiated himself in their new community while she had been run off her feet behind the bar. But people enjoyed the way he sat with them and got to know them. Although they never realised that when he ordered a drink for himself, there was no alcohol in it. He had made it a code behind the bar with Phyllis and Pauline that if he ordered a rum and coke or any kind of short that needed a mixer, they were only to give him the mixer. If he ordered a pint of lager, they would give him a shandy. He liked his wits about him, liked to listen to their drunken talk, not the other way around. Phyllis and Pauline had found it unusual that Alex wasn't a drinker. The truth was, he liked a drink, like anyone else, but he couldn't afford to let his mouth run free whilst under the influence.

'I've got onto the brewery and asked them about a delivery service. Everyone is doing it these days – takeaway Sunday lunches. They like the idea, and it's extra profit and good promotion,' Maggie said.

'Why would anyone want to do that?'

'Because people can't be bothered to get dressed up and come out on rainy days. It's much easier to sit in front of the television and chill out with your Sunday roast. Some people live on their own and can't be bothered to cook for one either.'

'I notice that Percy always seems to hang around near closing time; he thinks we're a food bank,' Alex scoffed.

'He comes in very handy, and giving him a plate of leftovers is no skin off my nose. They would only go to waste. Who wants yesterday's Yorkshire puddings? Do you know that in his younger days he was a fisherman on the trawlers?' Maggie smiled as though it was a secret. Percy bored everyone with his days as a fisherman, and his stories became more unbelievable with each tale.

Rolling his eyes to the ceiling, Alex sat on a bar stool and put his head in his hands. 'Yeah, I know. I've heard him say how cold it was. Icy in the Baltic apparently. I swear his stories change each time he tells them. Deana calls him "Uncle Albert" behind his back. You know, the old seaman from *Only Fools and Horses*. Well, he always started his sentences with "During the war", but Percy always starts with, "When I was on the trawlers". She's a cheeky minx.' Alex burst out laughing. He thought it was hilarious because that summed up old Percy to perfection. Frowning, Alex looked at Maggie. 'But what do you mean he comes in handy?'

'Well, if you took any notice, Alex, you would have seen he is the unofficial glass collector. He puts the dustbins out before I have a chance to. God knows what time he gets up! And when he's after another free pint, he wipes down the tables in the restaurant. I think he's lonely.'

'He's a creepy pervert,' chipped in Phyllis, while busying herself polishing the already polished bar and clearly eavesdropping on Maggie and Alex's conversation. 'His eyes follow you, especially the ladies. I hate turning my back on him; he's always spying on your bottom. And why does he have three blue bins for recycling? How much cardboard does a single pensioner who never spends any money have?'

Raising his eyebrows, Alex looked at Phyllis's bottom, while Maggie gave him a stern, knowing look. Curiosity got the better of him, and he stood up, peering through the window at Percy's house. Phyllis was right; there were three blue bins outside. Everyone else stored theirs around the back of their houses, so it didn't make the street look untidy. But there, in full view, were Percy's bins lined up together. Furrowing his brows, Alex couldn't help but wonder why. 'You're right, Phyllis, he does, and in plain view. That's strange...'

'I told you he was weird,' she scoffed and left the room.

Alex walked over and stood behind Maggie, putting his arms around her waist and pressing himself against her, much more than he should. 'I think he must be weird if he stands at the corner of the bar admiring Phyllis's arse,' he whispered. 'I would much rather look at yours.'

'It's not you looking at my arse that bothers me, Alex, it's what you're pressing against it. That Latin blood of yours will get you into trouble one day.' She smiled, half-turning and kissing him on the cheek before Phyllis's cheerful humming made them quickly part.

'Deana,' Alex called up the stairs. Seeing her at the top of the landing, he beckoned her. Lowering his voice, he steered her out of the back door into the beer garden. 'Did you do as I asked?' he whispered.

She nodded.

'Good. Was it hard to bring here?'

'Not easy. No one expects a sixteen-year-old with a golf bag full of clubs on the bus, and it was bloody heavy!'

Like any good assassin, Alex couldn't be without his own guns. They were his work tools, and had saved his life many times. And although he'd had everything else taken away from him, he had been determined that they wouldn't take his guns. He'd known he would need them one day and that they would possibly save his and his own family's life one last time. With no one to turn to, he had swiftly hidden his guns at his golf club before the police could take them when they had emptied his house.

Informing for the police was a means to an end for Alex, a way to save his wife and kids. He'd always known the next bullet at the next shoot-out could be in his head. That was the world he lived and fought in. What he had done, by turning himself in and grassing up his associates, had been the only card he had left to play with.

He thought back now to the puzzled looks on the faces of the police officers who had ransacked his home but never found any weapons in the house. They knew who and what he was, but Alex Silva didn't have a gun? That was unbelievable. He'd also reasoned with himself that one day it might be mentioned in court that no weapons had been found at his house, casting a small shadow of doubt that he was known as the 'Silva Bullet'. An assassin without a gun was like night without day.

These guns were his armour, his friends. Part of his makeup, almost. Knowing he would probably need them someday, now he had a bounty on his head and any gunslinger would want to take their chance for a huge payout, he wanted his faithful friends with him. How could he fight fire without fire of his own?

'That's my girl. Bring them to me later then, while you're working in the restaurant. I'll meet you outside the fire exit in the kitchen. Be careful; you don't know who's watching.' Alex looked through the hallway to the bar and glimpsed the first of the customers: Percy. Shaking his head at the thought of another trawler story, he retreated to the cellar. Although Maggie and the others thought he was clearing it up, he actually found it was the perfect place to read his newspaper in peace, but first, he had something to do.

* * *

The restaurant was busy for a midweek night, the locals popping in for a catch-up with their neighbours. It had become the end of the day meeting place to share gossip. It was never going to make a fortune, Alex mused to himself, but passing trade was pretty good.

Deana was wandering around gathering plates, and she bumped into him. 'Sorry, Dad.' She smiled and quickly cocked her head, indicating for him to follow her.

'Oh Deana, I've got gravy on me; I'd better come and clean up.' Joining in with her playacting, he followed her out through the kitchen to the exit. Deana ran behind a tree and dragged a large golfer's bag, full of golf clubs sticking out of the top, towards him. 'Here,' she panted. 'How are you going to get it inside?'

'Round the back, there's the outside entrance into the cellar the draymen use. I've got an old barrel to stash everything we need in.' Picking it up and throwing it over his shoulder, Alex looked around furtively to make sure no one was around. Deana ran around the back and opened the cellar shutter and walked down the stone steps that led into the cellar underneath the pub. It was dark and full of cobwebs, and Deana searched for the light switch in the darkness. Only a light bulb hanging on a baton in the middle of the ceiling lit up the room.

'That barrel in the corner, under the stairs, the lid is loose; take it off.' Doing as she was told, Deana waited for her father to join her with the golf bag. In turn, they reached inside and took out all kinds of guns, rifles and ammunition, filling the barrel to the hilt.

'My babies.' Alex held up a handgun and kissed it. 'Thanks Deana, I appreciate it. Did you get there okay?'

'Getting to the golf club was the easy part. Carrying the bag across the green and hailing a taxi for the train station was hard. But the bloody bus after! Oh my God, these bags weren't built for buses. They take up so much space and everyone moaned. Still, it was nice seeing parts of London again and the old golf club. Reminded me of the old days when you taught me to play golf on a Sunday morning.' She grinned. 'But when you asked me to do you a favour Dad, I didn't expect this.' Rolling her eyes at the ceiling, she looked down into the bag and took out a few golf clubs to get a better view of the contents. 'Look, they're all here, just as we left them all that time ago. Christ, I wasn't sure they would be, Dad.'

Alex scratched his head. 'To be honest Deana,' Alex whispered. 'I wasn't so sure either. I feared they might have been thrown out, but it just goes to show what a shithole that place really was, doesn't it?' He grinned, flashing a perfect row of white teeth. His heart was pounding in his chest. He couldn't believe it, here was his salvation.

'Nah! This just means they haven't had any new members! I can't believe the caretaker or someone hasn't tried getting into your old locker before now though. For all they know it could belong to some member who died. How long were they going to leave it?'

'Who the fuck cares? Let's just be grateful for their oversight. Now give me a bear hug, Deana Silva!' Hugging each other tightly,

Alex felt more at peace with himself, as his eyes brimmed with tears. Deana had always been his wingman. She was like him and had the same survival instinct. He had taught her and eventually Dante how to handle a gun, but he'd shared secrets with Deana that he knew he shouldn't have. He didn't want to frighten or bother Maggie any more than need be, so he confided in Deana.

'Take this and put it in your room. Hide it well, so that your mother doesn't find it when tidying up in there.' Alex put a magazine in the bottom of the gun and checked that it was loaded. 'The safety catch is on, but be careful, love.'

'I know, Dad, you don't have to tell me. What about Dante? He's a crack shot.'

'I'll cross that bridge when I come to it. For now, it's just you and me. No one knows I had these stashed away at the old golf club. Did anyone see you picking this up?'

'I don't think so, Dad. There was no one around, but I couldn't swear on it.'

'Well, let's hope they didn't. What matters now is that I can protect you all. I feel like a sitting duck knowing there's a bullet out there with my name on it and nothing to protect myself with. Sorry to lay this on you Deana. You and Dante have had more than your fair share to deal with. You are innocents in all of this.' He hugged her again. Mentally, Alex felt like he had made such a mess of his life, and more to the point his kids'.

'Dad, did something happen when those coppers visited the day of the opening?' she whispered. Watching her father nod his head, she sighed. She'd known something was troubling him, and when he'd asked her to go to his old locker at the golf club, she had a fair idea why. 'It would kill Mum if we had to leave here. She loves it.'

'I know. How do you think I feel? It's the first home we've had in ages. You're settling in at your new college, and Dante likes his new school. But, with these in the house, I feel safer. Put some of those old crates on top of the barrel to disguise it.'

Deana put the gun Alex had given her in the front waistband of her jeans, carefully hidden behind her kitchen apron, and disappeared up the stone stairs again.

Alex blew a kiss to the barrel loaded with guns and went up the stairs that led into the pub, carrying a crate of mixers. 'Here you go, love, you looked like you were running short.' Frowning, Phyllis looked along the bottom shelf of the bar and saw that it was fully stocked. Catching her eyeline, he played the fool. 'You did say mixers, didn't you, Phyllis?'

'No, I don't remember saying that.'

'Oh God, what am I like? I thought I heard you say mixers. What a waste of time that was,' he sighed dramatically. 'Anyway, you take your break now; I'll cover for you.'

As Phyllis left, Alex went to the front of the bar and asked the usual crowd what they were drinking, pulling their pints of beer with a contented feeling inside of him. Thank goodness Deana had an old head on her shoulders, and he had taught his children well. They would be safer now. Alex was going to make sure of that.

* * *

Waking up and yawning, Alex looked at the bedside clock. It was just after 5 a.m., and he could hear the dustbin truck. Realising it was blue bin collection day, Alex jumped out of bed and moved the blinds from the window to peer across at Percy's house. His bins – all three of them – hadn't been put out for collection. Finding it odd that none of them were full or needed emptying, Alex decided to mention it to Mark. If anyone knew the secret behind it, Mark definitely would. Running his hands through his black hair, he lay on the floor and began his morning push-ups. He had always exercised and hated being without a gym at his disposal, but for now, this would suffice.

Bleary eyed, Maggie glimpsed the clock beside the bed. 'For God's sake, Alex, do you have to do that first thing in the morning every day?'

Panting, he looked up from beside the bed. 'Would you rather I did my push-ups closer to you?' He winked.

'Not this early, and doesn't your dick ever have a day off? You're like the emergency services – always on alert!' Turning on her side, Maggie tried dozing off again, even though all she could hear in the background was Alex puffing and panting while exercising. 'Talking of exercises' – Maggie turned back over to watch Alex – 'Olivia mentioned that the old publican used to let them have use of the pub when it was closed for a Zumba class. I think she's hinting that we do the same – what do you think?'

'A Zumba class – where?'

'Well, I suppose we could put the tables and chairs aside; it would give them enough room. He used to let them use one of the rooms up here, but we couldn't do that now. He used to charge them £50, and Olivia's friend does the classes.'

Sitting on his haunches, Alex took a breath. 'If you want to do it, then do, but I wouldn't charge that amount. Why don't you say, if there are more than ten people, you take twenty pounds, or a pound for every Zumba queen who turns up? That way the woman will make money, and Olivia will be eternally grateful. Between 10 a.m. and 11 a.m. would do it, then the cleaner will have done her stuff, and after all their hard exercise, I am sure they would need some form of drink to quench their thirst. Can I get on now?'

Starting his push-ups again, Maggie gave a wry smile. Realising she was never going to get back to sleep, she pushed back the duvet and got out of bed. 'I'm going to put the kettle on. I was thinking,' she laughed as she opened the door, 'the Zumba queens, as you call them, have a personal trainer on site. Maybe you could be the Zumba king.' Looking down at Alex on the floor, she saw him raise his head and glare at her underneath his dark eyelashes as the sweat poured down his face. She couldn't help laughing as she went into the kitchen.

6

THE MYSTERY UNFOLDS

During his days, all Alex seemed to have to do with his time was observe and watch the neighbours. It was a lovely area, he had to admit, but it had hidden depths, he was sure of it. Seeing Mark with his head under another car bonnet, he strolled over. 'How's it going Mark?'

'All right Alex, trying to fix this.' Raising his head from under the bonnet, Mark rubbed his oil-stained hands with a rag.

'Isn't that your mobile van for call-outs?'

'Yeah, it's broken down again. I need to sort it out. I'll pop in for a drink later. Oh, by the way, do you have a spade? We have, but it's a bit bent at the end. Percy asked me earlier if he could borrow one.'

Thinking to himself, Alex nodded. 'I think there's one in the old shed. What does he need it for?'

'Apparently he wants to plant something or other, pretty big by all accounts and he needs a big hole. He's got a heart problem so I've offered to dig it for him; I don't suppose you fancy giving me a hand?'

Still looking at Mark's battered old mobile mechanic van, Alex couldn't help wondering why a man who advertised fixing other people's cars had problems with his own. Was Mark a mechanic who couldn't actually fix cars? That puzzled him. 'Yeah, I'll give you a hand. Let me find that spade and I'll give you a shout later. It will get me from under the women's feet. That bloody Zumba class is driving me bonkers, even Phyllis and Pauline turn up early to join in, then they all turn purple and sweat. I thought it would be all young birds with everything in the right places, but, God no. It's all wobbly bits flying in every direction and none of them know their left from their right, and that includes your wife!' Alex grinned.

Mark burst out laughing. 'It wasn't Olivia's brain I married her for, it was definitely her tits!' Mark winked and laughed. 'She knows left is the side she wears her watch on, but if she ever takes it off, she is well and truly stuffed!'

* * *

'How's Mark? I saw you talking to him,' Maggie asked as Alex arrived back at the pub.

'Old Percy has a hole he needs digging; I'm going to give him a hand. I've seen an old spade in that shed, it will keep me out of mischief.'

'Have you seen that bloody dog of his?' laughed Maggie. 'It's got three legs, cancer tumours all over its stomach and it sounds like it has a smoker's cough. Emma said he's refused to have the dog put down, but I'm surprised it's still standing. And to make it worse, it's called Skippy!' Maggie had tears running down her face she was laughing so much.

Frowning, Alex looked at her. 'I didn't know he had a dog; I've never seen him walking it.' Alex's curiosity was well and truly piqued. 'I'm going to get the spade now; this is something I really have to see.'

* * *

'Mark! I've found that spade. Do you want to do it now? It shouldn't take long. What's he planting?'

'Yeah, why not? While it's daylight.' Leaving the bonnet of his van up, Mark rubbed his hands on a cloth that was more oil stained than his hands.

Walking around the back of Percy's garden, Alex grimaced. It was a total mess. He had old sofas and washing machines piled high. The grass wasn't cut and he had planks of old wood scattered everywhere.

'Where the hell are we going to find a place to dig a hole in this scrap yard? His front garden looks tidier.'

'Percy! Get your arse out here. Where do you want this hole?' Mark shouted.

Coming out of his back door into the garden, Percy sported an old grey vest and tracksuit bottoms which looked like they had belonged to someone else, while holding a mug of tea.

Grimacing at the sight, Alex glanced towards Mark. 'Hasn't he ever heard of soap and water? And seeing those wrinkly man boobs under his vest makes me want to run home.'

'Yeah, well, it gets worse in the height of the summer, believe me,' Mark laughed.

'I need the hole at the back there.' Percy pointed to the side of some old washing machines stacked against the fence. 'It has to be deep though.'

Sighing, Mark and Alex walked over to the appointed area and started digging. After a while, Alex stopped and rubbed his back. 'What are you putting in this hole anyway, Percy?'

'Yeah,' Mark butted in, 'what is it? An old oak tree or something?' Puzzled by Percy's furtiveness, they both waited until he went indoors and came out holding a long, thick parcel wrapped in black bin liners. 'It's my dog.'

'What?' exclaimed Mark. 'You've had us both dig a hole for your dog? What is this, the bloody pet cemetery? You can't go burying dogs in your garden; isn't it illegal these days? What about when you die, and the next tenants come in and decide to sort this garden out and end up digging up its carcass?'

'Never thought of that, but it needs doing.' Percy lit his roll-up, which was perched safely on his bottom lip as always.

Flabbergasted, Alex mopped his brow. 'Why don't you ask the vet to take it away? They'll sort it properly.'

'This is its home.' Percy laid the dog in the hole they had both dug. 'I think it needs to be a bit deeper,' he muttered.

Mark shook his head in disbelief. 'Well, we've started Alex, we might as well finish. Though God knows what anyone else moving in here is going to think.'

Both of them were amazed at Percy's nonchalance as he waited for them to dig a deeper hole. 'Maybe that's the only way they're going to get the garden cleared. If they report it to the police, they will dig up the garden!' he laughed.

'I've got my court case coming up soon, so it was best old Skippy died,' said Percy out of the blue.

'Court case? For what?'

'Had a bit of trouble with the law. I could end up back inside prison.' Poker faced, Percy stared at them both.

'What kind of trouble?' Alex cast a furtive glance towards Mark, who shrugged his shoulders.

'My friend in prison asked me to throw some mobile phones over the wall and I did. But I didn't realise they had them CCTV cameras outside and they saw me.'

Amazed, Alex and Mark looked at each other and then back at Percy, their jaws almost dropping at this confession.

'Did you kill your dog in case you go back in prison?' Alex asked. When Percy nodded, he shook his head. 'You old bastard. The vet would have done it for nothing, you know.'

'I know, but this is its home. No one would foster it or take it in because it's old and has cancer. They wouldn't be able to find it a new home. This is for the best.' Percy took a sip of his tea, while Alex and Mark stood there amazed. They couldn't believe their ears.

Alex was just about to throw his spade down and walk away, when Magda, the young Polish woman from next door, popped her head over the fence and waved a piece of paper in their direction. 'Mark, Mark come here.' She beckoned.

Alex had long realised that anyone with a problem seemed to go to Mark; he was like the godfather of the street.

Walking over, Mark took the piece of paper out of Magda's hand and read it. 'It's an electricity bill, what of it?' Mark scoffed and passed it to Alex for inspection.

'Have you seen how much they want to charge me for three months?' Magda almost shouted, in a state of panic. Both Alex and Mark looked at the sum owed and let out a loud whistle. 'Three thousand pounds. What the hell! Blackpool illuminations doesn't cost that much, I'll bet. You need to get on to the electricity company. They have obviously made a mistake.'

Tears rolled down her face in despair. 'Will you ring them for me? My English isn't so good. Help me Mark, please,' she begged.

Glancing up, Alex saw Percy blush slightly, and his gut instinct told him he had something to do with it, or he knew something about it.

Mark took out his mobile and after a lengthy conversation, the electricity company informed him that the amount was correct, but they would send someone around to check the meter. Satisfied with another good deed done, Mark smiled. 'Sorted Magda, it's probably three hundred, don't panic. They are coming tomorrow.' Relief washed over her, and she couldn't thank Mark enough, which built his ego even more. 'Christ, no wonder I never get any work done around here. I'm like the Samaritans,' muttered Mark.

Alex picked up his spade again and turned back to Percy. 'And you, you weird old bastard, can sort your dog out yourself, I'm having nothing more to do with it. Come on Mark, we've earnt a drink.'

Alex felt Percy had deeper dimensions than just being the old man across the street. Instinct told him that things were not right, and his instincts had usually been right in the past. That was what had saved him and made him dodge a bullet in his past life.

Walking into the pub, Alex shouted, 'Maggie, whether it's opening time or not, we're having two pints and a smoke out the back. What a bloody morning.'

'Well, don't think about bringing those muddy trainers in here; this carpet's just been hoovered,' Phyllis remarked and folded her arms defiantly. Like two naughty schoolboys, they took their shoes off while Phyllis poured their drinks.

'Where's Maggie?' Looking around, Alex couldn't see her, and usually on hearing his voice she appeared.

'She's got visitors out the back. Brewery I think.'

Curious, Alex excused himself from Mark. 'I'll just pop to see if she needs me.'

Alex stopped dead as he entered the room; it wasn't the brewery but the police inspectors he had spoken to the other day.

'Hello Alex,' one said. 'Just thought we'd pop in to see how things were.'

Alex rubbed his hands together and smiled, hoping they hadn't mentioned the murder of the family they had previously spoken about. 'Everything's fine here. Just been doing some gardening.'

After their usual chat and Maggie's eternal tea and biscuits, they got up to leave. Suddenly a thought occurred to Alex and as he walked them out the back entrance, he pulled them to aside and whispered, 'That Percy bloke over there, do you know him?'

The police officers glanced at each other and then back at Alex, making him realise that there was more to Percy than met the eye. 'Why, what do you know?' they asked furtively.

'Oh nothing. He has some strange ways that's all and apparently he has friends in prison that he's throwing mobile phones to. It's not a secret and I'm not grassing anyone up. It seems everyone knows.'

'Don't worry, Alex. He won't go back to prison. For one, he's too old with heart problems and secondly, he works for us. He'll get a slap on the wrist and a fine that he'll never pay.' They were about to walk off, when Alex stopped them again.

'What do you mean he works for you? Who the fuck is he? I need to know; my family's safety is on the line,' he spat out.

Sighing and looking at each other, they realised Alex's anxiousness. 'He's an informer. Don't worry about it – he's not your problem.'

Alex was gobsmacked at this revelation. 'An informer? Does he know about me?' The detectives shook their heads. 'No, not unless you've told him, which means the deal is off.' Alex watched them as they casually walked away and got into their car. He thought about good old Percy; the neighbourhood watch who helped everyone and gathered information. But he was curious to know why Percy was on licence from prison in the first place. He doubted anyone knew and for the time being his lips were well and truly zipped, although he did wonder if Mark knew anything. He seemed to have his fingers in a lot of pies when it came to people's business.

'You okay Maggie? What did those two have to say?' Alex asked when he walked back inside.

'Just the usual Alex. They wanted to know if anyone has

contacted us, just chit chat really. You know they have to come and check on us. Stop worrying, we're okay. Well, for now anyway.'

Satisfied that the police had said nothing else to upset Maggie, he smiled.

Maggie smiled back. 'I'd better get on; thirsty people out there.'

Alex's mind was in turmoil. He now knew Percy couldn't be trusted with anything, although he wasn't going to tell him anything anyway. Musing to himself, he rubbed his chin. This wonderful suburban neighbourhood had so many secrets once you scratched the surface. He would wait and see what the next bomb-shell would be. Maybe Mark would turn out to be MI5 or something.

7

BOUNTY

Walking down the iron staircase and along the landing surrounded by prisoners in blue uniforms, the prison guards walked on either side of Paul Pereira, one of the Portuguese mafia bosses awaiting trial. Now in his late sixties, with his grey hair swept back from his face, he still had an authoritative air about him. His uniform was freshly ironed; his highly polished shoes that one of his lackies in the prison had spent their time doing shone almost like glass; and the Windsor knot in his tie gave him that added extra something. Pereira ran this prison; no one dared cross him, and other inmates divided themselves, leaving a walkway for him to pass through. A well-built swarthy looking man, his body was powerful, and he walked straight and upright almost like a sergeant major, staring at the other inmates as he passed them with his dark piercing eyes.

'This way Mr Pereira.' One of the guards held out his hand, indicating for him to walk towards the left corridor.

'Who is my visitor? Is it my lawyer?' asked Paul in a heavy accent.

'I don't believe so Mr Pereira; family I think.' Although he was in custody, the guards still called him Mr Pereira. They all knew of his reputation and none of them wanted to get on the wrong side of him. Their jobs weren't worth it. Taking him into a solitary room with a table and two chairs, Paul looked up and frowned. He could see it wasn't his lawyer, but one of his associates. He wasn't sure how he had introduced himself and so kept silent.

'Cousin Paul, it's good to see you.' The visiting man before him stood up and held out his hand to shake his.

Paul turned to the guards. 'Leave us, I wish to talk to my cousin alone.'

Glancing at each other, the two guards nodded. 'No funny business Mr Pereira, please,' one said.

'Funny business? What am I? A fucking clown!' snapped Paul at the guards and pulling his chair out, he sat down. 'No problems.' Lowering his tone, although without a smile, Paul nodded his head. 'Go take a piss, everything is okay here.'

Once the guards had left the room, Paul grabbed hold of the man in front of him by the shirt collar. 'What the fucking hell do you think you're playing at?' Struggling to release his hold, the man stood back.

'I'm sorry Mr Pereira. It was just an accident. The family fitted the description and they lived at his old address. It made sense.' The man's eyes widened with fear and he was pleased they were inside prison walls, because he knew for sure that Paul would have killed him otherwise. Beads of sweat appeared on his brow and he stood staring at Paul, waiting for his next move.

'Alex Silva is not that stupid! Do you really think he is going to return home? I am in here for extortion, racketeering, murder and drug smuggling, all because of him. He has betrayed me and now I want his blood! I don't intend to die in a shithole like this. He has a fifty-million-pound bounty on his head, and it's rising the closer the court case looms. Surely you can get it right for that sum of money. For Christ's sake, can't anyone do anything right these days?' Once his rant was over, Paul sat down on his chair again. Feeling somewhat safer, his visitor sat down too.

'The last we heard Silva was in France with his family, then he just disappeared. Once we heard about the family at his house, we thought... well.' The man stopped talking and stared at Paul nervously.

'You, Tommy, are a hitman. That is your job and you can't organise a simple thing for me. Silva is under witness protection. He turned evidence against me and the other families. The police need him to put us away and are hiding him until he has served a purpose and then they will drop him. But that will be too late for me. He cannot go into that courtroom and give evidence against us – do you hear me? God only knows what he has spewed to them already!' Paul said, banging the table with his fist.

Tommy looked at Paul's face as it became red with anger. 'We'll sort it boss, I promise. I came to apologise about that family. We're human, we make mistakes!'

Lowering his voice, Paul looked up from under his lashes. 'Those human mistakes you talk about, come back to me. Everyone knows I want Alex Silva out of the picture, so any mistakes that *you* make come back to me. I wish it was you they were looking for because Alex would have found you and buried you by now. If nothing else, that slimy bastard was a professional.'

Squirming in his seat, Tommy looked down at the table. He'd known this wasn't going to be an easy visit. Someone had to tell Paul that the family that had been assassinated wasn't Alex Silva's. It was a misjudgement – a tragedy – but where the fuck was Alex Silva? He'd disappeared into thin air.

Paul's voice was almost a whisper and he seemed to have composed himself again. 'Somebody knows where he is Tommy and he can't hide forever. This case has been going on for over a year while they gather more evidence against us. They have shut down my brothels, my drug business has been busted; do you know how much money I am losing every day that I am in here? Thankfully, I have partners on the outside who are looking after my affairs. But that means I am relying on motherfuckers like you to get me out. Shit, they may as well throw away the key.' Paul sat back in his chair and sighed, rubbing his hand through his hair.

'Boss, you own the streets, you have people out there, but no one has come up with anything.' Tommy felt he was pleading his case too much, but he desperately wanted Paul to see reason.

'He killed my brother. For that alone I want him dead. He waited while he got out of his car, shot him in the head, and then pulled his pants down, cut off his balls. He told the police that it was at my orders. Some police think my brother had it coming, but, for fuck's sake, it was in broad daylight and there isn't one witness against him. I want justice, not only for myself, but for my brother.' Paul hit the table with his fist again.

'Yeah, but didn't your brother...' Realising that his mouth had run away with him, Tommy stopped short. He could have bitten his tongue off.

'Didn't my brother what? Finish your sentence, Tommy. You've obviously heard the lying rumours. Say what's on your mind.'

Almost trembling with fear, Tommy put his hand on his leg to stop his knees from shaking. He didn't want to speak, but didn't want to incur any more of Paul's wrath. 'Some people say...' Tommy swallowed hard and moistening his dry lips, he knew he had to finish the sentence. Paul sat there stony-faced, staring at him. 'Some people say that your brother tried raping Alex's wife... although, I know that's rubbish. But people like to make up stories, don't they.'

'Yes and some people like to repeat them.' Glaring at Tommy, Paul pushed his chair back, sending it screeching across the floor. He stood and walked towards the door at the end of the room and knocked on it. Instantly the guards opened it to let Paul out. Tommy sat in the empty room staring at the door, in case Paul came back in. Rubbing his face with his hands, he took a huge breath. His heart was pounding in his chest and he couldn't wait to get out of this miserable place.

'Everything okay?' one of the guards asked as Tommy stood up to leave.

'Yes, everything's fine thanks. Now get me out of here.'

'Here, have one of these, you look like you need one.' The guard took out a packet of cigarettes from his jacket pocket and handed Tommy his lighter. Taking it, Tommy smiled. 'Thanks, I left mine in the car.' Inhaling on the cigarette, Tommy could feel his nerves settling. He felt better already.

'Come on, let's go,' the guard instructed as he marched Tommy out of the room.

The guard's eyes started watering slightly, and Tommy suddenly complained of feeling dizzy and asked to sit down, but the guard ignored him and walked him towards the exit, and almost threw him out of the door. Once out into the open air, Tommy staggered and leaned against the wall as he tried to fill his lungs with clean air, while tossing his cigarette butt aside on the pavement. Feeling sick and disorientated, he looked towards the car park for his car. Feeling pain in his chest and finding it hard to breathe, he was tempted to bang on the door of the prison again to seek help from the guards. It felt like he was having a heart attack. Unable to think straight, he swayed back and forth as he walked towards his car. His head spun and he felt woozy and his instinct was to try and get to the hospital. Through his clouded brain, he knew he was having a heart attack or possibly a stroke, possibly brought on by the stress of seeing Paul. Paul's anger had frightened him, and he knew what he was capable of, even though he was inside prison. With his mind in turmoil, he considered he might even be having a panic attack, but the pain was too severe for that. He needed to get help, but his mind was a blur, his eyes felt heavy and he almost fell inside the car as he opened it, his head falling backwards onto the headrest as he let out a laboured breath. Blinking hard to stay awake, he started up the car, gripped his chest and breathed heavily.

Turning towards the passenger seat, he noticed his packet of cigarettes that he had left in the car. His mind wandered back to his meeting with Paul. Suddenly, as clear as day, he thought about the cigarette he had been given by the prison warder. It was rumoured that Paul used cyanide and often boasted about it to his friends and family and joked about not eating anything he'd cooked. Through his haze, Tommy realised what was happening to him. Since when did prison warders hand out cigarettes? Stupidly, he cursed himself for accepting it. Tommy knew he was dying; he didn't have long. Sweat poured down his face and behind the blur of confusion, he knew he had to get to a nearby hospital. As he put his foot on the accelerator, the last thing Tommy heard was the sound of a crash as he hit another car and his head fell forward against the steering wheel. His lifeless body was slumped forward, with blood running down his head and face.

Paul was in the prison corridor where the telephones were situated. Making a call, he looked at his watch and then spoke. 'Tommy came today. He won't be coming back. He implied my brother was a rapist. I leave this urgent matter in your hands now.' With that, Paul ended the call. Turning towards the prison guard, he held out his hand. 'Nice work Mr Barrow, you learn fast.'

The guard handed him the packet of cigarettes containing cyanide. Paul liked cyanide, it couldn't be easily detected, and it worked swiftly. It had become a code between himself and this warder. Paul always carried his own cigarettes, but when he asked Barrow to fetch them for him, they both knew it was his 'special packet' for his enemies. Paul looked at Barrow with distaste, but he came in handy. He was greedy, like all other men he had known. Still, Paul thought to himself, at least his wine and his own food was smuggled in by this man, so he served his purpose. Maybe one day he would be sharing one of his special cigarettes. After all, he didn't want this warder finding a conscience and loosening his tongue to the authorities.

Paul smiled. 'Check your account, I've made sure you've got your money.'

The guard looked at him and nodded. 'I have to see you back to your cell now Mr Pereira, is that okay?'

'Sure thing, let's go. Did my red wine get delivered today?'

Nervously, the guard answered. 'Yes Mr Pereira, everything is waiting for you in your room.'

Satisfied, Paul followed him back to his cell. Anyone could be bought, Paul thought to himself. No one was above the law and sooner or later, someone would tell him where to find Alex Silva. He picked up a glass of red wine that had already been poured for him and rose it in a toast. 'Rest in peace Tommy.' Then he took a huge gulp.

'Barrow. The governor wants to see you.' The young prison guard stood before his senior. Frowning, Barrow looked at him quizzically. 'Did he say why?'

'No sir, he just sent word that he would like to see you in his office.' Once the young guard had delivered his message, he walked away, and Barrow's mind swam with all kinds of thoughts. He knew some of the other senior warders knew that he paid special attention to the needs of Mr Pereira. Most guards had their favourites, and Mr Pereira was a very generous man. Barrow just hoped that this hadn't come to the governor's attention.

Barrow walked along the landing until he eventually stood outside of the governor's office. Straightening his tie and rubbing imaginary fluff from his jacket, he stood upright and knocked on the door. His mouth felt dry as he swallowed hard, not knowing what to expect.

The governor was sat at his desk with two policemen stood at either side of him. 'You wanted me, sir?' Barrow was doing his best to keep his voice calm and steady.

'Indeed, Mr Barrow. It seems there has been an accident outside the prison in the car park. A man is dead. He was visiting prisoner Pereira, a despicable man.' The governor scoffed. 'I believe you were there during his visit. Did you notice that he didn't feel well or anything? Apparently, it looks like he's had a heart attack in his car and then crashed it. I wondered if you could shed any light on it?'

Looking at the policemen, Barrow felt on safer ground. 'Well, sir, he did visit prisoner Pereira.' He looked around the room as though deep in thought. 'And he did say he felt a little warm, but he didn't want any water or anything and then he left. There was no heated conversation or anything, if that's what you mean. All seemed well.' His mouth felt dry, and he licked his lips, waiting for the next line of investigation.

'There you have it, gentlemen. We know nothing, apart from the fact that he visited a prisoner and left in one piece.' The governor looked towards each of the police officers.

'The problem is, Mr Barrow, it seems there were a few passports in his glove compartment under different names. We've checked which name he signed the register with and the visiting order that was sent out to him, but have you ever seen this man before?'

'No, sir.'

The police officer nodded. 'Mr Barrow, would you make a statement about the visit? How the man looked and what they talked about? I presume you were in earshot of their conversation?' The policeman stared at him suspiciously. Barrow looked like a scared cat, desperate to get out of the office.

'Of course I will sir, but, as I say, there is nothing to tell. The man in question visited prisoner Pereira. All seemed well and then he left. I know nothing about passports or anything else.'

The governor nodded. 'You can go now, Mr Barrow. If I need to speak to you again, I will send for you.' As an afterthought, the governor looked towards the policemen. 'That is, unless, you want Mr Barrow to go with you now to the police station to make a statement?'

'That won't be necessary at the moment, but, if we need to, we will be in touch. Although, maybe we could speak to Mr Pereira. He knew the man who died. Perhaps he can tell us who he really was and why someone would have so many different passports in different names. I would say Pereira knew him very well. He was probably one of his men.'

'Do you want him brought up now to speak to him? Mr Barrow could fetch him for you.'

One police officer shook his head. 'No, that won't be necessary yet. We need to look into this first. I am sure this man's fingerprints are on our system somewhere, whoever he is.'

Taking his leave, Barrow turned and left the office. He was glad to be out of there and he rubbed his finger along his shirt collar which seemed tighter than normal. His hands felt sweaty, but he knew his first port of call would be Mr Pereira to inform him about the police investigation.

The last thing he wanted was for all of this to blow up in his face and for him to end up in prison himself, sharing yard space with some of the people that hated him the most. He'd heard stories of how prisoners had treated coppers and other guards in prison and they'd made his blood run cold.

Inwardly he cursed himself; how quickly he had been drawn into Pereira's scams. Especially the cigarettes. Paul had told him about his lethal cigarettes, and should he ever ask for them, Barrow was to bring the cyanide tipped cigarettes and offer one to whoever Paul instructed. Again, he cursed himself. Paul had never handed one of his lethal cigarettes out himself, it had always been Barrow. He had murdered them, not Paul. His hands felt sticky, and he flexed them as he hastily walked up the stairs and along the landing towards Paul's cell.

Barrow's mind was in turmoil when he realised how stupid he had been without even realising it. There was no turning back now; he knew that he was in way too deep. And now there was this investigation into the man's death. He could only hope that it would blow over quickly.

Hopefully Paul might have the answers to his concerns. He seemed to have an answer for everything. Standing outside of Paul's cell, he found himself knocking and coughing before he entered. His heart was pounding, but he needed reassurance.

Paul was lounging on his bed with his arms behind his head, watching television. Although he looked up, he said nothing, not even turning the television down.

'Mr Pereira, I've just come back from the governor's office. It seems your visitor is dead and the police are making enquiries about him.' Pausing, he waited for Paul to make a comment, but none came. 'It seems the police found a lot of different passports in his car.' Giving a nervous laugh, Barrow looked at Paul who was still ignoring him and continued staring at the television. 'It seems he had a lot of pseudonyms and he died in our car park. It's a shame it wasn't somewhere else.' Again, he laughed nervously, and shifted from one foot to the other.

For the first time, Paul looked up. Nonchalantly he plumped his pillow. 'Why are you telling me this Barrow?'

'Well, he was your visitor. They will be asking you questions. And they'll be asking me.' Looking at Paul's face questioningly, he waited. There was a silent, nervous tension in the room. 'What should I say?' Swallowing hard, Barrow felt the sweat on his brow and took off his cap to wipe it.

'You have had enough money out of me Barrow to come up with something – that's your job. Of course, if you feel your world is crashing around your feet, you can always take a break and have a cigarette.' The smug smile that crossed Paul's face sickened Barrow. 'Now, if you don't mind, I want to watch the end of my series.' Picking up the remote control, Paul turned the volume up a little louder. Accepting his dismissal, Barrow walked out.

Walking along the landing aimlessly, he realised Paul wasn't going to help him. As far as he was concerned, he'd been paid his money and whatever happened to him was his problem. Barrow knew he was doomed if the police dug a little deeper and found he had been taking money from Paul and doing him favours. It all seemed such a mess now.

'Are you okay Mr Barrow?'

He looked up. Seeing the young guard before him, he tried to sound more casual than he felt. 'I'm good, lad, I like it up here on the top landing. It gives you a better overview.' Nonchalantly, he rested his elbows on the metal rail of the balcony and looked over. 'Come here.' He beckoned the young guard over. 'Look at all these men; every day is the same for them. No sooner will they leave than they will be caught doing something again and be right back inside. Some of these men find life on the inside easier. They have been institutionalised for so long they don't know how to survive on the outside. Three meals a day, no rent, no council tax and they don't have to apply for benefits. They do education courses to pass the time, but they will never get a job on the outside once employers find out they have been in prison. Would you let one of these prisoners be the manager of your bank?' Laughing slightly to make light of the situation, he slapped the young guard on the back. 'They talk a lot about equal rights and this diversity business son, but does it really exist, or do people just agree to what people want to hear?'

The young warder looked at Mr Barrow who seemed to be rambling. His face was ashen and he didn't look well. 'I'd like to think everyone deserves a second chance sir.'

'That's because you're young and starting out. When you have been in this game as long as me you will feel the same. Go about your business sonny, everything is fine.'

Barrow just wished he could believe it was.

8

LIVING WITH THE PAST

Putting the telephone down, Maggie squealed with excitement and turned to Alex who was standing behind her listening in. 'Did you hear that, Alex? That was the brewery.' She beamed. 'We're actually making a profit, especially on the carvery. Oh my God, I am so pleased.' Stamping her feet and clapping her hands together, Maggie did a jig.

Alex smiled. Maggie was beautiful and seeing her this way touched his heart. She was beaming with happiness; she loved the pub and the neighbours, and the kids were happy in school. This was normal family living, and they were all happy and that was what mattered – wasn't it?

He laughed and reaching forward, he kissed her gently. 'I knew you'd be a superstar, Maggie. This is your world. Your hard work. You have turned a sow's ear into a silk purse. The pub has its regulars, and they love you, even Pauline and Phyllis. The chef makes amazing food, and I'm not surprised you're making a profit.'

'You're amazing, too Alex. All the regulars love you and your playful banter, and I don't think Mark has ever had a real friend before. By the looks of it, all the people that hang around him always have an ulterior motive. You know Alex, you're the only person who hasn't asked him for anything and I think that means a lot to him.'

'He likes holding court, Maggie. But he's a gentle giant really and Olivia rules him with a rod of iron.'

'She's just feeling insecure because she's going through premature menopause apparently. That's why she hardly lets him out of her sight. If some woman smiles at him, she's jealous and he's in the dog house until he convinces her that she is the only woman for him.'

'And have you smiled at him to make her jealous?' Alex smiled.

'Good God, no! Well, not in that way. He's not my cup of tea at all. You're my cup of tea and my coffee and after last night's little performance you're my drinking well, too.'

Raising his eyebrows, Alex smiled. 'Little performance?'

Playfully, she punched him in the arm. 'Oh, you know what I mean. Go and wash your car.'

'Car? It's a clapped-out old banger. It's what old ladies drive, but the police don't want me driving something more noticeable.' He swept his hands through his dark hair and rolled his eyes. 'Sometimes I miss the old days, Maggie. The cars, the money and the lifestyle. Sometimes I feel I have totally fucked up and taken you with me. I'm surprised you've stuck it out this long.'

'Don't be silly.' Putting a hand on either side of his face, she looked deeply into his dark eyes. 'We've done the right thing. Living that kind of life only has one ending. I know it's boring in comparison Alex, and not what you're used to, but this is us now. Our new lives together. Sooner or later, this will all be over with and we can concentrate on just being ourselves, living in the suburbs like boring people. Not sleeping with a gun under your pillow or the police stood there with a warrant searching the house. This is how normal people live Alex. You're amazing and brave.

Our pub is amazing with its amazing staff and food. What more could we ask for?'

'Well, you could have mentioned your amazing kids.' Standing at the top of the stairs with her arms folded, Deana started stomping down each step before pushing them out of the way sulkily.

'We love you too. You're amazing Deana, especially if you help me wash that heap of junk they call a car!' Alex shouted after her. Waiting for her usual response, he saw her turn and stick her finger in the air at him. 'I take it that is a no then!' He grinned.

'Mark has a pressure washer, use that.' Alex and Maggie looked up the stairs and saw Dante walking down them. 'He's always out there either with his head stuck under the bonnet or washing that camper van. Have you seen his camper van?'

'Christ, you two are like cockroaches just coming out of the woodwork. Where are you going?'

'Me and George are going to watch Pete cut that nurse's grass. It's really funny, because he hasn't sussed out she already has a lawn mower yet. Although he must know she has because her grass is so short.'

'And your life is so sad, that you're going to watch him?' Alex shook his head in disbelief.

'Oh no Dad, you have to see this. He has just bought a wireless lawn mower that he has to keep charging up. So, he does a small patch and then the battery runs out, so he goes back to his own house and plugs in the charger. That nurse says hello and then goes back into her house and shuts the back door on him. Last week it took two days for him to cut her grass because the battery needed charging.' Dante couldn't contain himself and burst out with laughter. 'If you want fun Dad, come and see Pete try and charm her. She knows what he's up to and takes full advantage of it. Last week he knocked on her door with a bowl of ice cream and half a bottle of sherry. He asked if she needed company. She said no, she was busy but took the bowl of ice cream.' Again Dante burst out laughing.

Frowning, Alex turned to Maggie and then back at Dante. 'Is it just me but who takes a half bottle of sherry to a woman's house hoping to get into her knickers?'

'Well, Pete obviously does.' Maggie laughed. 'Poor bugger, he's lonely since his wife died last Christmas Day. He must have been devastated.'

'His wife died on Christmas Day?' Alex's jaw dropped. Although he had kept a close eye on the neighbourhood, he'd obviously missed some things.

Phyllis arrived and took off her coat. 'That's right, selfish bastard he is. Couldn't believe it when I heard it.'

Alex rubbed his dark stubble. 'Do you want to extend the conversation a little Phyllis? Why does his wife dying on Christmas Day make him a selfish bastard?'

'Because he ate his dinner first before calling the ambulance – did you know that? She'd cooked the turkey and everything and then just collapsed and died on the kitchen floor. Pete was upstairs and when he came down and saw that she was already dead, he didn't want to waste good food so ate his Christmas dinner first. I know this because he went to Olivia's for some gravy. It was Olivia who called the ambulance while he sat at the kitchen table eating his turkey. He told her there was no point in rushing because she was already dead and the ambulance would be busy, especially on Christmas Day. Can you believe it!' Phyllis almost shouted with disgust.

Shocked, Maggie stood there with her jaw open, while Alex wanted to burst out laughing. He saw the funny side of it, but now was not the time to point that out.

'Oh my God, that's awful Phyllis. Was he sure she was dead?

What if she wasn't and he could have saved her?' asked Maggie, astonished and shocked at Pete's dark side. He was such an amiable man; but this, this was too much.

'Oh yes, we'd all expected it for some time. She was an alcoholic and on borrowed time anyway, but that's not the point is it?' Standing there with her arms folded, huge Phyllis almost towered over them all, apart from Alex. Her face was set in stone. 'Since then, he's been chasing anyone in a skirt.'

'Well, how did you escape his seduction techniques Phyllis? You're a hard woman to ignore.' Alex grinned and winked at Dante.

'I moved!' she shouted as she walked into the kitchen and switched the kettle on.

Alex, Maggie and Dante burst into an uproar of laughter. The whole story was bizarre, and no one would ever believe it, but coming from Phyllis they knew it was the truth. She never made jokes.

Maggie winked at Phyllis who was now handing each of them a cup of coffee. 'Right, I can smell the cooking, it's time me and Pauline sorted out that bar and opened up. There are a lot of bookings for the restaurant today which means they'll be spending time at the bar drinking.' Taking her mug with her, she walked into the bar, leaving the three of them alone.

'I'm going to call for George and watch Pete,' shouted Dante as he ran out of the door.

'And I'm going to wash my car Maggie, so that you can actually see the number plate. Somebody wrote "wash me" on the back of it, so I am taking the hint. Where has Deana run off to?' Taking a sip of his coffee, he waited.

'Where she usually goes... Wendy's from college, although I do believe Wendy has an older brother and I feel that could be the attraction.' Seeing Alex's face drop, she laughed. 'Oh my God, don't scowl like that, no wonder she hasn't mentioned it. She is still Daddy's little girl.'

'How much older is he? What does he want with a young girl? She's only sixteen.'

'Oh, I think he's about eighteen and just for the record he has a girlfriend, but that doesn't stop Deana window shopping, does it?'

A smile spread across Alex's face. 'I suppose not. I'll take my coffee with me. See you later.' Giving her a peck on the cheek, Alex walked out of the door, although it bothered him that his family was growing up fast and he hadn't realised it. He knew they were all young adults now. Time was the one thing you couldn't stop and he hadn't spent enough of it with his family in the past. In some ways he felt envious of Mark. He seemed to have it all. He had spent every waking day with his son. He had all his friends nearby and didn't venture far from the community. He seemed to have plenty of money, even though Alex had never seen that mobile mechanic van move more than ten inches from his drive. Maggie was right, he decided, these were normal people with normal lives, well, kind of.

'Hey Syl... I mean, Alex!' Mark blushed. 'How's it going?' Wearing his usual vest, jeans and worker boots, Mark wandered over. His hands were covered in oil and as usual he was wiping them with an oily rag. Alex wondered if Mark actually possessed a shirt.

'What did you call me?' Alex asked.

'Syl,' Mark laughed. 'That's what her indoors calls you. She thinks you look like Sylvester Stallone.'

'Is that before or after he gets beaten up in the boxing ring?' Alex laughed, smiling at the compliment.

'I don't think it matters, but that's what they all call you behind your back.'

'Oh yeah, well, it's better than some I've had. What's your nickname?'

'What do you mean, apart from loud, fat bastard who's useless at fixing cars? No idea mate. I don't think I want to know. You going to wash that car of yours? Be careful; once you take the dirt off it might fall apart. The dirt is the only thing holding it together. I'm selling that Range Rover down my drive if you're interested.'

Alex knew the Range Rover he was talking about and he knew it didn't work. For days he'd seen Mark under the bonnet trying to get it started. It was falling apart and even the tyres weren't the right ones for the car. Even if Alex wanted to, he knew the police would never allow him to register it. 'Nah, I like my old rust bucket, it suits me,' he lied. Alex winced inside as he remembered his old red, E-type jaguar. Now that was a car.

'Tell you what though, if it helps. Some people pay me instead of their car insurance. As a mechanic I'm insured to drive a lot of cars. If the insurance money is a problem I can do it for around five hundred pounds if you're interested?' Alex couldn't believe his ears. People actually went through his insurance to save paying a proper company? Shit! he thought to himself. Are there any more surprises in this neighbourhood? Maggie is deluded that these are normal people living boring lives, he mused. Maybe that's because she wants to be.

'I'll think about it Mark, thanks, but I doubt this old heap is worth five hundred pounds.' Mark was now looking at the Polish woman's house, totally oblivious to what Alex was saying.

'Do you remember Magda throwing a wobbly over her electric bill the other day?'

Recalling the hysterics, Alex nodded. 'Sure, it was a mix up or something, wasn't it? Didn't she owe thousands of pounds?' Alex recalled Magda waving her electricity bill in the air before them.

'Yeah, well, Percy's meter is going backwards and he's had a cheque for a refund. They're sending someone out to take a look, but in the meantime, Percy comes to my house saying he doesn't have a bank account and would I take the cheque and I give him the cash. Can you imagine someone who doesn't have a bank account?' Amazed at the prospect, Mark scratched his shaved head.

'How does he get his pension then?' Knowing what he knew about Percy, the lack of bank account intrigued Alex. Most informers were paid one way or another, so how come Percy didn't have a bank account?

'Who cares? I charged him for exchanging his cheque though,' Mark laughed, then furtively looked up and down the road and then scratched his head again. 'I think it's got something to do with the Liverpudlians; have you seen them? Flash cars, Rolexes. Real bruisers,' he whispered. 'But why on earth would they mix with Percy?'

Before Alex could answer, Mark walked down the side of his driveway to his back garden before reappearing with his infamous power washer. Winking at Alex, he started it up and handed him the hose. The noise was almost deafening, and Alex looked down at himself and saw that he was soaking wet as the water gushed out at full speed.

Mark stood closer to him while he sprayed his car. 'That's better. No one can hear us now. The Liverpudlians are gypsies, although now they are known as travellers or something. Into drugs and stuff, really hot stuff by all accounts. Percy works for them. Not sure what he's doing for them, but they are using him good and proper – weird really. Keep an eye on Percy, he's a dark horse. Not as stupid as he makes out.'

Alex remembered he had noticed a 'flash car' as Mark described it, cruising around the neighbourhood. It had stood out like a sore thumb and had immediately raised his suspicions. He remembered that car from somewhere but couldn't place it. From then on, he'd looked for it daily, expecting the knock on the door from his enemies. But something nagged his mind about that car and now Mark had mentioned the Liverpudlians... Yes, he knew these men. In a roundabout way, he'd had dealings with them. They were drug dealers, Mark was right about that, and trying hard to think back, as Mark talked on, Alex vaguely remembered having to go to Liverpool once to collect money that was owed by these men. They had owed two hundred grand and it had been Alex's job to collect it or shoot the boss and teach them a lesson if they didn't pay. When he had arrived, it was that car that had been parked outside. Now it all came flooding back to him.

There had been a couple of men leaving the building and as he had walked in, he'd seen that the safe door on the wall was ajar. Once he had introduced himself and explained why he was there, there had been a bit of a scuffle and an exchange of insults, including someone calling him a Spanish prick! Alex had realised that he had more or less walked into an ambush and Alex now realised that the tip-off had probably come from Matteo. He didn't have the guts to kill Alex himself, but was more than happy for someone else to do it.

After frisking him and taking his gun from the inside of his leather jacket, they had laid it on the desk before him. Alex had noticed that the leader of the three had two front gold teeth, which had made Alex smile – he'd obviously already had them knocked out by someone. Alex, trained in martial arts, had lashed out at the other men, but had taken a beating. During this, the man with the gold teeth had looked at him like dirt and walked out, leaving his men to finish him off. But Alex had managed to grab his gun and firing it at one of the men, had killed him. The other man had fled, fearing for his own life. Breathing heavily, and with his nose bleeding, Alex had opened the safe door and taken out wads of cash that were owed to him and after firing more shots into the air, he had left the building. And it had been that very car that had started up its engine and attempted to run him over as Alex had run to his own car. Fortunately, Alex had seen it coming and to avoid impact had jumped onto the bonnet, doing a body roll onto the floor as the car drove away.

As Alex thought about that day, his mission now was to see the driver of the car and see if it was the same man with the gold teeth. He had vowed to pay that bastard back one day, and here he was driving down his street.

Above the blast of water while he wrestled with the hose, Alex glanced at Mark and wondered just how much Mark knew about Percy and if he was testing him. 'What has Percy got that they want? He's not exactly a mastermind, is he?'

'Maybe not, but something's going on, that's for sure. Why do they always go to his blue bins and drop off and pick up cardboard? He is touting drugs for them, I'm sure of that.'

Alex looked him square in the face. 'Is that where you get yours from?' He could have bitten his tongue as soon as the comment left his mouth. He didn't want to offend Mark; he'd been a good friend and it was nice to have grown-up male company again.

'Nah Alex, I get mine from my brother-in-law. There is another guy I know but getting hold of him is a pain. You text him, are you working tonight and if he answers he does and if not well, you don't get anything, do you.' Mark laughed. 'Not exactly reliable. Olivia uses speed as part of her slimming routine. Apparently it kills your appetite.' Sweeping away the splashes of spray from his face and head, Mark shrugged. 'I'll fill it full of car cleaner now you've got the shit off it.' Again, Mark walked away, returning minutes later with a bottle of car wash. He proceeded to put it in the power washer. Now, it not only sprayed water, but soapy water and lots of it!

Hearing a noise drown out Mark's chatter, Alex looked up and saw a helicopter above them. Frowning, he watched it hover above the rooftops and then fly away. That had been the second time he had seen it. The previous time had been while Maggie had been asleep the other night, and he'd heard the noise and got out of bed. Just like now, it seemed to hover above them and then disappear.

'That helicopter has been flying around a lot lately. It's bloody noisy and puts me off when me and Olivia are in the midst of passion. The hospital's not far away, so I presume it's one of those air ambulances. It seems to fly off in that direction.' They both looked up at the sky, which was now empty. Again, Alex's curiosity rose. There had been no logo on the side of the helicopter to indicate it was an air ambulance. No, he thought to himself, there was more to this than met the eye. It was none of the emergency services as far as Alex was concerned because it was unmarked. A fleeting thought crossed his mind and he wondered if it was an unmarked police helicopter keeping an eye on him. It was a possibility, but he felt it was a bit over the top. The plot thickened as far as Alex was concerned. There were more mysteries in this place than an Agatha Christie novel, he thought to himself. Only time would tell.

Avoiding Mark's gaze, Alex carried on spraying his car. Alex's cynical side rose to the surface. Was Mark testing him? And if so, what did he want from him? Or was he just a giant idiot, who liked to look as though he was in the know and impress his friends, to make him feel important.

Looking up, Alex saw Deana just about to cross the road. Seeing his wet appearance, she looked him up and down, and walked in a big circle around him. 'I didn't realise it was raining. I'd have taken my coat,' she scoffed, and as per usual, strutted passed them both laughing.

'You have your hands full there Alex. Christ, I've never seen a young girl fight like her before. I was amazed.' Alex stopped pressing the lever on the power washer and turned to Mark. A frown crossed his brows. 'What do you mean fighting? Who was she fighting with?'

'I was driving, and I saw her jumping in the air with karate kicks or something. She looked like a ninja warrior. Didn't she tell you? Oh shit, have I dropped her in it? I thought you'd know.' Mark squirmed, and his face looked troubled.

Brushing it off nonchalantly, Alex smiled. 'Oh yeah course, she took lessons when she was younger. Just another phase kids go through. But why was she fighting in the street?'

'Dunno Alex, but let her know if I ever piss her off, she should give me the chance to apologise first. She is one mad, angry woman!' Mark laughed.

Alex's mind wandered as Mark continued to talk the hind legs off a donkey. He remembered teaching Deana to fight when she was just a young girl, first it was kickboxing, then judo and she had taken to it like a duck to water, even to the point where she had entered tournaments and won. It all seemed a world away now, but obviously Deana had kept it up. He wanted his children to be able to protect themselves, knowing the world he came from. They had to be tough to survive. Dante had taken his lead from Deana, but he preferred boxing to Deana's high kicks, although you wouldn't think it to look at him. Most people described Dante as geeky, with a shy persona and horn-rimmed glasses. It was a good disguise for what was inside.

Alex still worked out, too. He knew there would be trouble to come, and he wanted to be in shape and ready for it. Letting his mind roam into the past, he saw himself in his sharp suits alongside Paul Pereira and the other mafia families. His gut feeling told him that it wouldn't be too long before Paul and his spies would track him down. He'd given the police enough information about gangsters they already knew about, and police inspectors that were on the payroll. Sooner or later the police would have enough ammunition to walk into the courtroom and imprison them all for a very long time and the last name they would all remember would be Silva. Half of him wanted it over and done with, even if that meant they shot him. He thought about how happy Maggie was these days. At least if he was dead, she could carry on – hopefully. There were no guarantees though.

He loved seeing her happy, but they had been moved around a lot lately for their own safety and her getting so attached to this place unnerved him. How would she feel if the detectives that looked after them suddenly turned up and said they had to move again? Maggie was busy making a home for them here and he hated the idea of them leaving like thieves in the night, in the back of an unmarked police car to God knew where. It would break her heart and she would finally resent and hate him and that was the one thing he feared most of all. She was his heart and soul; his reason for turning on his fellow criminals. Losing Maggie would break him. He hadn't wanted to get attached to this place or the people, but strangely enough fate had stepped in and he'd been swamped with friends. Sighing to himself, he knew they wouldn't be friends for long once they found out he'd been lying to them and just what kind of a man he was.

'Hey Alex, wake up mate, you're miles away. You've nearly washed the colour off that car of yours and I've got a water meter. You need a drink?' Playfully, Mark slapped him on the back and went inside his house with the intention of appearing again with a couple of bottles of beer.

Shrugging, Alex looked at the now dripping car. 'Wing it Silva, you always have in the past. Don't stop now...' he said to himself.

9

UNRAVELLED MYSTERY

While the restaurant and its waitresses, including Deana, were running around with plates of food, and the eighties music in the bar blared out, Alex had felt stifled by it all. This wasn't his life, this was someone else's life he was living and to be honest, sometimes it bored him. He missed the excitement of his former life; the buzz and adrenalin that had soared through him while he was on a job had made him feel alive. Mr Suburbia, he was not. He wasn't a chameleon like Maggie and found it hard to adapt, although he was giving it his best shot.

Leaving everyone behind, he had walked into the dark December frosty night. Looking up, he saw the sky was clear, but the icy breeze made him shiver. Sometimes he liked being alone and letting his mind catch up with the things that ran around it. Avoiding the beer garden, which was usually full of people smoking, he walked closer to the pavement and lit a cigarette. Looking up he noticed a silver BMW driving slowly before stopping and flashing its headlights. Turning his head, Alex noticed a larger vehicle coming from the opposite direction. He couldn't help himself; call it habit, or stupidity, he walked across the road where the BMW was parked, and knocked on the window. Seeing the confused look on the face of the middle-aged man driving it, Alex waited while the electric window was wound down.

'If you're doing a drugs drop, you're way too obvious,' Alex remarked.

'And what would you know? You're the publican bloke that just moved in aren't you?'

Alex smiled at the scouse accent. Considering the expensive suit this man was wearing and his very groomed experience you would expect him to speak more eloquently. 'I am, but whatever your drop-off is, it's not good.'

'What the fuck has it got to do with you? I don't see anyone else butting their nose in my business. Do me a favour mate – fuck off.'

'I will.' Alex grinned. 'If you tell me how you have wired up Percy's electric meter to the neighbour's. Because that is what you've done, isn't it?' It hadn't taken long for Alex to work out that someone was using Magda's electricity and that was why her bill was so high. It was an old trick, but it did come with consequences. In the short term you could get away with it, but you eventually got found out if you were too greedy.

Alex looked up at the night sky. 'It's a clear night tonight mate, and whatever it is that you're lighting up and keeping warm in old Percy's house can easily be spotted. Just a tip.' Inhaling on his cigarette, Alex stood up, away from the window, and started to cross the road towards the pub. Hearing the car start up and feeling its headlights behind him, he moved aside thinking the driver was going to run him over, but instead it stopped beside him, and the driver leaned his head out of the door. 'Who are you mister?'

Turning his head and holding his hand up to his eyes to stop the glare of the car's headlights, Alex laughed. 'You know who I am, you've just told me. Have a nice evening.' Flicking his cigarette to the pavement, Alex walked back to the pub. Alex congratulated himself on his calmness. He was right, as soon as the driver of the car spoke to him, he saw his gold teeth. What a small world, he thought to himself. The man had shown no sign that he recognised or remembered Alex even though he had attempted to run him over and have him beaten up. Now, Alex thought to himself with a grin, this was his chance to turn the tables and surprise this would-be small gangster. Vengeance was always best served cold!

Inside the pub, he saw poor old Dante had been roped in to help wipe tables. Cocking his head to one side and catching Dante's eye, Alex grinned and saw the exasperated look on his son's face.

Alex looked around and instinctively knew that something was missing. He scanned the busy pub again, and realised Percy was missing, which was unusual, considering he usually did a bit of glass collecting for a few beers and a free meal. Maggie also gave him a few quid for his help, but tonight Alex couldn't see him anywhere. Why wasn't he there claiming his freebies?

Strolling into the restaurant area, Alex knew something was wrong, but he was missing a piece of the jigsaw. Then he saw Deana rushing past him, her blonde hair pushed back into a pony-tail and her faced flushed as she carried an armful of dirty plates towards the kitchen. 'Deana, wait a minute.'

'A minute, I haven't got a minute. Did you know that Mum and the brewery were doing a "buy one get one half price" night with an alcoholic drink thrown in? Fuck, I'm run off my feet. Poor old Dante is wiping tables as quickly as Mum's filling them again. It wouldn't do you any harm to help!' she snapped.

Relaxing his stance, Alex smiled, flashing a set of white teeth. Putting his hands into his leather jacket pockets, he stood back.

'Now why would I do that, Deana? If I helped you, you would have nothing to complain about. Have you seen Percy?'

Still balancing the gravy-stained plates that were starting to drip slightly as they wobbled, she frowned. 'Percy? He's not here this weekend, is he?'

'What do you mean? I didn't know he went away for dirty weekends.' As he tried to make light of it, Percy's absence intrigued Alex even more.

Thrusting the plates towards him as she heard her name being shouted, she turned around and then back at Alex. 'Look, you take these; they piss me off in the kitchen barking orders. I have to help clear the other tables, and as for Percy, yeah, he's gone to do that night fishing or something. Gone with a friend; he will be away all weekend. Ask Mark, he'll tell you. Apparently, he does it a lot.'

Flustered, Deana marched off towards another row of tables and started gathering plates. Alex took the plates he was holding and walked through the kitchen swing doors and put them on the long metal worktop. Spotting the poor young kitchen apprentices emptying and filling the dishwashers, Alex's mind wandered, and he rolled his eyes to the ceiling in thought. Why were those Liverpudlians at Percy's tonight? If it was a pick-up or a drop-off, as Mark called it, why was another car there and why were they signalling to each other?

Going through the back exit without being seen, Alex walked towards the street again, then stopped short. Parked directly in front of Percy's house on the pavement was a large white van. From where Alex was standing, it blocked Percy's house from sight from his side of the road. You couldn't see it at all.

Back in his younger days, when he had first started breaking into houses, they used to park a van outside the house they were going to burgle. All the vans they used had side sliding doors. This way you blocked anyone's view while you burgled a house and put your booty straight into the side of the van. No one saw you, or the house being burgled. Other times, they had used vans with delivery or plumbing logos on the side. It was easy to get these things printed out and stuck on the side of a van. It sounded simple, but it had worked many times and no one ever saw or suspected a thing. His favourite, Alex smiled to himself, had been using the local council workmen logo. No one took any notice of it. The bigger the large transits were, the more invisible they seemed to be.

Treading carefully, Alex could see there was no one around. It seemed to him that once everyone got home from work, they either spent the night in front of the television or went out for a quick meal to save them cooking and then spent the night in front of the television. It might be Maggie's idea of heaven, but to him it was bloody boring! His past life had been so full and so busy, sometimes he didn't have time to catch his breath but here, he walked, he helped out in the bar and was permanently watched, supposedly for his own good, by the police. He felt confined and felt like breaking out, but there was nowhere to break out to. Now, at last, something had sparked his interest. He knew this kind of work; it was second nature to him.

Walking further up the street away from the pub, he put the collar of his black leather jacket up and put his chin down to try and hide his face. A few yards away, he turned as though walking down the street towards Percy's and was surprised that there was no action. Confused and intrigued, he found himself walking closer to the van and Percy's house. He had been right, the van had a side sliding door, but it was firmly shut. Now he knew something wasn't right; none of this added up. If someone was burgling Percy's or dropping off drugs they would have been gone by now. Standing there he lit a cigarette, knowing that someone would notice him if they were watching. But there was nothing. His mind worked overtime as he walked back to the pub. Even an hour later when he looked out of the window, the van hadn't moved.

'Oh my God Alex, I'm glad that's over,' Maggie sighed as she put the bolt across the pub door. 'Bloody hell, if that was a trial run for the Christmas bookings we have, we're going to need some extra agency staff for the bar and the restaurant. I'm absolutely shattered. Pauline and Phyllis have worked their socks off. I know you laugh, but they are bloody good at their job.'

Alex turned towards the optics and picked up two glasses and got them both a brandy. 'You look like you need one of these; it will help you sleep.'

'I don't need any rocking tonight love, and if you've got any ideas about action down those trousers of yours, you're definitely wrong. I'd probably fall asleep while you were doing it.' She laughed and took a sip of the brandy he held out to her.

'Thanks for that Maggie, it's good to know I keep your interest.' Smiling, Alex walked forward and put his arms around her and held her tight, letting her head rest on his shoulder. He had other things on his mind tonight, so sex was definitely out of the question. 'I love you Maggie, you know that don't you?' he whispered.

'And I love you Alex, my Portuguese prince, but if this is the start of your seduction tactics, don't bother. If you love me, let me sleep,' she laughed.

'Go on, up to bed. I'll switch the lights off here and put those few glasses in the dishwasher. You've done enough. Go on, off to bed woman or I might change my mind and let my Portuguese snake appear!' Slapping her bottom, he let out a huge laugh.

'You're shameless Alex Silva. But thank you, I'll see you up there.'

Finishing his brandy, he did as promised and had a last tidy up around the bar, turning everything off. Checking his watch, he saw that it was only just past midnight. He had an unsettled feeling about tonight, and something inside him told him to check the van out again. He didn't like involving Deana, but she was wily and could be trusted. Walking upstairs he saw that Maggie had gone straight to bed and was already wrapped inside the duvet snoring. Then he walked to Deana's bedroom and without knocking, he opened the door. She was lying on the bed, still clothed with her headphones in. Touching her shoulder, she opened her eyes with a start, shocked look.

'I did knock,' he lied.

'What is it? What's wrong, Dad?' Sitting up, she took out her headphones and waited.

Alex put his finger to his lips and whispered, 'Mum's asleep and I need back-up. Come with me.'

Sliding off the bed, she frowned. 'Are you okay?' she mouthed.

Beckoning her to the bedroom door, he put his finger to his mouth again and instinctively Deana followed him. A hundred things passed through her mind at once. Her first thought was that they had been found and it was going to be some kind of shoot-out. She shivered at the thought and her blood ran cold, but she trusted her father.

Seeing her shiver slightly, Alex looked around and saw her fleecy dressing gown on the back of the door and handed it to her. Tentatively, they crept down the stairs and unlocking the back door, they walked out into the street.

'What's going on, where are we going?' she whispered.

'Percy's. I have a hunch and I need a lookout, are you up for it?'

'He isn't there; why are you going to his rat hole?' Wrapping her dressing gown firmly around her, she followed her father up the street, mentally thanking herself for still being dressed. It looked like it was going to snow and the air was freezing cold.

Following her father as he walked up the street and around the back of Percy's house, she was intrigued. Percy had nothing worth nicking that was for sure, so why was her father coming here in the dead of night in secret?

Deana could hardly see her father, he was dressed all in black, even his hair was black, but she could see he was wearing gloves. Old habits die hard, she thought to herself. Now curiosity had got the better of her so she waited. Her dad tried the door handle and they both turned to each other when the door opened. She could only presume somebody was in there, but they'd come this far and they weren't turning back now.

Once inside, Deana held her nose. 'Fuck,' she whispered, 'this place stinks of BO and dog piss.' They wandered into each downstairs room to check them out, but there was no one around, which made this more intriguing. Maybe Percy had just gone away and not locked the door. After all, who in their right minds would come in here to steal anything!

Deana followed Alex into Percy's bedroom, which made her want to curse even more at the state of it. 'God, do people actually live like this?' she exclaimed. She had forgotten to whisper out of her shock of the smell and the state of the place and Alex glared at her. Percy's bedroom was small and his double bed barely fit the room. Suddenly, Deana grabbed her dad's arm tight. 'What's that?'

They both stood in silence looking at each other. Their only lighting was the streetlight outside as it shone through the bedroom windows. Holding their breaths to listen, both of their hearts were pounding in their chests. And then they heard a low moan. Sharply, Alex looked around, but he couldn't see anything.

Again, they heard the faint, low moan and Alex and Deana followed it, their ears pricked as they waited for the next sound. Alex noticed it was coming from on old wardrobe, which almost looked antique. Opening the door, Alex put his hand inside. There were a few clothes on hangers but nothing else, and then they heard it again. 'It's coming from behind it, Dad.' Alex nodded and looked at the wardrobe. How the hell were they going to move this wooden mountain? To double check, Alex opened the wardrobe fully, well, as best as he could considering the limited space. It was taller than him and moving the old hanging shirts out of the way, he went deeper inside to put his ear to the back of the wardrobe to listen. Confused, neither of them could understand where the noise was coming from. Alex trailed his hand along the back of the wardrobe. There was no back on it! Knocking on the wall behind it, he heard a louder moan and looked back at Deana.

'That's a false wall. No wonder this room is so bloody small. It's been divided. Someone is behind there.' Walking to the side of the wardrobe, Alex knocked on the wall, ignoring the moans. He was right, he thought to himself. Behind this mismatched wallpaper was plasterboard and on the inside of the wardrobe, hidden from sight by Percy's belongings, was the entrance. This had been well thought out. Pulling out Percy's coat hangers, he threw them on the bed. 'Come on, Deana.'

'God no, it could be a dead body Dad.' Deana's eyes widened. She didn't know what was behind there, but her own instincts told her it wasn't good.

'Corpses don't moan. Someone is behind there and by the sound of it they are in pain. Come on, man up!'

Annoyed at being told to man up, she followed her father who seemed to disappear into the back of the wardrobe, then she heard his low whistle. Crouching down, she hurried after him and almost knocked him over with her speed. Shocked, she stood up in amazement and wonder and looked at Alex. 'This is like that book, *The Lion, The Witch and The Wardrobe.* We've just entered another world.' The pair of them looked around the secret room. It was lit up with UV lamps, keeping rows and rows of cannabis plants warm. It was just what Alex had expected, but not to this extent. This was a professional job, not Percy earning a few quid on the side. He was obviously the keeper and the gardener, making sure the plants were watered.

'Did you know this was here, Dad?'

'Yes, and no.' He shrugged and shook his head. 'Strange men in sharp suits and big cars have been hanging around, and that Polish woman's electric meter has been going around at a hundred miles an hour by all accounts. They've wired the electricity to her mains. I had my suspicions but not on this scale.'

Deana walked along the rows of trestle tables holding a host of potted plants. Some were in full bloom, larger than life, others were seedlings. 'It looks like a bloody forest. You never see Alan Titchmarsh planting these on any of his shows.' They heard the moan again and followed the noise to one of the trestle tables holding the plant pots. Alex looked underneath it, then looked up at Deana. 'Give me a hand.'

Clasping her hands over her eyes, she squirmed. 'Is it a dead body?'

'No, it's a live one, you silly cow. I told you corpses don't moan. Now give me a hand to get him out. I'm bloody roasting in here, it's like being on a sunbed.' Sweat had started to pour down both their faces, and Deana wiped her brow with her sleeve. Kneeling down beside her father, she saw a young man who was bleeding and had obviously taken some kind of beating. His knees were up to his chest, and he was bound and gagged. Without disturbing the plants, Alex pulled him out. The young man tried to wriggle away from him in fear, but Alex used his full force until he was out from under the table. Pulling off the brown tape from around his mouth, Alex threatened him. 'Not one word sonny, or this goes back on and you're on your own. I'm sweating to death in this forest.'

The young man nodded and acknowledged Alex as best as he could through swollen slitted eyes. Taking out his Swiss Army knife, Alex cut the ropes that bound him and noticed his clothes were dripping wet with sweat. He could feel his own shirt starting to stick to his back.

'Go back through there Deana, and get some water for him to drink. He's dehydrated. Use whatever you can find; the bathroom is next door.' Alex waited while Deana left.

'Can you stand, son?' Seeing the young man nod, Alex put his hand underneath the man's arm and helped raise him to his feet.

Deana rushed back through with a plastic jug. 'Sorry mate, but it's all I could find.' Deana held the jug to his mouth as he gulped it down.

'Get him some more while I find him somewhere to sit. There is an old stool over there, I bet that's where old Percy the Gardner sits,' Alex scoffed.

'I'll get it.' Deana pulled the stool up for the man to sit down on. 'And I'll get the water now.'

Crouching beside him, while he sat on the stool, Alex looked at the young man. 'We're not the police, unless they wear fluffy pink dressing gowns, and we're not whoever it was that left you here. So, tell me your story son – what is your name?'

'Luke,' the young man blurted out, his eyes wild as he scanned the hole in the wall waiting for Deana. His lips were cracked and swollen, not only from the beating he had taken, but from thirst. Deana struggled through with a washing up bowl full of water and the jug. This time the man had enough strength to pull the jug of water out of her hands and drink it down. Alex scooped his hands into the washing up bowl and poured water over the young man's head to cool him down and bring him to his senses. 'Keep drinking Luke, we'll talk later.'

'No!' Luke shouted. 'They are coming back to finish the job. I know them, they will have either hoped I've already died, or they will finish me off themselves and I will be buried in this hell hole.'

Water spewed from his mouth as he tried to drink and talk at the same time.

'How do you know they are coming back? Did they say so?' A puzzled frown crossed Alex's face.

'Yes, they think I grassed them up – I didn't, I swear,' Luke pleaded. 'I bet it was that old bastard that lives here.'

Knowing that Percy was a police informer, Alex nodded. 'So do I Luke. No need to plead your case with me.'

'They are coming to move the stuff. The police have had a tip-off.'

'You been creaming it off the top, Luke? I take it you're a dealer then?'

'No, I'm a businessman. I see opportunities and use them.'

Instantly, Alex liked the young man. He reminded Alex of himself in his younger days. He was a thief and a scallywag, but he was honest. He made easy money where he could. That was the name of the game and the world he came from.

'I know people who like to buy the stuff and yeah, everyone creams a little bit off the top, it's expected, but I was the last one to pick up from here and they think I've tipped the police off about this garden.' Feeling more himself now, Luke was more coherent for Alex and Deana to understand. 'I've got a gun; I'll shoot the bastards for this.'

Alex gave him a wry grin. 'I bet they've got a bigger one Luke. Do you even know how to shoot a gun?'

'Not really, but it can't be too hard... you just pull the trigger.'

'And if you're lucky enough to hit them, you maim or even kill them and if you miss, you're dead meat,' Alex laughed.

'Who are you two?' Luke asked.

'We're your friends. Friends who have an idea and you're going to get off your arse sharpish and help us with something. You're going to die tonight, Luke.' Seeing the fear in Luke's eyes, Alex reassured him. 'As far as they are concerned, you're going to die. There's a van parked outside – I take it that's what they brought you in?' Alex watched as Luke nodded.

'Well, we're going to fill it full of plants and take them somewhere safe. There will be a police raid tonight. You said yourself, they are coming back, so we had better hurry up. Come on, there is a lot to clear.'

'You do know you're crazy. That bunch don't fuck about mister and this isn't just a bit of weed, there's hundreds of thousands of pounds here. Take a look. Look how many plants there are.' Luke stressed.

'Yup, so get moving. We have a lot to do. I'll go and open the van. Deana, start bringing those plants. Oh, and we'll take a few of those lamps as well.'

Quickly and carefully, Luke loaded the plants into some nearby crates and passed them through the hole in the wall towards Deana and Alex. They had formed a chain gang and it was working brilliantly! Even Alex hadn't realised how many plants there were and they almost filled the van to capacity. There wasn't a soul about in the street, and each house light was turned out. The van blocked them from view and Alex was grateful for that, because he knew a few of the neighbours had cameras. Once Alex saw how full the huge van was, he knew it was time to call it a day. The men it belonged to could come back at any time. Now it was time for Luke's untimely death.

Going into the kitchen, Alex saw that Percy's cooker was a gas one. This was what he had hoped for. Pulling it out slightly so that he could see the pipe, he slightly dislodged it, knowing the gas would escape. All the worst accidents happen in the home, he thought to himself.

Deana and Luke met Alex back at the van and jumped inside. Then Alex slowly started to drive away.

Once they had got to the top of the street and turned on to the main road, Alex nudged Luke and Deana who were squeezed up in the front seats beside him. 'Look who's coming.'

Luke peered out of the windscreen and saw the silver BMW. 'Fuck, we've just made it. Do you think they've recognised the van?'

'Doubt it. It might dawn on them afterwards, but not right now.' Handing Luke his cigarette packet and lighter, Alex smiled and drove on.

10

A NEW ADVENTURE

Pulling up outside a large family house surprised Alex. The area looked a bit glum. This was definitely the dark side of Kent. It was a typical estate with high rise tower block flats, that looked grey and daunting, but in between there were houses. 'Are you living in the flats Luke?' Alex asked.

'No Alex, but the crack den is up there. It doesn't belong to anybody, well it does, but nobody knows who. People just come and go, buy what they want, and they have a safe place to use it, if they want.'

'A squat, in a tower block for druggies. That's predictable.'

'It gets raided every two weeks or so but after that people come back.' Luke half smiled through his swollen face.

Alex took hold of his face and looked at him more closely. 'Your jaw's not broken, but I would say your ribs are by the way you're breathing and holding them. You'll soon be on the mend Luke.' Alex looked out of the window at the four-bedroom house they were parked outside. 'This yours then?'

'It's my mum's, but she's ill and I look after her. She bought it from the council for fourteen grand. It's worth four times that if we ever wanted to sell. She's left it to me, so yeah, I guess it's mine.'

'Nice profit. People pay for postcodes these days.'

'So, what do I do now Alex? You said I was going to die...?'

'Just keep your head down. Look after your mother and do some healing. How are you going to stash all these plants without your mother noticing she lives in Kew Gardens?' Alex laughed.

'There's a basement. She never goes down there. Plus, it's always warm in the house because Mum is always cold, and the heating is always on full. That and the heaters should keep them going.'

'Good luck Luke.' Alex held out his hand to shake his.

'Thanks Alex, erm I mean both of you,' Luke stammered.

Alex yawned. 'Come on then, let's unload this van so I can get home. There will be hell to pay if my wife has turned over in bed and I'm not there.' Alex got out of the van, prompting Deana and Luke to do likewise.

'Just put the plants in the hallway, I can see to them now. You had better get off.'

'Yes, and I need to get rid of this van.'

Letting out a huge sigh, Deana turned towards Alex. 'Does that mean we're walking home?' she asked.

'Part of the way Deana. We'll torch the van. That way, it will get rid of any soil, leaves and fingerprints. Neither you nor Luke are wearing gloves and there is too much evidence to clean up, so yes, in answer to your question, we're walking.'

A mile or so from home, Alex turned into a side road. 'Is this close enough for you? Look, there's the answer to your prayers,' Alex laughed.

'What, where? Are we going to hot-wire a car?' she asked excitedly, not wanting to brave the cold after the warmth of the heater in the van.

'Nope, but someone has left two push bikes over there. We're going to pedal home. That will warm you up. Come on.'

Alex found an old spanner and used it to break the petrol tank. He watched the petrol start to flood out just as Deana came towards him with the bicycles. He held up his hand to stop her. 'That's enough, we'll need to pedal like hell, when this goes up.'

Nodding, Deana waited while he lit a cigarette and threw it on the ground. It burst into flames and led a trail to the main petrol tank. Alex ran towards Deana and they rode the bikes as quickly as they could as they heard and felt the blast of the explosion. They could hear a shattering of glass and see smoke in the air as they turned off the main road towards home. As they turned to each other, the wind blowing through their hair, they both smiled and burst out laughing. Alex had to admit, tonight had been the adrenalin boost he'd needed.

Leaving the bikes at the top of the street, they walked home and carefully opened the door. Everything was in darkness and there was no sound. He was glad of that. Creeping up the stairs, Alex blew Deana a kiss as she entered her bedroom. Once in his own bedroom, he looked at Maggie, who was still fast asleep. Walking towards the window, he noticed Percy's house was still intact. It confused him. He wondered if he had sorted out the gas pipe correctly. Maybe not, he mused to himself. It had been dark, and his visibility had been limited.

Leaving the bedroom, he went into the bathroom and discarded his clothing, leaving his usual T-shirt and boxer shorts on. Creeping into bed, he lay back on his pillow and thought about the evening's events. After everything that had happened, he was shattered and found himself drifting off to sleep.

'Alex! Alex, wake up love!' Bleary eyed, Alex tried to stir as Maggie shook him vigorously. 'For God's sake Alex, wake up!' Maggie shouted in his face. Sitting up with a start, he looked at her.

'Listen, outside there's shouting and police sirens. Have they found us Alex?' Frightened and almost crying, Maggie shook him again. Jumping out of bed, Alex went to the window and looked further up the street. Looking at the clock he saw that it was nearly 5 a.m.; he'd been asleep for a couple of hours, but it only seemed like minutes. Police cars were parked outside Percy's house and police, all geared up in helmets and bullet-proof jackets, were shouting to each other and banging on Percy's door.

'It's Percy's house Maggie. Come and see.' He beckoned. Maggie ran her hands through her hair and jumped out of bed to join him at the window.

'Oh my God, what's going on? Come on, let's go down and see.'

Alex quickly stopped her. 'No, there's a better view here.' His heart was pounding in his chest as he thought about the gas pipe and mentally, he was counting down as he saw the police with battering rams at Percy's door. Everyone in the neighbourhood was coming out and standing at their gates to watch the scene. As Alex predicted, once the police entered the hallway someone must have turned on a light. With one vast explosion, the police officers standing at the door seemed to fly into the air backwards. Alex closed his eyes and winced. Percy's house became an inferno as another blast followed. Alex held up his arms to his face and shouted for Maggie to get down as glass from shattered windows flew into their bedroom. Alex could hear shouts and cries from people outside running up and down the street.

Deana and Dante came running into the bedroom. 'Wait kids, stay there, there's glass everywhere.' Alex bent down to Maggie who was lying face down on the floor. 'Stay there Maggie, don't move. Deana, get me a pair of her shoes, any will do.'

Doing as she was told, Deana brought a pair back and threw them towards Alex. Bending down, he put the shoes on Maggie's feet. 'Take my hands Maggie, close your eyes and stand up. Your hair and nightie are covered in glass and you need to stand up and let it fall,' he instructed. Maggie was shaking, and tears brimmed in her eyes as she held out her hands and let Alex take the weight of her as she stood up, letting the glass fall to her feet. 'Are you two okay? How are the windows in your rooms?' Alex shouted.

'Fine, it was just the noise and the banging. We thought, well...' Dante trailed off. For so long they had been expecting this kind of intrusion into their home and had been living on eggshells for a long time, so no wonder they were all frightened. Out of shock, Maggie burst into tears and so did Dante. Only Deana and Alex stood there staring at each other. They both knew the truth of what had happened.

'You two go downstairs. Maggie, take your nightgown off. If you walk out of here, you'll trail glass everywhere.'

'What about you? You're covered in it.' Her lips trembled as she spoke, and her eyes were red from crying. 'Oh, Alex, I don't know if I can live like this any more. I thought we were doomed.'

Pulling her close to him, Alex held her. The stabbing pain he felt in his heart when he heard her anguished cries was unbearable. He had done this. His whole family lived in fear because of him and his lifestyle. 'I'm sorry. Maybe I should leave. Walk away and not drag you and the kids into this life again. I'm sure those police can arrange it.' Feeling his own tears brimming on his lashes, he sniffed hard to keep them at bay.

Standing back, Maggie looked at him. 'Don't you dare say that. Do you hear me? Never again. We all enjoyed the spoils Alex and now we all take the fallout. Don't leave us. Nothing is worth that. Promise me,' she begged.

'I promise, but I hate seeing you like this. Always looking over your shoulder – afraid of your own shadow.'

'I'm more afraid of you leaving me. I love you.' Wiping her face with her hands, she half smiled and took a piece of glass out of

Alex's hair. 'Glass is going to be hiding in that thick mane of yours for years.' Picking up her brush, Maggie ran it through her long blonde hair and heard the glass fall to the floor. Taking the brush, Alex turned her away from him and brushed it for her – he hadn't realised how long it had grown.

'Have you had your hair dyed?'

'Yes, about two weeks ago! And it's taken an explosion in the street for you to notice.' They both burst out laughing. Suddenly they heard a banging and shouting at the door. Instantly recognising the voice, Alex looked at Maggie and in unison they said, 'Mark!' and burst out laughing again. Alex walked downstairs to open the door.

'Bloody hell mate, don't tell me you slept through that.' Mark was standing in his boxer shorts only, which to Alex's eyes was offensive. Mark's hairy stomach and chest facing him at this time of the morning was enough to bring Alex out of his shock.

The street was already full of fire engines, more police and ambulances. 'Let's hope no one wants the emergency services Mark, because they are all here!' Alex joked. 'What's happened, do we know?'

'Whispers about a gas explosion or something.'

Despite just mentioning a gas explosion, Mark took out his packet of cigarettes, lit one and offered them to Alex who gratefully accepted. 'Is Percy okay?' Alex enquired innocently.

'He's not there the lucky bastard. He's fishing or something. Fuck knows. I think they are going to evacuate the area, which means us living with Olivia's mum and dad. What about you? You can come with us if you want, there's plenty of room,' he offered.

'Well, I don't know about lucky. Old Percy is going to get one hell of a shock when he comes home and finds his house is not there any more! As for the offer, we're okay, thanks. I don't know if the brewery will let us leave the pub – anyone could break in,' Alex lied.

Alex looked up at Percy's house. What had been an inferno was now being dowsed by water from the hoses of the fire brigade. It looked like a charcoaled shell; there wasn't a window left intact and the outside was black with smoke. Alex was pleased about that. Whatever evidence was in there had now gone.

Walking as closely as he was allowed to the scene, Alex saw people sat in the back of the ambulances being treated for cuts and bruises. Some were on oxygen, and some were covered in silver capes being treated for shock. Thankfully, no one was badly hurt. His thoughts turned to the police officers who had entered the building. The blast alone had blown them into the air. Thankfully, they had been wearing helmets which would have protected them. In normal circumstances he would have called it collateral damage, but mentally he cursed himself. They weren't the ones he'd intended to hurt. It had been meant for that Liverpudlian lot who had hurt Luke and had grown cannabis in a false room in Percy's bedroom – not innocent police officers going about their daily work.

Poor Magda next door. Alex felt almost ashamed as he looked at her shattered shell of a house. Hopefully she had insurance, he thought to himself. If nothing else, she was free of Percy and his mates stealing her electricity. It was little compensation, but it made him feel better.

As predicted by Mark, the police came round and said they were to move out for at least twenty-four hours while they made the area safe. They enquired if people had anywhere to go and if not, they would be put up in B&Bs. Olivia and Emma were already on hand coming out with trays of tea for everyone. Maggie had dressed and joined them outside Mark's house, as daylight broke through properly.

'Alex!' Maggie called, waving her arms to attract his attention. He walked across to the neighbours sitting around Mark's front gate on stools and chairs drinking tea. To Alex's mind it was like something out of the Blitz. It was crazy. 'The brewery has called. If possible, they would like us to stay here. They are sending someone straight away to fix the windows and sum up the damage. There is a problem with the phone lines apparently. Is that okay?'

'I presumed as much Maggie. There's a lot of money in there and burglars always find a way in even if they board the place up,' Alex said. He could tell Maggie was relieved that they were staying put.

Deana squared up to Alex while he was on his own. 'Well Dad, you have made your mark on the world – that's for sure. What now? I suppose those protection blokes will come sniffing around, but there shouldn't be any danger to us, should there?'

'No, I think we'll be okay. It's not a revenge attack on us, it's just one of those things. Deana,' Alex faltered, 'thank you for last night. I never got the chance to say before, but thanks,' he whispered.

'That's what families are for. Anyway, it was fun.' She grinned and walked away to join the others. Alex knew he couldn't have accomplished half of what he had last night without her help. She was trusting, strong and loyal.

The street was suddenly deserted. It seemed weird looking at the boarded-up houses and the police taping off the house and the end of the street. The police knew they were staying in the pub and had agreed to keep an eye on them. And, of course, their own team had contacted them and arranged a visit later that day. It was to be expected, but they were always under scrutiny.

Maggie sidled up close to Alex and held his hand. 'Well, that's a lot of money the brewery will lose with no one allowed down the street. It's Christmas in three weeks and we have bookings, what are we going to do?'

Putting his arm around her comfortingly, he looked down the street at Percy's house. Wincing inside, Alex knew this was all his fault. He realised now that he had gone too far. 'Don't go cancelling anything Maggie. Not yet anyway. Believe me, this will last a couple of days at most and will give you a chance to sort out your decorations. The neighbours will get fed up of sofa surfing and start to come home. They have their own Christmases to sort out. The only person really in shit street is old Percy and I'm sure he'll get sorted soon enough.'

'Do you think we should offer him a room here? He's an old man. Who knows if he has any family?'

Shocked at her idea, Alex quickly scuppered it. 'Definitely not Maggie. If we let him stay, we'll never get rid of him. Anyway, I don't think the brewery would let us have lodgers, or the police either. Let the authorities look after Percy, it's for the best,' he reasoned. Personally, he thought Percy had everything that was coming to him. He'd known something was going down this weekend, which was why he'd disappeared.

'Yes, you're right. It was just a thought.'

'That's because, my lovely, you're a kind-hearted woman, which is why I married you.' Kissing her on the top of the head, he pulled her closer.

'Is that all?' She laughed. 'I thought it was because you were fed up with having a "quickie" in my dad's shed after closing time.' They both burst out laughing. Alex thought back to the many times the handlebars of her dad's bicycle had banged his arse, or some other tool had fallen on his head during their frenzied passion. A smile crossed his face when he thought back to those days. Funny, but bloody uncomfortable!

11

PARTNERSHIPS

Almost ten days passed in the blink of an eye. Maggie felt happy again, because Alex had been right. Within two days Mark had drifted back into the neighbourhood and landed on their doorstep complaining about Olivia's mother who was 'a moaning, miserable cow'. He couldn't stand it any more apparently.

Slowly everyone had drifted back into the neighbourhood, and the police had taken down the tape that had cordoned off the area. Percy had been put up in a bed and breakfast for the time being, which he was quite happy about, considering his house and possessions had been blown to bits. He was getting regular meals, and it wasn't costing him anything.

Alex had waited for Percy's return and noticed when Percy had originally come back to the neighbourhood, unaware that there was nothing to return to, that he had no fishing rods with him when he had been dropped off. Musing to himself as he stared out the window, he wanted to laugh but couldn't find it in him.

Deana pulled Alex aside one day. 'Dad, I've got a bit of gossip for you,' she whispered and walked out of the pub. Following her lead, Alex followed her into the beer garden out of earshot.

'I know how they wired up Magda's electricity.' She grinned.

Puzzled and frowning, Alex waited. 'Well?' he prompted.

'Did you know she has a summer house at the bottom of the garden. Well, I say summer house, it's enormous.'

'How could I? I've never been down her garden.' Intrigued, he waited, knowing full well that Deana was pausing for effect.

'It's about twenty foot long and wide and is more like a granny flat. It's all kitted out apparently.' Deana nodded, clearly impressed.

'Deana, do you want to get to the point?'

'I've just mentioned the point and you've missed it. To go that far down her garden with electricity, she had to have a separate mains box put in, leading from the original one. The bastards have wired it up from her garden summer house, that's why no one saw the wiring. And the only person who knew she had a summer house was Percy!'

Alex was amazed. 'That's fucking genius Deana!' he exclaimed. 'Absolutely brilliant. Christ, I wish I'd thought of it,' he laughed. Seeing the angry expression on Deana's face, Alex changed his attitude. 'Is she okay? Her and her daughter, are they both all right?'

'Yeah, her daughter was staying at her dad's. And Magda sometimes works nights at the supermarket shelf filling for extra cash.'

'You're a nosey fucker who's found out a lot from a neighbour we hardly speak to.' He grinned.

Giving him a knowing look, she smiled. 'Maybe I'm more like my father than he realises. Oh, and by the way, I thought I would give you the heads up about Mum's Christmas plans. It's going to be big this year!' she laughed and walked away.

Slowly making his way back into the pub, Alex fought his way through tinsel, Christmas trees and even more lights and decorations. Maggie had gone mad decorating the place, he thought to himself. It was like Santa's grotto, but it had kept her mind busy. Seeing her behind the bar polishing glasses, he walked towards her and nonchalantly enquired about her Christmas plans for the family.

'Oh, I'm glad you asked that Alex, I was going to tell you, but, with one thing and another it went clean out of my head. None of our Christmas bookings have been cancelled; on the contrary, nosey buggers want to come and see what's happened since it was on the news. But I thought when we're finished in the afternoon and the last customer has left, we could have our own Christmas dinner down here in the pub and I've invited all the neighbours and staff. It's a goodwill gesture considering everything that's happened, and Chef is more than happy to pop another couple of turkeys in the oven, especially as he's staying too.' She beamed.

Alex's heart sank. 'Don't they have families they want to be with? Maybe we could throw a party afterwards.' The very idea of it made him squirm inside. He hated big social occasions and the fact that they weren't having Christmas together for the first time in a long time, made him wince. He knew the smile had disappeared from his face, but thankfully Maggie hadn't seemed to notice.

'I've said all are welcome and that includes their immediate families. Phyllis is on her own, so why shouldn't she stay? Pauline was going to her son's but likes the idea of staying here. It saves messing around on Christmas Day getting taxis or her son not being able to have a drink.' Maggie walked over to him and put her arms around his neck, giving him a peck on the lips. 'I knew you would be the Grinch. Which is why I didn't mention it earlier. And do you know the best part, Alex?' She winked.

Alex really couldn't see a 'best part', his mind was already swimming about trying to eat his Christmas dinner with everyone's kids running around the place.

'We are going to provide some bottles of wine and some soft drinks for the kids and after that they have to buy their own. And as we're opening Christmas night they will stay and fill the cash register. Plus, Phyllis and Pauline can work Christmas evening and I've got a couple of agency staff from the brewery to help us out with the bookings. See, I'm not just a pretty face.' She laughed and kissed him again.

'My God, you have it all worked out, don't you, Mrs Business Brain?' Alex had to admit, it was a good idea and she was right. 'You're a devious woman Mrs Silva, I'll grant you that.' Shaking his head with disbelief, he held her tight. She was his heart and soul and he loved her. The very nearness of her caused a stirring within him and if having a big Christmas party dinner made her smile, who was he to complain?

'You can keep that swelling in your trousers firmly away,' she laughed. 'I have things to do. Save it for later.' She winked, pushing him away playfully.

'Is that a promise, Mrs Silva?' The smile spread across Alex's face at the thought of the evening to come.

'Cross my heart,' she said, 'especially if you agree to wear the Christmas jumper I've bought you. There could be added bonuses.'

Alex held up his hands in submission. 'Count me in, your temptress.'

* * *

Within the blink of an eye, Christmas was upon them. The street looked as though nothing terrible had happened and everyone was surprised that things had been done so quickly before the Christmas period. They had even given Percy some kind of government grant so that he could buy bits of furniture from second-hand places and with Olivia and Emma emptying their households of things they supposedly didn't need he was up and running again. Everyone was in high spirits, and even Alex had to admit it was infectious.

Olivia and Emma were sorting out Christmas presents that had to be put under the pub Christmas tree that they would all open after lunch, making a real Christmas occasion of it. Dante had expressed concern, in case any customers pinched any of the growing gaily wrapped parcels, but Alex had assured him they would presume they were just empty boxes wrapped in Christmas paper for effect, which put his mind at rest.

Dante seemed pleased that he would be having his friend George to dinner on Christmas Day, and for the sake of his family happiness, Alex was going to step back and let them have their moment. Maggie had even gone so far as asking the witness protection police if they wanted to join them. When they had declined, she had made a point of buying them presents. They had kept them safe, and as far as she was concerned, they deserved a thanks in return for their hard work.

As always, Alex had gone to a local Catholic church for Christmas eve mass. His mother had always done it when he was a child and he kept up the tradition in memory of her. The family had tagged along, although he'd said they didn't have to, but it was nice to have them there with him. Afterwards, it seemed like they had only had a few hours' sleep when they heard Dante's bedroom door open and slam shut.

'I thought they were grown-ups now and didn't believe in Father Christmas,' yawned Alex. 'Bloody hell, can't anyone have a lie-in?'

'Come on grumpy, it's Christmas morning and it's snowed. If you and your family traditions hadn't kept us up so late, you would have slept longer. Merry Christmas darling.' Maggie cuddled up to Alex and nestled her head in his arms.

'Talking of Christmas, I have something for you. You can sort this while I go and put the kettle on.' Getting out of bed, Alex opened a drawer of the dresser and took out a mobile phone. 'Ring your mother. They can't trace this, no one knows about it. There are different SIM cards in there with different telephone numbers. Get rid of each one after you use it, then your mum can't be tempted to call you back. I know it sounds harsh, but it's for the best. Merry Christmas love.' Seeing the tears well up in her eyes, he knew he had done the right thing. This had made her Christmas.

'Oh, Alex love, I don't know what to say. Mum will say nothing, you know that. Thank you.' She was about to reach out for him, when she heard Dante's excited voice cry out her name. 'The joys of being a parent, Alex. Go on, I'll join you in a minute.'

Alex went to join Deana and Dante as they began opening their presents. For the first time in a long time, they had legal money to spend on their kids. All of Alex's accounts had been emptied because they had been classed as ill-gotten gains and they had been left absolutely penniless which had hurt Alex's pride. But now they ran the pub and had a wage, which gave them the chance to splash out and buy the family some proper new presents.

Dante had already taken off the big red sheet Maggie had put over the electric bicycle they had bought him. He was always unsteadily balancing on the back of George's bike and desperately would have liked one of his own and Maggie had made his wish come true. 'It's just like George's. It's fantastic!' he beamed, while sitting on it in his pyjamas. 'Can I go out and try it out and show George?'

Alex looked out of the window. 'Sure, why not, but don't you want to open the other ones first?'

'In a minute. Help me carry it downstairs. I've not had an electric bike before. They are ace, but heavy,' Dante laughed.

'I know Dante, I carried the bloody thing up.' Alex walked over and ran his hands through Dante's black hair, which resembled his own. 'Don't you want to put some clothes on first? It's snowing.'

Looking down at his clothing, Dante smiled and left the room while Alex carried the bike downstairs and opened the back door, quickly followed by a hastily dressed Dante. Going back upstairs, Alex saw how radiant Maggie looked. She had obviously made her call and it had made her day. As far as she was concerned, Father Christmas really did exist. 'Well, Deana, aren't you going to open any of yours?'

'I'm not a kid any more, I can wait until you're both here,' she scoffed, 'although I do like the look of that slim, long box.' Reaching out for it and ripping off the paper, Alex and Maggie saw the excitement on her face when Deana realised, she had a new laptop. She had moaned for weeks that she had to go to the library to use theirs or stay behind at college to finish essays. Now she had her own and Alex and Maggie knew they had made the right decision coming out of hiding and trying to make a new life for themselves. Things like this made it all worthwhile. Family first, no matter what.

'Here's your jumper Alex. Remember you promised to wear it and wear that frown upside down,' laughed Maggie, handing Alex his present.

'Any other presents under there for me? Such as any bonuses if I wear it?' His dark eyes twinkled naughtily as he winked at her.

'No one gets a bonus until later today, or tonight in your case. So maybe, just maybe, there might be something extra in your stocking.'

'Or in yours love. I prefer my stockings on you.' He grinned, then looked towards Deana, who plainly wasn't listening. She was too busy looking at her laptop.

Maggie laughed. 'Come on, we need to get up and at 'em. Chef's coming earlier than usual, and we need to get sorted out. First sitting for lunch is twelve.'

* * *

Alex couldn't believe his eyes when the army of customers started coming through the doors on Christmas Day. The brewery had sent two agency staff to help them, one for the bar and kitchen, but even then, they were still struggling. So Olivia and Emma rolled up their sleeves and came to the rescue – all in the spirit of Christmas.

'Are you Spanish?' Julia, one of the agency workers, suddenly asked Alex.

'No,' answered Alex swiftly. He felt it was unnecessary for a temp to be so nosey. 'Why, are you prejudiced or something?'

'Oh no,' she blushed, 'it's just the accent, it reminds me of when I was on holiday in Spain. Yours just comes out now and again, doesn't it?'

Not answering her, Alex walked behind the bar and started serving customers. The people that were staying behind for lunch had also come early to have a drink before their dinner.

When the last customer finally left, everyone pushed tables together to enjoy their own Christmas lunch. The chef had left it as a carvery so that everyone could help themselves to whatever vegetables and extras they wanted. The tables were overflowing, and spirits were high as more drinks were poured. Alex had to admit, he was thoroughly enjoying himself. It felt good to be surrounded by neighbours and friends.

Presents were handed around and then they all sat back groaning and loosening their belts. They had eaten and drank more than their fill. The pub looked like a bombsite. Christmas paper, streamers and the remains of pulled crackers were everywhere, not to mention the mountain of plates overflowing with gravy.

'We had better get cleared away,' groaned Maggie. 'Oh my God, I don't think I can move.'

Mark burst out laughing. 'I wouldn't move that quickly; most of the people that are coming in here tonight are already here. Come on you lot, you've had your fun, now it's clean-up time. Get some bin liners Maggie.'

Alex nodded. 'To be fair Maggie, he does have a point. Just unbolt the door and we'll clean as we go.' With the army of people offering, the place was tidy within an hour. No one had come through the door and so Maggie decided to let Phyllis and Pauline go home. 'Go on then, before I change my mind. You have both earned it.' Waving them off, she turned to Alex. 'All in all, I'd say it's been a good Christmas, wouldn't you?'

'Much better than expected. Come on, let's have a drink with the others. No one else seems to be coming in.'

No sooner had Alex opened his mouth and stood at the bar with a very loud, drunk Mark and his pals, than Father Christmas walked through the door.

'You're bloody late!' shouted Mark, nudging his friends, and spilling lager on the carpet.

Alex's suspicions rose, and he felt a sick feeling in the pit of his stomach. This Father Christmas, in his long red coat with a hood firmly over his head almost covering his face, bothered him. Holding a bag over his shoulder, he stood at the bar. 'Orange juice please,' he asked, while ignoring Mark's witty remarks.

Alex rushed behind the bar, stopping Maggie from serving, and poured the customer a drink. 'You go and take the weight off your feet love, you've earned it.'

The customer turned his back towards the others, and, facing Alex, reached up and pulled his hood back slightly.

Alex's eyes widened with shock – it was Luke!

'Meet me in the beer garden.' Luke gulped back his drink, waved to Mark and his crowd who were shouting to him and laughing, and left by the front doors.

Alex sidled up to Maggie. 'Just popping out for a quick cigarette love.' Without waiting for an answer, he walked out the back to the garden. He spotted Luke sat on one of the garden benches.

'What the hell are you doing here?' he whispered angrily.

'Disguised as Father Christmas and bringing your gift,' Luke answered and held out the bag he was holding.

Alex stood there confused, staring at the bag. 'What is it?'

Luke proffered the bag towards him again and put it on the ground. Alex knelt down. Curiosity had got the better of him, but he was cautious. Unzipping it slowly, he looked up at Luke who seemed to be smiling.

Blinking hard to take in what he was looking at, he looked up at Luke again. 'Money?'

'To be more accurate Alex, your money. Your share for now...' Luke stood looking very pleased with himself. 'Great disguise this outfit. There must be a million Santas out there; no one is going to take any notice of one more.'

'My share? What are you talking about Luke? I never expected to see you again.'

Still on his haunches, Alex looked from the bag to Luke again. He could see there was a few thousand pounds in there.

'That is what me and my gardener have made in three weeks. There is eight grand in there. It's your share.' Luke looked almost proud of himself.

'You've made eight thousand pounds out of those plants?'

'No Alex, I've made twenty grand out of a few of those plants. I had to pay the gardener and the drivers who drop it off, but the rest is ours. It's Christmas and people want to be as high as a kite as they party. Supply and demand. We've been rushed off our feet.'

Stunned, Alex stared at him. 'You have made twenty grand in three weeks on weed?'

'Yeah. Like I said, I'm a businessman. I see an opportunity and take it. I've also got a nice sideline too if you are interested in that?'

'Thanks for the offer, but I'm not in any position to get involved. It's good of you Luke, but thanks but no thanks.' About to walk away, Alex stopped and turned back to face Luke. 'What's the sideline?'

A big grin crossed Lukes's face. 'I knew you'd be interested. My sideline is this... I know a couple of old dears and they get all kinds of pills and painkillers. They use half and sell the rest on to me. I've got one old lady, she's been on a cruise. She knows she hasn't got long left and wants to enjoy her life while she can. Cruises have doctors on board and food and she enjoys the company and sunshine. Better than wallowing at home. To be fair Alex, I think she's going to live longer than us with all that vitamin D.' Luke laughed.

Shocked, Alex just stared at him open mouthed. 'You're selling prescription pills?'

'Yes, so what? They get a fair price and they're happy. I'm happy, my customers are happy and everyone's a winner.' Luke shrugged.

Alex couldn't believe what he was hearing.

'When they do eventually die, there is always someone else to take their place. Families are left with cupboards full of pills and they sell them to me.'

Lukes's nonchalance surprised Alex. He couldn't believe his ears. 'Look, I've got a pub full of people pleased with their bubble bath or bike from Santa and now he turns up with eight grand in a bag for me. I must have done more than just sit on his knee. Christ, I must have given him a blow job!'

'You saved my life, Alex. I wouldn't have made any of it without you. I don't know why, but you saved me and dropped me off safely at my house no questions asked. I doubt you ever thought you'd see me again. But whether you like it or not, this is yours. Take it.'

Ideas swum around Alex's brain. If he and his family had to flee in the night, what would they live on? Where would they go?

Maggie was happy with the pub. The police were happy, hoping to get the result in court, to put Paul Pereira behind bars. But what did he get out of it? He had nothing, apart from his freedom and even then, he had been told he might still have to do a few years behind bars. He wanted his family to be financially secure in his absence and fate had lent a hand and Father Christmas had stepped in. Why shouldn't he take it? This was cold hard, untraceable cash. It could never be deposited into a bank, but it would be on hand if ever he needed it in a hurry.

'I can't really leave the pub for periods at a time Luke, so I'd be no good as a partner. I couldn't help you.'

'Why can't you leave?' Luke asked curiously.

'Got a tag on,' Alex lied, 'and no, I'm not raising my trouser leg to show you. I got into a bit of trouble, that's why the pub is in Maggie's name not mine.'

'Fair enough, plenty of my mates wear ankle bracelets,' Luke laughed. 'I think that's a better name for them, don't you?'

Alex's business brain started working. 'Of course you have an alternative option.'

Frowning, Luke shrugged. 'Go on, I'm listening.'

'Sell the rest back to the people who own them. Who are they going to tell?'

'Are you fucking crazy! What am I going to say? Here's your stuff I nicked while you were trying to kill me?'

'Let me think about it. Keep some of the seedlings for your gardener and get him to take some cuttings.' Alex grinned.

'So, does that mean we're partners then?' Luke asked.

Apprehensively, Alex thought about Luke's words. What harm could it do? Alex reasoned. And there was a lot of money at stake. He needed to think about it. Holding out his hand, he picked up the bag and held his other hand out to Luke. 'Partners. Let me work something out about those plants. How do I get hold of you?' Alex was feeling much more relaxed now.

'You know where to find me Alex.' Luke shrugged.

'Indeed I do. I'll be in touch. I had better get back; they'll wonder where I am.'

'Speak soon, I've got my reindeers parked at the top of the street with false plates on, so I had better go too. I'm glad we sorted that out.' Shaking each other's hands, they walked in opposite directions. Alex had to laugh to himself. Reindeers, indeed. He liked Luke.

Going down into the cellar, Alex stuffed the bag behind some barrels. Standing back, he could see no sign of the bag. That will do for now, he thought to himself and walked back up to the bar with a smile on his face. This was the best Christmas he had ever had!

12

GOLDEN OPPORTUNITIES

Mark's phone rang during the pub's New Year's Eve party. Answering it, his face dropped. 'Sorry mate, no can do,' Alex heard him say.

'What was all that about? Trouble?' asked Alex.

'Sort of. Someone has broken down in town and rang for help. I am entitled to a few days off, aren't I?'

'Mark, you're a good mate, but I think you have more than a few days off. Your van has been stuck in your drive for weeks. When was the last time you actually went on the road and fixed a car?'

'Fuck, I could have charged double, too,' Mark laughed and took another gulp of his drink. Spying him closely, Alex could feel an idea forming in his brain. It was worth a chance.

'I could do it. I haven't had a drink tonight. If it's double money, you could give me half. I know a bit about cars; what did they say was wrong with it?'

'Nah Alex, they want a professional. Proper mechanic like me. They said it wouldn't start. Totally dead apparently.'

'Well, if they want a proper mechanic, why are they calling

you?' Making light of it, Alex burst into laughter. 'Sorry Mark, you walked into that one.' Seeing the smile appear on Mark's face meant no offence had been taken. Then Mark's phone rang again; it was the same person, begging him to go, even offering more money.

'You sure you're sober Alex? It's New Year and the police are about, looking for drunk drivers.'

'Haven't had a drop.'

'If you will go, I'll give you half. But do a proper job mind,' Mark warned. Alex couldn't help laughing, because he knew whatever he did he'd do a better job than Mark. The complaints he had about his work were unbelievable. Even the reviews he got online were abusive with people wanting their money back.

Once Mark had said he was on his way, he handed Alex the keys to his van. 'Everything you need is in the back. Any problems, give me a call.'

Going out into the dark, he opened Mark's van. There he found Mark's giant waterproof coat including his woolly hat with an LED light on the forehead. The coat was too big and covered him almost to his shins. Pulling up the collar and hood, he started the van and drove off to the address Mark had given him.

A distressed woman and her friend flagged him down once they saw the logo and the orange light flashing on top. The rain was now pouring down on them, so he told the women to get back into the car. Once he'd looked under the bonnet, he saw that it was a straightforward job, but decided to take his time and give the women their money's worth.

Raking through Mark's untidy van, he found the jump leads and, in an instant, started the car up. 'Hope you ladies haven't been drinking. You can't drive if you have. I can tow you somewhere if you want?' he offered.

'No, we haven't. We've been to see a musical at the theatre and it's quicker to take the car at New Year. I need a large drink when I get home though. This has been a nightmare.'

'You need to join a rescue scheme and not hope for the best.' Taking his advice on board, the women opened their purses and between them found three hundred pounds in cash.

So, Mark was all cash in hand then, he thought to himself. 'Thanks ladies. Now, go on home and have that drink. If you need us again, you know the number.' Alex grinned and after waiting until they drove off safely, drove home himself. This could be his get-out-of-jail-free card, he thought to himself. He was a mobile mechanic, and he could go anywhere. He could even pop to Luke's, if and when he needed to... Now that was a good idea.

Once home, he looked to see if the police surveillance car was around. They drove past a lot and sometimes sat out there for hours on end watching him. He was their precious cargo for now. In time, he knew they would drop him like a hot potato, but for now, he felt like a goldfish.

Once out of the van, he walked straight into the pub. Still wearing Mark's coat and hat, he handed Mark the money.

'Was it okay? Could you fix it?'

'Yeah, just battery trouble like you said. You really know your stuff Mark.' Alex knew to appeal to Mark's ego and flattering him was the only way to get the little bit of freedom he had enjoyed.

Grinning from ear to ear, Mark pulled him aside, counted out the money and gave Alex his half. 'Give me the coat Alex, you're dripping all over the carpet. I'll put it back in the van.'

'Oh, sorry Mark, I wasn't thinking. I should have done that.' Alex watched as Mark left the pub and put his coat back in his van. It was perfect. If the police were looking, it would be Mark they saw putting his clothing in the car, not Alex. The perfect alibi, Alex mused to himself. All he needed was for Mark to take the bait and come up with a great idea. Although even he had to admit, it would take a little nudging, because he wasn't the brightest lightbulb in the box.

Furnishing Mark with another drink, he grinned. 'I enjoyed that, Mark. It got me out from under the women's feet. I get bored in here sometimes. It's been a while since I was under a car bonnet. It took me back to the good old days.' Alex had now dropped the bait, and was waiting for a drunken Mark to snap it up.

'Good old days? When was that then? You don't speak a lot about your life before here.'

'Oh, didn't I tell you my dad was a mechanic? I used to help him out a lot. Cars are my first love; pubs are Maggie's, and she doesn't really need me here.' Alex saw Mark spying him closely between gulps. He could see Mark's brain drunkenly forming an idea that would suit them both.

'How come you're not working love? I thought all agencies wanted extra staff at this time of year.' Barrow undid his tie, casting it aside. It had been a hell of a day at the prison. It always was this time of year. The inmates tried making the best of Christmas, but it hit home more than usual just how much they missed their families.

'No, nothing for tonight. I had my fingers crossed that pub I worked at on Christmas Day might need someone.'

'Yes, I remember you saying. Maybe you didn't make a good impression,' he joked while kicking his shoes off.

'Well, I liked the landlady, she was nice, but her foreign husband Mr Silva didn't take too kindly to me.'

Although tired, the name struck a chord in his brain. He had heard that name before. 'Foreign husband? From where?' he asked, trying not to cause suspicion.

'Well, I thought he was Spanish, and I asked him, but he

ignored me. A bit shirty if you ask me, too big for his boots in my opinion. How he got a nice caring wife like that is beyond me.'

'The same could be said about you Julia. Unusual name though, Silva...' Walking into the bathroom to have a shower, he pondered on what she had said, and knew it was of some importance.

In bed later that night, Barrow suddenly remembered where he had heard the name before. Paul Pereira had said it many times. This was apparently the man who had put him behind bars. The very man Pereira was trying to find. Barrow felt as though he couldn't breathe. He had found the very man that Paul was prepared to pay millions in bounty for. This was his lottery ticket out of work. No more walking landings and sorting arguments between inmates. The money he could get for this information was unbelievable. There was a bounty on this Silva bloke's head, and he would claim it. Paul would be more than grateful and eager to pay, and more than that he would be forever in debt to him for saving his neck. Mentally, he was already spending the money and picturing himself on some yacht in the middle of the Mediterranean with some young woman.

The money he had already had out of Paul he had put into a separate account his wife knew nothing about. He wasn't prepared to share it with her and her greedy family who were always borrowing money. A wry grin crossed his face when he thought about his good fortune. This was definitely a new year and a fresh start. At last there was something to look forward to in life. He couldn't wait to get back to work and spill the beans. That Silva bloke, whoever he was, was his ticket to freedom.

* * *

After a couple of days, Mark approached Alex.

'Alex mate, I've had an idea I want to put to you, if you have a minute.'

Instantly, Alex's ears pricked up and he strolled over, his hands buried deep in his pockets. This could be what he was waiting for.

'What's up Mark?'

Mark looked at him. 'Well, I've got a proposition for you. That job you did the other night; the woman you helped called and said you were brilliant and she's going to recommend us to their friends. Do you fancy doing a few more jobs for me? I can't be arsed sometimes.'

Alex beamed; this was just what he was hoping for. 'Oh, Mark mate, that would be great. To be able to get from under the wife's feet once in a while would feel like an escape. Sure, call on me whenever you don't feel like doing a job.'

'You haven't asked how much yet Alex, and I don't intend paying all that tax and insurance stuff. It's zero hours and cash in hand.'

'I don't need to know Mark. We're mates, aren't we? I'd prefer evening work though; that way Maggie is firmly busy behind the bar and can't moan if I'm not around.'

'Even better, because I like a drink in the evening, and I hate these dark nights. I can't be bothered to go out in the evenings any more.'

'That's a done deal then.' Alex and Mark shook hands on their new partnership. For Alex, it was a dream come true. Disguised as Mark, he could now travel anywhere he liked!

Stubbing out his cigarette, Mark looked up and saw Percy hanging around and hovering as usual. 'I see old Percy's moved back into his place properly. I bet he misses that bed and breakfast though.'

Alex turned his head and saw Percy walking towards them. 'Yeah, well, I suppose it was company for him as well.' Alex had been wondering how to instigate a meeting with Percy, and this was the perfect opportunity.

'Shit! I'm off. I can't be doing with any more trawler stories or how he survived a bomb blast. Stupid old bastard probably left the gas on. See ya, Alex.' With the wink of an eye, Mark had gone in and shut the door firmly behind him. Smiling to himself, Alex knew he would have done the very same thing, except he had an ulterior motive for wanting to speak to Percy. Taking out his packet of cigarettes, he lit one, knowing full well that Percy would do his usual scrounging act when he saw them.

'Hi Alex.' Percy's eyes went straight to the cigarette packet he was holding. 'Don't suppose you have a spare one of those, do you?'

'Of course, Percy, help yourself. How are you anyway?'

'I'm okay. My house still needs sorting out though. Got furniture and stuff but it needs decorating inside. I've got to wait for the plaster to dry properly first before the council can paint it. I'm still in shock; all my personal possessions over the years, just gone up in a puff of smoke. The fire brigade says the gas pipe was faulty and leaking.'

Alex frowned, showing fake concern. 'Well, don't the council or that housing association that own your house do regular inspections of appliances?' Alex was interested to know exactly what the outcome was and if the investigations were firmly over.

'No, they just check the heating and a gas fire if you have one. The cooker is my responsibility.' Mournfully, Percy looked down at the ground aimlessly. 'Mind you, I had had that cooker for ten years and I got it second hand when I came out.'

'What were you inside for Percy? If you don't mind me asking...'

'I got twenty years for murder; well, it was reduced to manslaughter. I suppose everyone knows, it was in all the papers.' Percy shrugged and took a drag of his cigarette. Alex's mind swam, and he swallowed hard. Percy seemed so nonchalant about it.

Mentally, Alex now understood how he had become an informer for the police. It was part of the deal to freedom.

'So,' Alex joked, 'who did you murder then? Or are you having me on and this is all part of a New Year joke?'

Wide eyed, Percy shook his head. 'It's not a joke, Alex. I killed my wife.'

Seeing Percy had nearly finished his cigarette, Alex handed him another one. Quickly, Percy took it and put it behind his ear while finishing the one he had. 'Go on, you were saying Percy mate?'

'Oh yes, my wife. Well, I was on the trawlers, gone for six weeks at a time we were.' His slow monotone voice started to annoy Alex, especially as he felt another fisherman story coming. 'The trawler office used to give your wife half your wages each week while you were away, to make sure the rent is paid and there's food in the cupboards, you know what I mean.' Percy reached up for the cigarette behind his ear and held his hand out for Alex's lighter. Intrigued, Alex handed it over. He felt there was a lot more to come.

'Well, when I came home from sea, I went to our house and discovered my wife had moved. I didn't know anything about it; there had been no message left for me at the office. Anyway, a neighbour saw me and told me where she had moved to. They were good friends and kept in touch. When I got to the new address, I tried the door, and it was open so I walked in. I could hear a noise coming from upstairs and so I shouted and walked upstairs. She was having sex with a bloke in our bed! I froze in the doorway, and they were just as shocked to see me. Apparently, she had moved in with this bloke and he was shouting at me to get out. I was blazing angry, I don't mind telling you,' he spat out, as though remembering that day vividly in his mind. 'When I walked back down the stairs, I saw a cricket bat behind the door. She always had something behind the door in case of intruders, you see,' Percy explained, while delaying the punch line. Alex felt he knew what was coming and he had a sick feeling in the pit of his stomach. He stood in silence, listening to Percy's confession.

'I didn't mean to hurt her but I was so angry, I saw red. I hit her with it while she was still naked on the bed, time and time again. I couldn't help myself,' he stressed. 'I didn't know what I was doing, and then her bloke tried grabbing me from behind. I was a lot younger and a lot stronger in those days and I had muscles,' Percy said while flexing his arm in the air for Alex to see.

'The bed sheet was red. My God when I think back it makes me shudder. Anyway, her new bloke tried grabbing me and pulling my hair from behind. The window was half open. It was one of those sash windows and with all of the strength I had in me, I turned and grabbed him, pushing him out of the window.' Percy looked down at the pavement, as though disgusted with himself.

Alex's jaw was on the floor as he looked at good old friendly Percy. The neighbourhood's friend! He was rooted to the spot as Percy carried on with his story.

'Once my anger calmed down a bit, I sat on the edge of the bed near my wife. Her head was caved in. There was no point in running. I knew someone would have called the police when her bloke fell out of the window. So, I lit a cigarette and waited for them to come and arrest me.' Percy shrugged. 'They said it was murder, but as I hadn't gone to her house with the intention of hurting her or knowing she had a new bloke, they said it was the heat of the moment. In France, it would have been a crime of passion and I wouldn't have gone to prison at all.' He scoffed. 'I was the innocent party in this Alex. It was her who was using and cheating on me. She was still collecting my wages and keeping that bloke and my hard-earned money!' Alex could almost see the anger still bubbling in Percy when he thought about it. A chill ran down Alex's spine, and he knew he wasn't one to judge anyone, but, this was something else. He felt sorry for the friend who had given him his wife's new address. He wondered how she felt all these years on.

'I met some good mates inside, never had any trouble in the showers.' He smiled and laughed at his own joke.

'A bit like that bed and breakfast you stayed in I suppose.' Alex could well imagine that Percy would take to prison like a duck to water. He wouldn't have had to think for himself – or pay rent! The prisoners had probably looked after him and kept him in cigarettes.

'Yeah, I didn't mind prison, because of what I was in for. When I got parole on licence, the housing association came up with this place and I never looked back. My son has only just started speaking to me though. He blamed me for everything, but kids do that don't they. I was an innocent victim in all of this though, Alex. I loved my wife.'

Seeing Percy had smoked his second cigarette, Alex handed him another one. Moistening his own lips with his tongue, he didn't know where to start. When he had first seen Percy, Alex's plan had seemed easy, but now he wasn't so sure. He wondered if he would ever get this chance to ask him again though and decided to throw caution to the wind.

'Actually Percy, this isn't my business, but I've been asked to give you a message. It's a bit cryptic, probably so I won't understand it, but you might,' Alex stammered. He couldn't believe he actually felt nervous broaching the subject. 'The message is from your friends. They said to tell you that they entered your house when they saw the fire and thought you were in there.' Alex shook his head. 'Then they said to tell you that they saw the hole in the wall and rescued some very expensive items that they think you will want to buy back...' Swallowing hard, he waited for Percy's response, which was much faster than he expected.

Percy's eyes widened. 'Who was it, Alex? Who said it?' he pushed.

'I can't tell you that, I promised. I don't know what it's about, but if people want to sell you your old table lamps back or your war time medals, then the deal is there to be had. I've passed on the message and that's it. The rest is up to you.' Alex was about to walk away when Percy stopped him.

'How do I contact these people, if I do want to buy these things back?'

'I suppose I could always pass a message on if that was the case... you just let me know, Percy. Now I've got to go, the wife's waiting.' Alex cursed himself inwardly for that last sentence. What a stupid thing to say to a man who has just confessed to murdering his wife!

Wandering back into the pub, he saw through the open bar door that everyone was busy, and crept up the stairs. His mind was swimming with information and he needed to get his head around it. This bloody neighbourhood! This was supposed to be one of the posh parts of Kent and people paid a fortune to buy a house here. But scratch the surface and the people surrounding him were worse than he had ever known.

He had always mixed with criminals and there wasn't anything he hadn't come across, but they admitted what they were and never pretended to be anything else, including himself. But these people acted as though butter wouldn't melt in their mouths. Good hard-working citizens. Yet, they were all Jekyll and Hyde-type characters with dark secrets of their own. It was unbelievable, Alex thought to himself, and he wondered if he should tell Maggie. Maybe not, he mused. Maybe he should leave that on ice until he found out if Percy passed his message on and if the Liverpudlians wanted to buy their cannabis plants back.

Slowly he was forming a plan in his mind of how he would deliver their plants, which he knew they would definitely want back. They must have been gutted once they realised they had lost everything. He still couldn't understand why the helicopter had been flying over, which hadn't been seen since. If the police were going to raid the place, it was to find the plants and the only person that had known they were there was Percy and the people who had put them there and wired up the electricity.

Trying hard to fathom it out, Alex realised it must have been Percy who had grassed up his mates to the police and had wanted to look innocent by going fishing. If those men ever found out Percy had informed on them, he would be dead meat!

Smugly, Alex sat back on the sofa. Being an informer was one secret Percy would never confess over a couple of cigarettes in the street! But Alex officially had Percy by the balls. He would have to do his bidding from now on.

13

MASTER PLAN

Almost skipping as he walked along the tiresome prison landings, Barrow saw them in a different light today. Suddenly walking along these landings held a new future for him. He was itching to get away while the breakfast was sorted and the prisoners made their way to whatever work or education classes they were assigned to. He looked up, almost to the top of the prison, or what other prisoners called the penthouse suite. Paul Pereira's cell was up there, and he would be getting himself smartly attired for the day.

Walking up the staircase, Barrow made a mental note of the lackies leaving Paul's cell. The shoe shiners, the runners so that he could place his horse bets, and of course the usual grovellers that were on hand should he need anything. Paul had built his own empire in prison and although officially the governor made all the decisions, it was Pereira who ruled the prison with an iron fist. No one crossed him.

Today, Barrow mused to himself, he would claim the bounty on Alex Silva's head. Straightening his tie and making sure there were none of the other guards about, he knocked on Paul's cell door and then walked in. He was shocked to see that Paul was being measured up for a new suit by one of the inmates, who used to be a tailor.

'Got to look our best Mr Barrow, uphold the reputation of the prison.' Paul grinned.

Clearing his throat, Barrow looked directly at Paul and straightened his own tie again. 'If I could just have a word in private Mr Pereira?'

Feeling the importance in his manner, Paul brushed off the tailor and waved him away. 'Come back later,' he commanded. They both waited while he left, and Barrow shut the door.

'Well, Barrow, what is it? If it's about the investigation into the car park tragedy I'm not interested. You're beginning to bore me.' He yawned, emphasising his disinterest.

'No, it's not about that. But I might have something for you; that is, if I have heard you correctly. The man you say put you here – am I right in thinking his name was Alex Silva? A Portuguese man, like yourself?'

Intrigued, Paul looked up at him. This wasn't the line of questioning he had been expecting. He had found Barrow to be a weak, spineless man who used his prison authority like some trophy badge. He came in handy, but now he was getting tiresome and greedy.

'You would be right in thinking that Barrow. What of it?'

'Am I also right in thinking there is a huge bounty on this man's head? And something, dare I say,' Barrow coughed nervously, 'you would pay handsomely for information about?'

'Whatever it is Barrow, spit it out. I don't play games; surely you know that by now.'

Barrow stiffened before speaking again. 'My wife works for an agency, working as a barmaid as and when, if you know what I mean...'

'For crying out loud, I am not interested in your wife's working day. What has it got to do with me?'

Barrow blurted out his winning hand. 'Well, she worked for Alex Silva over the Christmas holidays!' Seeing Paul's stunned face, Barrow squared up to him. 'But if you don't want to know then I will keep it to myself.' He turned and made to leave.

'Officer Barrow, wait a minute.' Paul's thick accent seemed to get stronger suddenly. It was clear to Barrow that Pereira had been unnerved and was trying his hardest to cover it up.

Barrow turned and looked down at Paul. 'So, am I right? Is there money to be made for information of his whereabouts?'

Slowly, Paul began to speak again, his eyes glancing furtively around the room, while trying to think. His mind was swimming with thoughts and the excitement at finding his arch enemy before his trial made his heart pound in his chest. He could scarcely breathe as he waited for the rest of the story. All he could do was nod his head in agreement.

Raising his eyebrows in a cocky manner, Barrow continued. 'Does it have a lot of zeros on the end, Mr Pereira?' Arrogantly, Barrow folded his arms and Paul nodded. This had certainly taken the wind out of his sails.

'Well, he is here in England. He's using his own name and he and his family are running a pub.'

'And how do you know it's him – my Alex Silva?' Paul poked himself in the chest with his finger while he spoke, his anger rising. If this was some kind of joke or revenge for what Barrow had suffered lately at the hands of his workmates, he would gladly wring his neck himself.

Standing back, fearing he would lash out at him, Barrow decided to play down his information. Paul was notorious for his fiery temper, and he didn't want to be on the end of it. 'Well, Mr

Pereira, there aren't many men called Silva are there? Well, not in this country anyway sir.'

Hearing the respect in his tone, Paul nodded. 'If your information is correct Barrow, you will be paid in full. But first I have to check it out. I am not paying for mistakes... do you understand?'

'But if I give you his whereabouts, Mr Pereira, you will know where he is and I won't get anything out of it. I want a retainer for my information, or I could get you photo evidence, if that would suffice?'

Waving his hand in the air, and shaking his head, Paul dismissed the idea. 'I don't want you wandering around taking photos. You do realise he will be under the police's watchful eye and if they see you taking photos, they will ask questions. What are you going to say, that you're part of an amateur camera club?' Paul narrowed his eyes. 'Do you not believe I am a man of my word? I have always paid you for your services in the past, haven't I?'

'You have, but by all accounts, this is a very large sum and sometimes when people get what they want, they forget who gave it to them... if you know what I mean. And I don't intend hanging around here. I'm finished with this place. So, the way I see it, you're going to pay me for my freedom, and I am going to give you your freedom. As for trust, do you think I would lie to you about a thing like this?'

Weighing up the argument, Paul nodded. 'A retainer of five hundred thousand pounds. Would that suit you for now and the rest on confirmation?'

'Make it one million, that's goodwill. Just how much is this bounty?'

'It's worth millions, but there is also the cost of hiring a hit man to finish the job, unless you want to do it?'

Red faced, Barrow looked down at the floor. 'No Paul, I'm no hitman, just a businessman with something to sell. So, what is the final price?'

'We would go as far as fifteen million. The rest would be for the man who finishes the job.' Hardly able to contain his excitement, Paul agreed to Barrow's one million. 'Take me to the phone and I will ring my lawyer.'

Barrow stood rooted to the spot; he couldn't believe his good fortune. One million now and fourteen to follow. 'Right, when you're ready then, I will escort you to the phones.'

Barrow listened closely as Paul gave out the instructions over the telephone and felt a deep satisfaction inside. He was already rehearsing his resignation speech for the governor. No curtesy or politeness; he would tell him and the others to shove it up their arses!

'Right Barrow, you've had your retainer on trust. Now you give me the information I want to hear, and it better be worth a million pounds.'

'He runs a pub in Sevenoaks. His wife is the publican, and it's her name above the door. Silva is tall with dark hair. Muscular. The missus said he was quite a handsome man, but he was also arrogant and rude. Recently there has been a gas explosion near where his pub is. It was in the papers, that might give you more to go on,' Barrow stressed.

Paul burst out laughing. 'That sounds like my Alex. Always the lady's man! They loved him with his charming ways. Crikey, he could charm the knickers off a nun, apart from your wife of course. He obviously didn't want to impress her.' He laughed again. Once Barrow had given him the name of the pub, both men smiled at each other. Paul knew the information was correct. But he would never pay Barrow the full amount. He hated giving this cretin anything else. He had sponged long enough, Paul thought to himself. Once Barrow had left him to go back to his cell alone,

Pereira thought about the information he had been given and knew he had to tread carefully.

Alex's demise had to be planned out. He was still in witness protection and the police would be crawling all over him. 'The bastard!' Paul cursed himself. The last he had heard, Alex was somewhere in Switzerland, then France... According to his informers he had been everywhere. Absolutely everywhere except Sevenoaks in Kent!

He didn't like Barrow much, and the last thing he wanted was him coming back for more money or boasting about his find while under the influence of drink. Men like him always bragged about their own importance, and it gave Paul an uneasy feeling. Barrow's ego would be the death of him and Barrow would always remind Paul that it was he who'd freed him from prison. Barrow also knew his intentions towards Alex Silva, and so when the inevitable happened, Barrow would know it was Paul who had issued the order. The consequences of leaving Barrow alive could be fatal. No, Barrow would have to go, he decided. But first he would have this information checked out, and if it was wrong, which he doubted, he would want his money back in full.

* * *

'Alex mate, I know it's sooner than you probably expected.' Mark stood on the doorstep looking sheepish, rousing Alex's suspicions.

'What's up Mark? You look fed up, come in.'

'Well, it's like this mate.' Mark took out his packet of cigarettes and offered Alex one. 'You know we've been doing up our camper van?'

Alex nodded, recalling the cheap transit Mark had bought thinking he could turn it into some amazing camper van, complete with kitchen and all. It was a disaster on wheels and rusty on the outside. He'd acquired it at some auction in part exchange for some other vehicle that didn't work. Day in, day out, they had watched Mark and Olivia insulate the van on the inside and put in an Ikea sink and kitchen workplace. They had a water tank, but best of all was the bed space. Dante had been roped in by George to help out and had nearly wet himself when he'd told them all. Mark had basically built a square wooden frame, put some hardboard on it and put a mattress on top of that. Underneath, Mark had made cupboard space and a small freezer box. Alex had shuddered when he thought about the safety of it all. It was a death trap, but they were proud of it.

'Yeah, well, Olivia wants to give it a trial run. She wants to go to Scotland for a long weekend and there's some stuff I need to do under the bonnet. It's our wedding anniversary you see.' Alex nodded, and knew what Mark was asking. 'And you want us to look after George, is that it? Of course we will! Him and Dante have become best mates. Don't give it a second thought.'

Frowning, Mark looked at him, puzzled. 'Oh no he's coming with us! No, it's the mechanic business. There have been a couple of MOTs come in. I don't have the garage space, but my mate does. So, we work it between us. One of the cars needs work. I think it's the alternator. So I would normally go, get it started up and tow it back to the garage. Do a bit of work and my mate sorts out the MOT certificates.' Mark winked.

'So, if your mate has a garage, why doesn't he pick the cars up or get them started?'

'Come on Alex, we work it between us. These people need certificates, so we patch them up and give them one.'

'So, they could be driving death traps. Is that what you're telling me?' Alex laughed.

Blushing slightly, Mark inhaled on his cigarette. 'No Alex, the car is roadworthy. The tyres could be shit, but all these people are interested in is it passing an MOT. Anyway, would you look after the business in case any calls come in while we're away?'

For a moment Alex couldn't believe what he was hearing. This was what he wanted: a ticket out of here to meet up with Luke and discuss business. The garage and MOTs all sounded very dodgy, but it wasn't his business so why should he care? He'd done worse, hadn't he?

'Course I will Mark; you go off and have a good time. I'll do my best for you, you know that.'

'Fifty-fifty on the money Alex, like before. And, we'll have a drink later. I've got to get my head under that van and make sure we make it as far as the motorway,' Mark laughed and left.

As an afterthought, Alex shouted after him, 'What about all your gear Mark? You know, the waterproofs and stuff.'

'Yeah, all my gear's in the back, use what you want. Oh, and will you feed the cat while we're away? I'll give you the spare key later.'

Grinning to himself, Alex waved. This was even better. He could come out of Mark's house and into the van and no one would know it was him. It was the best alibi ever.

14

SHADOWS IN THE DARK

Dante ran upstairs to the living quarters, bubbling with excitement. 'Dad, can I go to Scotland with George? He's asked me to go along with them and I think it would be great fun.'

Sat reading his paper, Alex looked at his son over the top of it and gave him a knowing look. 'Nope,' was the only answer he gave before looking back at his paper.

Dante stood there defiantly, hands on hips.

'Nope,' Alex answered again, without looking up.

Maggie came through from the kitchen. 'What's up with you Dante, and you Alex, what have you done?'

'Dad won't let me go with George to Scotland. He's just mean. I never go anywhere.'

Casting a furtive glance at Alex, Maggie leaned forward and pulled his newspaper down. 'Tell him the truth, Alex. He can't go because the police would never agree to it. We can't go walking off away from each other. I'm sorry Dante, it's just not possible.'

Standing up, Alex walked towards Dante and put his arms around him, hugging him tightly. 'Well, personally, Dante, I'm saying no because I love you and that bloody van is a death trap. It's got no safety certificates and it's still licensed as a transit van not a camper van, which means it has no real insurance. If Mark wants to kill his family, that's his business, but me… definitely not. He drove it around the block the other day and the wheel fell off! I like Mark, he's a gentle giant with a big heart, but he has ideas above his station. I love you Dante, and if you're going to be maimed and killed it's not going to be by his hands.'

Dante hugged his dad back. 'Sorry Dad, I love you too.'

Maggie took a sigh of relief, and Alex looked across at her.

'Talking of Mark, he's asked if I can take the calls for his mechanic business while he's away.'

'What, he wants you to answer the phone like his secretary? Can't he do that on his mobile?'

Alex hadn't told her he might do the odd job for Mark. He wanted that to be kept under his hat, so she wouldn't be involved in any way.

'We're mates and I said I'd help him out.'

They were interrupted by Deana walking in nonchalantly and slumping down on the sofa beside Alex. Deana attempted to pick up Alex's newspaper but he swatted her playfully.

Maggie looked around her nicely furnished lounge, full of warmth and her family and she couldn't have felt happier. She had given herself the night off, which felt like the first night off since they'd arrived. The pub was open and being run by Phyllis and Pauline excellently. Chef and the kitchen staff all knew their jobs and had slipped into a routine. For the first time in a long time, Maggie felt like her life was running smoothly. She was happy. Looking across at her handsome husband, she felt herself almost bubbling over with love for him. He was her rock and always backed her up with whatever she wanted. He was the love of her life and always would be.

Reaching for her purse, she took out two twenty-pound notes

and handed them to her kids. 'One for each of you to go out and amuse yourselves. Don't rush back.'

'Thanks Mum.' Dante grinned. Almost snatching it out of her hand, Deana stood up. 'Come on Dante, it means they want some together time!'

Looking across at Maggie, Alex smiled, showing a perfect row of white teeth. 'So Mrs Silva, what do you have in mind?' he asked when they kids had left. 'Do you intend using and abusing my body for your own gratification?'

Standing up, Maggie took his hand. 'I most certainly do, Mr Silva. First, we're going to take a soak with some wine in a hot bubble bath, while I massage you and you do likewise. Then, we will see what happens. Come on big boy.'

Sinking into a warm bubble bath with a cold bottle of wine, they chinked their glasses together. 'Here's to you Maggie. You have turned this place around and made it a success. Cheers!'

Seeing his slightly tanned body and the dark hairs on his chest, made wet by the soapy water, Maggie admired her husband. His muscular body and his well-shaped arms stirred something inside her. Taking a sip of her wine, she watched how his strong hands swept his wet wavy hair from his face. His dark eyes, with long dark lashes, seemed to swallow up his whole face.

'You're bloody sexy Alex. I'm sorry if I've neglected you of late.'

'Nothing to apologise for Maggie. Although I think I should tell you that isn't my big toe you're toying with.' He smiled. As she leaned forward to meet his lips, she could feel his own body harden to her touch. The warm steaminess of the bathroom was nothing in comparison to their love making which followed in the bedroom. They felt like naughty teenagers considering everything that was going on downstairs in the pub. Each time their damp bodies met and locked together in rhythmic pleasure, their need for each other grew more and more until they both reached their peaks. Gasping for air, Alex lay beside her, both of them breathing heavily.

'God, that was good,' Maggie panted.

Raising one eyebrow, Alex smiled. 'Really? Well, I haven't finished yet.' Turning towards her he playfully flicked her nipple with the tip of his tongue. His hand traced her long slim body. 'You're beautiful, absolutely perfect. You're like one of those marble statues and better still, you're mine.'

Turning towards him, Maggie mounted him and slowly moved her body on top of his, feeling his thrusting manhood. She felt dizzy with excitement, until a slow moan escaped from her lips and she cried out in pleasure. Lying in each other's arms afterwards, they both drifted off into a contented sleep.

* * *

The next morning, Maggie felt an extra skip in her step, especially as she thought about the morning's encore of love making. A smile crossed her face as she counted out the float for the cash registers.

'Phyllis put everything in the safe last night Mum, and I helped her lock up. She said you must be really tired, and that it was time you put your feet up, considering what you do for everyone else. That's nice isn't it?' Deana smiled and kissed her on the cheek. 'She is right though. You always help other people out without a thought for yourself.'

Puzzled and suspicious at Deana's mild-mannered way, Maggie waited for the punch line. 'Okay Deana, what do you want?'

'Nothing Mum. I was just talking to Phyllis last night. She makes a lot of sense. You deserved a night alone with Dad. You don't get much time together, and it's only right that you do. Sometimes it's easy for us kids to forget that you're still a married couple who want to be alone. Even though it did cost you forty quid! I hope he was worth it.' Deana laughed and walked away.

Biting on a piece of toast, Deana heard a knock at the back door. Opening it, she saw Percy standing there looking rather sheepish, with his roll-up resting on his bottom lip. 'Whatever you need Percy, we haven't got any. Haven't you heard of supermarkets?'

'It's your dad I want,' he muttered.

'Dad!' Deana shouted up the stairs. 'Percy's here again!' Pushing past him, Deana flounced out as her dad arrived. 'I'm off to Wendy's.'

'What can I do for you this early in the morning, Percy?' Alex yawned and looked at his watch. It was only 8.30 a.m. and he didn't remember getting a lot of sleep last night.

Furtively, Percy ushered Alex into the beer garden. Looking around to see if anyone was listening, Percy said, 'Those people you told me about, who asked you to pass that message on. Well, it wasn't for me, it was for some people who were storing some stuff at mine. So I passed it on and they'd like to meet.'

Alex's ears pricked up. 'Look Percy, I don't know what this is about and I don't want to get involved,' Alex lied.

'But you are involved Alex; you're the middleman like me. My people are interested in buying back, or claiming back what they have lost, if you know what I mean.'

Alex knew he had to play this carefully. They were treading around each other tentatively. 'If you want, I can pass the message on, Percy.'

'Fair enough. But tell them that my people want to arrange a meeting.'

'I'll see what I can do, but I'm making no promises.' Alex walked away, his mind working overtime. He wasn't sure how to arrange this meeting. He couldn't reveal his own involvement, yet he wanted to make a deal. While getting showered and dressed, he had an idea. 'Dante, come here, son. I want you to write me a note.'

'Why can't you do it? I've got to go out.'

'Because if it's ever checked, I don't want it to be in my handwriting.' Handing him a pen and a piece of paper, Alex dictated the message.

'Why don't I type it and then we can print it out? That way it's in no one's handwriting.'

'Fair enough Dante, let's do that then.' Alex waited while Dante typed and printed out the letter which was short and to the point. It was a big chance Alex was taking and he knew it, but it sounded like those Liverpudlians badly wanted their stuff back and he had to strike while the iron was hot.

> I went to save old Percy, and while there I came across his gardening equipment. I have twenty plants that were saved. I can either sell them on, give them to the police or give them back to their rightful owner – for a price. Knowing the street price, I would say it's a bargain at a hundred thousand pounds in cash. If you agree, I will leave them in a car in Chatham. There is a main supermarket there and I will give you the details and the time once the price is agreed.
> Your friend

Alex put on Maggie's rubber gloves as the letter came out of the printer and picked it up, folded it and put it in a self-sealing envelope. Alex grinned as he caught Dante watching him. 'No fingerprints son, means no DNA.'

Alex waited until opening time, when the pub was full of its usual lunchtime regulars. Just as he'd anticipated, Percy soon entered.

'He must save a fortune on heating bills,' scoffed Pauline as she went to serve him.

Stopping her and picking up a bar towel, Alex stepped forward. 'I'll serve him Pauline, I know you hate the smell of him.' Alex nodded to Percy to meet him at the end of the bar. Still holding the bar towel, he took the envelope out of his pocket. 'Someone left me this to give to you.' Alex saw Percy look around the pub, scanning the faces of everyone to see if anyone was watching, but they weren't.

'Who sent you this, Alex? And how do we contact them?'

'Honestly Percy, I don't know. This was left on the mat this morning after I spoke to you. I haven't opened it, but I can see the postman hasn't brought it as there's no stamp, so I presume whoever it is, will be watching you and may make themselves known to you. I don't want to know Percy. I like a quiet life.'

Nodding and shoving the letter in his pocket, Percy left.

'Crikey Alex, I've never known him leave so quickly before. Whatever you said, I must remember it,' laughed Pauline.

Alex's heart was pounding, but he knew the first part of his plan had been put into action. Tonight he was supposed to be picking up some cars for Mark. If all went to plan, he would drive to Luke's, pick up the plants and put them in one of those cars.

He went down to the cellar. Looking around, Alex felt as though it was becoming his workshop. He'd even brought some tools down here without arousing suspicion. Over the last couple of days he had gone down there a lot. When Maggie had mentioned it, he had laughed and told her it was to get some peace and quiet, a place to read his paper. But Alex wasn't just sitting on his arse – he had plans and the cellar was the perfect place to get things done privately.

Alex had wondered whether Gold Teeth would take the option of buying back his plants or whether he would try to steal them back. With this in mind, Alex had spent his time in the cellar making a bomb to make the car explode. He'd already wired up the bomb with a remote control and a timer, so he wouldn't be anywhere near it when it went off, but he needed to put it in a safe spot in the supermarket car park, away from as many shoppers as possible. The only victims he wanted from this were Gold Teeth and his mob. Weighing things up in his mind, he decided not to tell Luke about his 'Plan B'. That was best left as a surprise. Chuckling to himself, Alex wondered how many stoned shoppers there would be if the car went up in flames with all of that cannabis inside!

'For God's sake Alex, you're like a cat on hot bricks,' Maggie laughed a little while later. 'What is so interesting outside that you're staring out of the windows?'

'Just watching Mark and Olivia pack up the camper van. It's comical really,' laughed Alex. 'I think I'll just pop and see if he needs a hand. Oh, by the way, he's asked me to pick up a car for him later, as he's going to be away. You don't mind, do you, love?'

'Of course I don't mind, so you go when you like. We're fully staffed here anyway.'

'Well, it will be this evening,' Alex explained, 'because apparently the people don't finish work till later on, so I am at your disposal all day, for you to do whatever you want to me.' He grinned and winked at her.

Folding her arms, she cocked her head to one side and grinned back. 'Is that an indecent proposal, Mr Silva? I do hope so.'

'You're damned right it is! What else have I got to think about all day?' Reaching forward, he tweaked her nipple. 'That's just a taster,' he laughed, seeing the glint in her eye.

'Go away Alex. You're too much of a distraction. Go and get some air and cool down, before my customers think you've grown a third leg overnight.' Pushing him away and shaking her head while laughing, Maggie went about her business.

Knowing that he had the green light from Maggie to do as he pleased, he could put the rest of his plan into action. Only how to pass on his next message? Suddenly a flash of inspiration crossed his mind. He typed out another note, putting today's date and the time of his drop-off and put it in a self-sealing envelope.

Once outside, Alex walked in the opposite direction of the pub. He saw a young man delivering leaflets – takeaway menus, supermarket deals, the usual rubbish that went straight in the bin. Alex stopped him. 'Do you want to earn twenty quid, mate?'

'Doing what?' asked the sullen young man, who obviously hated his job.

'By putting this envelope inside one of your leaflets and posting it through that letterbox. I'll be watching, so don't bother dumping it. Oh, and if anyone asks, you never got it from me.'

Puzzled, the young man looked at the letter in his right hand. 'What is it?'

'Do you want the money or not?'

Snatching the money out of his hand, the young man shrugged. Digging out one of the leaflets in his bag containing pictures of supermarket deals, he put the envelope inside. 'That house there,' Alex said, nodding towards Percy's.

The young man walked away, posted a few leaflets through the doors of the houses running up to Percy's and then put the leaflet through Percy's door. Looking up the street, the young man turned to see if Alex was watching and nodded. Walking away, he carried on posting his leaflets down the street. Alex hoped he had put the leaflet containing the envelope through the right door. But at least no one had seen Alex delivering it. Taking off his gloves, he smiled to himself. The only fingerprints on that envelope would be the delivery boy's, Alex thought to himself.

15

LUKE'S PRIZE

After lots of waving and goodbyes Mark, Olivia and a very disgruntled George set off in the camper van. A thought crossed Alex's mind that the only fly in the ointment would be if the camper van never reached the top of the road.

As darkness fell, Alex made his excuses and walked to Mark's house. The van was parked right down the driveway and getting inside, Alex immediately donned Mark's long waterproof coat, but this time he had brought a balaclava so no one could see he didn't have a beard. The weather was still bad, and it was drizzling with rain, so he knew he wouldn't look suspicious.

His first port of call was Luke's house, and Alex hoped he would be home. Thankfully when he drove up, he saw the lights were on. He decided to knock on the door and if Luke didn't answer he would claim the wrong address and leave.

Luke answered the door. 'Yeah, what do you want mate?' Looking past Alex, he saw the mechanic van with its headlights on parked out front. 'We don't need a mechanic – piss off.'

Alex pulled up his balaclava. 'You're not the only one that can dress up Luke.'

'Alex mate, come in. What's with the disguise?' Luke laughed.

'Do you still have those plants?' Luke nodded and opened the door wider for Alex to come in. Surprisingly, the house was a little old fashioned, but clean and tidy.

'It's only one of my mates, Mum! I'll bring you a cup of tea in a minute,' Luke shouted to one of the rooms, then cocked his head to Alex to follow him.

The huge house had a basement and going down the steps towards it, Alex held his arm up to shield his eyes from the light. 'Bloody hell, it's like Blackpool illuminations down here.'

'There they are Alex, in all their glory and they are growing. Even the seedlings are growing great.' Luke beamed.

'We need thirty of them tonight. Don't ask questions, I'll tell you later, but help me put them in the back of the van.'

Luke knew better than to ask questions, so he walked forward to the plants. 'Let's take a mixture of the large plants and the seedlings – mix and match. Where are you taking them?'

'Chatham. There is an Asda there, but I have to make a stop first and time is of the essence.'

'Chatham? That's a bloody warzone Alex. Shit, I'm coming with you. Let me take the old lady a cup of tea and then we will fill your van. Five minutes.'

'I'll start bringing some of these upstairs, then, while you go and make the tea.' Alex was sweating; the whole basement was like a sauna and wearing a large heavy coat and woolly balaclava didn't help.

Alex started loading up and Luke returned swiftly to help him. Between them they put thirty plants of mixed sizes into the back of the van. Luke got in and pulled up his hoodie. 'Where to first?'

'To start with, we're on a mechanic job, picking up a car to take it to a garage, then we are going to put these plants in the car.'

'I didn't know you were a mechanic. I thought you were a publican?'

'I'm not and I'm not. My wife is the publican and my neighbour's the mechanic, although I probably know more about cars than he does,' Alex laughed.

'So, who are we taking the plants to?' Luke smiled and lit two cigarettes.

'We're selling them back to the people we stole them off. The very people who wanted you dead.'

Luke paled. 'What the fuck for? They can't see me or I'm dead meat.'

'Nobody is going to see anybody Luke. Do you think I want to be seen?'

'Suppose not, but how do you know they are going to pay up? They aren't going to hand over money when they can put a bullet in your head and take them for free.'

'Watch and learn Luke. And stop asking questions. Come on, it's here.' Alex turned into a side road. Just as Mark had said, the car was parked in the driveway of the address given. Telling Luke to stay in the van, Alex knocked on the door, while pulling the hood of his coat way over his eyes and making sure his balaclava covered his face.

A woman answered the door. 'Mark, thanks for coming to pick up the car,' she babbled and reached up to a key holder at the side of the door and handed him the car keys. 'Okay, got to go,' Alex mumbled. The woman looked quite shocked at his abrupt manner.

The woman hovered at the front door, wrapping her cardigan around her and watching Alex attach the car to his van, waving as he drove off with it.

'Blimey, that was easy. What a way to steal cars, eh?' Luke laughed.

Alex heart was pounding in his chest. Looking at his watch, he knew he was stretched for time – towing the car had slowed him down, which he hadn't thought about in his planning. Once at the supermarket car park, he pulled over and turned to Luke. 'Start unloading. We need to put the plants in the car.' Jumping out of the van, Luke asked no questions but did as instructed.

Next Alex opened his jacket and pulled out the homemade bomb he had made earlier. Looking to make sure Luke was busy with the plants, Alex lifted up the bonnet of the car and attached the bomb to the battery and put a timer on the steering wheel of the car, with a red light flashing, so whoever entered would see that the car was wired up to something.

'You all done there Luke?' Seeing Luke mop his brow and nod, he told him to go and sit in the van and wait until he saw him leave. Then Alex swiftly walked away and into the doorway of the supermarket, which was surprisingly busy, considering the time. Mingling in with everyone else, Alex made his way to the toilets. He was sweating, and wet from the rain. He knew people would be on the alert looking for whoever had dropped off the car. In fact, they were probably already there; maybe his cover was already blown.

Seeing the disabled toilets, he noticed a notice on the door explaining that to use the toilet you had to get a key from customer service. Shit! He hadn't counted on that. He had expected it to be open.

Deciding to buy something, Alex purchased two large bags and some cigarettes and ignoring the cashier's odd look, he also asked about the key to the disabled toilets, explaining his disabled mother needed to use it. Thankfully she was too busy to see if he had a disabled mother with him and handed it over. He went back to the toilets, all the while checking his watch. This was taking more time than he had estimated. There he took off his coat and balaclava and stuffed them in the large bag for life and walked back out of the supermarket. If anyone was watching and had seen him go in, they definitely hadn't seen him come out. Mark had been the one to walk in and Alex had walked out. After the heavy weight of the coat, he welcomed the coolness of the rain. Now standing in the shadows, he could only wait.

Looking up, Alex saw the familiar BMW enter the car park and circle around twice, and instantly he knew they had got his second note detailing the time and the car's location and registration number. He had instructed that the bag of money be left in the disabled toilets, before anyone opened the car. The bomb gave them only fifteen minutes once the car door was opened before it went off. If the money hadn't been left before they emptied the car, then Alex would use his remote control to blow the car up. Crossing his fingers, Alex hoped he had covered everything. His stomach was doing somersaults.

He watched a man walk into the supermarket carrying with him a leather holdall and from what he could see it looked heavy. Then he saw the others open the car door and start transporting the plants into their own car. To the outside world, it looked like they had just bought plants from the supermarket and no one paid any attention to what they were doing. Waiting for what seemed a lifetime, he saw the man who had taken the holdall come out of the supermarket empty handed. This was now the trickiest part of his plan because Alex needed to go to the toilet to see what was in the bag without causing any suspicion. The bag could be full of nothing and he would have failed. Only time would tell.

Nonchalantly, Alex walked back into the supermarket and to the disabled toilet. It was still unlocked and he opened the door cautiously. The holdall was tucked away under the sink and he snatched it up quickly. It was promisingly heavy. Looking at his watch, he saw twelve minutes had passed already and he needed to look in the bag and get outside. Undoing the zip slightly, he saw there was some money inside but he didn't have time to look any further. He swiftly put the holdall into the other large shopping bag he had purchased earlier, left the toilet and made his way outside. From what he could see, the men had already emptied the car and left. As he started walking towards the car, an almighty explosion erupted, and the car burst into flames. Turning around, he hastily made his way back to Luke who was waiting for him in the van. He could hear screams and shouting from shoppers and jumping into the van, he quickly started the engine.

Luke's eyes were wide. 'Where the bloody hell have you been? I presume that explosion had something to do with you?' Luke peered through the windscreen. The light from the fire lit up the sky and Alex knew the fire brigade would soon be on its way. He hoped no one had been hurt. The parking bay had been empty when he had last seen it, so hopefully not.

'Open the bag Luke,' Alex commanded as he drove away. 'Just look in the fucking bag!'

Nervously, Luke did as he was told. 'Fuck Alex, it's full of money!' Luke swirled his hand around the bag and took out a fistful of notes. 'Shit, they have paid up. I can't believe it!'

'Let's see how much they have paid when we get back to yours. First, I have another car to pick up and drop off.'

'What the bloody hell are you going to tell the owner of that one?' Giving a nervous laugh, Luke looked at Alex.

'I'm only supposed to pick up and drop off at a garage, leaving the keys in the glove box. Cars get stolen all the time. Shit happens!' Alex laughed.

'Let's go and pick up your other car first, before we go back to mine. Where did you get the bomb from?' Luke asked suspiciously. 'That was a bomb wasn't it, not some petrol leak? Is that what you were doing while I was loading up?'

'What do you care? More to the point, why do you care? But if you must know, I made it Luke. Does that satisfy you?'

Luke cast a glance towards Alex in the darkness of the van and said nothing. What was there to say? They had left mayhem behind them, and had blown up some poor woman's car for a bagful of money. Some things were best left for another day, Luke thought to himself and looked at the road ahead.

Once they had picked up the other car and dropped it off on the forecourt of the closed garage, they drove on to Luke's house. Once inside, Luke steered Alex towards the kitchen and checked on his mum who had fallen asleep in her chair.

'Let's take a proper look Luke.' Alex picked up the bag and emptied the contents onto the kitchen table, some notes aimlessly falling onto the floor. Luke couldn't contain his excitement and he burst out laughing. 'Oh my God, you've done it. There must be thousands there.'

Alex grinned from ear to ear. 'A hundred thousand pounds is what I asked for; let's count it partner, then we'll split it fifty-fifty.'

'You mean half of this is mine?' Luke asked, surprised. 'Seriously Alex, you're giving me half of this?'

'You said it yourself, we're partners.' Without thinking, they hugged each other.

'For fuck's sake, we're rich!' exclaimed Luke. Adrenalin ran through their bodies as they sat and counted the cash, discovering to their joy that it was all there as Alex had requested. 'It's like monopoly Alex; I've never seen so much cash at once. Christ, I can't believe it. You've got balls, I grant you that.' Luke laughed almost manically.

Alex looked at his watch. 'I have to get back.' He stood up to leave. 'Put my half in the bag.' Luke scooped up Alex's half and was about to put it back into the leather holdall when Alex stopped him.

'Not in there; that's their bag and will be easily recognised. You destroy the bag here and I'll take the shopping bag with the cat on it,' Alex laughed. 'Next, we need to get some mobile phones, just for you and me. You buy them and I'll drop by in a day or two to collect mine from you.'

'I'll sort it. See you later Alex.' Without thinking, Luke gave him another hug.

As Alex turned into his street, he drove slowly as he approached Mark's drive and parked the van. Once out of sight, he took off the coat along with Mark's heavy boots and walked back to the pub.

'Where have you been? You've been hours,' asked Maggie, who looked rushed off her feet.

'I picked up those cars then thought I'd watch the football at Mark's. A bit of peace and quiet. I could see you were busy. Didn't you hear me shout to you?'

'What? Above all this noise,' Maggie laughed. 'Watching the football indeed. I bet you fell asleep.' She winked.

Alex had purposely left his bag of money in Mark's van. He had nowhere to stash it yet without Maggie seeing him so he'd decided to hide it in the early hours, when everyone was asleep. It had been one hell of a night, and he needed a stiff drink to calm him down. Pouring himself a brandy, he handed Maggie a glass too and he put his arm around her shoulders. 'Cheers!' he shouted to the people stood at the bar. He felt happy and smug with a job well done. Now his family had financial back-up, if they ever needed it.

16

A NEW DISCOVERY

'Is he right? Did you see him?' Standing in the empty corridor of the prison, Paul fired question after question at the man on the other end of the phone. His brow broke out in a sweat as he eagerly waited for the answers. He had dreamt of this moment, but didn't dare believe it, until his trusted friend could confirm Alex Silva's whereabouts.

Furtively, Paul glanced around to make sure no one else was in line waiting to use the phone, although he knew they would be going about their daily work routines. With the back of his sleeve, he wiped away the sweat forming on his top lip.

'Yes boss. It's that low life Silva and his family. Him and his missus are playing publicans in the posh part of Kent. Real suburbia, with hanging baskets and everything.'

Stunned, Paul felt rooted to the spot. He couldn't believe what he was hearing. His number one man, now his arch enemy, had been right under his nose all this time. 'Are you sure it's that bastard?' All of the pent-up anger he had felt from his betrayal and incarceration came spewing out in venom down the phone.

'Boss, I've drunk with you and Alex. I've eaten at his table. I am

telling you, whoever your informant is, they were right. It's definitely him. Do you want me to send a hitman and get rid of the lot
of them?'

Paul's eyes darted around the corridor. Now he had his wish
come true, he couldn't think straight. As much as he wanted Alex
dead at this very moment, he knew he had to think and leave no
trail leading to himself. First on his list would be that guard Barrow.
He needed to be able to walk out of prison as clean as a whistle. He
knew he was guilty and so did the police, but if they couldn't prove
it, any of it, they would have to let him go.

'No, just keep a tail on him. The police will be watching and
protecting him... We need to know his every move, who he sees
and where he goes. When we make our move, it has to be clean and
quick without any hiccups. I have some business to attend to here
first.' Paul laughed loudly, leaving an echo running down the corridor. He couldn't stop laughing, even when the guards walked by
and gave each other odd looks.

'It's okay, sirs.' Paul smiled at the guards and brushed away the
tears brimming in his eyes. 'It's just a funny joke my friend is telling
me about his wife.' Winking, he grinned widely at them. He could
afford to be gracious today. Today was a good day.

Once back in his cell, he shut the door and lay on his bed,
looking up at the ceiling. He had imagined all kinds of deaths for
Alex. He wanted him humiliated, tortured and to suffer a long slow
death. Or a quick one with lots of bullet holes, making him scarcely
recognisable. His blood boiled knowing that Alex was in reaching
distance. He would have liked the chance to kill him himself and
watch him die, but he knew that wasn't possible. Alex had to be
dead before Paul could be released. Either way, he mused to
himself, he would piss on Alex Silva's ashes.

Alex Silva had been only a young man when they had first
met. He had always been mixed up with the wrong crowd as a

kid, thieving and scamming with his friends. Paul remembered when his youngest brother had introduced Alex to him. Alex had been a young tearaway wanting to make quick money to get him out of the slums where he lived with his family. Alex's father had never worked but made damn sure that Alex's mother had three jobs. She scrubbed floors, waited tables and took in washing from the hotels, but Alex's father drank all the money away. Paul winced inside when he remembered the day that Alex had said, 'Paulie, you're more than a boss to me, you're like a father to me. The best dad in the world.' He had smiled and hugged him. Paul had put him on collecting the drug money or doing drops with his brother. They were just young kids, and Paul knew the police wouldn't do much if they were caught. Sometimes they collected money from the brothels, and Paul knew that Alex and Matteo sampled the goods too. Alex was a ladies' man and they all loved him. The very thought of it made him smile when he recalled how many times he had caught Alex with his trousers down and turned a blind eye, calling it a perk of the job. In those days it had made him laugh and he had warmed to Alex instantly. He was a very likeable, charming man who had always showed respect.

Even as a kid Alex had been quick to learn and had kept his mouth shut. From the money he was earning, he was able to make his mother's life easier, even though she still left the house every day so her husband wasn't suspicious. And Alex was loyal too. Even when he had been caught making a drug drop-off and had served eight months in a young offender's prison, he had never broken his vow of loyalty to Paul. He had pleaded guilty and kept his mouth shut and once he came out, Paul and the other families had made sure he had a job for life. He had gone a step up the ladder and the others, Paul included, felt that collecting wasn't good enough for Alex. He was a foot soldier and his time in the young offender's prison had hardened him and made him grow up faster than his years. He was sharp as a razor and hungry to learn.

As Paul surveyed the cracks in the ceiling, his heart sank. He realised now that his fatal mistake had been favouring Alex more than his own brother. Alex had been funny, charming and what was more, he was fearless. Whereas Paul's own brother was sloppy and loud-mouthed. He liked to drink and pretend he was some fearless gangster with the backing of the families. He demanded respect in the family name and acted like a spoilt child when no one showed him any. As loath as Paul was to admit it, his brother annoyed him, but blood was blood and so he had stood by him.

When Alex's father had taken his belt to Alex's mother again, Alex had made sure it was the last time. He had begged Paul for a gun and after a while Paul had given in thinking he would never use it. But Alex had been true to his word and had shot his father at point-blank range in the head. Paul and the others had all been surprised when they realised that Alex hadn't done it in the heat of the moment, but had created an alibi for himself and his mother, which had cleared them both of any suspicion. Alex had shown no remorse, which had given Paul the idea that he would make a perfectly good hitman. He was calm, calculating and as cool as a cucumber when interviewed by the police.

It had been at this point that one of the families had some drug deals going on in London and had needed some fresh faces to help see over things. Paul had felt it was best for Alex to escape for a little while just to take the heat off a little and the rest was history. Alex had become Paul's right-hand man, and when Paul had eventually come to England, they had eaten and drunk together, like a family. Paul could see that everything was running smoothly, and Alex did his job well. There was never a penny missing from the dealings, unlike Paul's own brother who helped himself constantly, which Paul had to cover up. If the other families had ever found out he was skimming from them, they would have shot him themselves. Rule one: you never steal off each other. Rule two: you don't shit on your own doorstep.

A fly in the ointment had been Maggie who had been beautiful, blonde and cheeky. Both Paul's brother and Alex had admired her, but she had chosen Alex. Paul had expected it all to blow over – they were all still so young, but Alex had announced that he and Maggie were getting married.

Alex had made Paul godfather to his children, who had quickly followed the marriage, and everything had seemed to be running smoothly with business booming. Until the day Paul's brother had been alone with Maggie, and having had too much to drink, not only had he made a pass at Maggie, but he had also beaten her and attempted to rape her. Paul had been determined to sort it out eventually, but thought a warning to his brother might have been good enough for now. Alex had taken the law into his own hands and had killed his brother horribly. There was nothing more that Paul could do than to put out a contract on Alex for the sake of the family name. Alex was a dead man walking and so was his family. It was a sorry affair, but in revenge, Alex had handed himself in to the police, informing them of all the dealings, accounts and murders that Paul had asked him to commit. He'd even told them where the bodies were hidden, and when drop-offs were being made, for the sake of his own family's safety. He had been angry that Paul hadn't stood by Maggie, and so the battle lines were drawn.

And now Paul was behind bars pending a trial and Alex was in hiding. Was it worth it? he thought to himself. He doubted it. Alex's hot blood and love for Maggie had spurred him on, and Paul's own family loyalty and the Pereira name had done likewise. Only now it was personal. Alex had betrayed him and put him in prison.

A knock at his cell door brought Paul out of his reminiscence. Sitting up, he saw the door open and Barrow stood at the opening.

'I just came to see how things were? It's been a while since we last had a chat,' Barrow said.

Paul knew Barrow wanted to know if his story had been checked out and whether he would be getting his payment in full. 'Close the door,' he whispered. On doing so, Paul nodded. 'You have done well my friend, and you will definitely get what is coming to you. You can be certain of that.' He smiled. Satisfied, Barrow turned and left his cell.

Paul looked at the back of the closed cell door. He had to create a diversion and make sure Barrow would never be able to speak again. No one particularly liked him, and so it wouldn't be too hard to get someone to finish him off accidentally. Alex could wait, he mused. This needed sorting now.

Walking out onto the landing, Paul looked down. He could hear some argument had broken out below him and two prisoners were fighting. It was a daily occurrence, but a thought crossed his mind. There was the diversion he needed.

'*Ola*,' Paul greeted the other prisoners in the dining hall. Everyone stood back, letting Paul walk through unhindered. They were surprised to see him; he never joined them for meals in the hall.

He reached a table, and everyone sitting down stood up to leave.

'Not you.' Paul spoke to a Jamaican man just about to stand up. 'We need a little chat.' Everyone else hastily moved on, silently thanking their lucky stars Paul hadn't wanted to speak to them. 'I hear you have a grudge against one of the men in here.'

'No offence to you Mr Pereira, but that is our business. It doesn't involve you.'

'Indeed, it doesn't. I am not interested in your petty squabbles, although I am surprised you haven't taken it further. You're like a pair of housewives scrapping in the street. Handbags at dawn as it were.' He laughed at his own joke.

'I hear you're due to be moved out of here to another prison. Aren't you going to make your mark before you leave? Other prisons could be harsher than this one, but if your life was made more comfortable, with a few home comforts, these places can be bearable.' Spying the man, Paul knew he had him hooked.

There was a silent pause between them and the man picked up his plastic mug of tea and took a sip. 'What do you want me to do?'

Pulling his chair closer, Paul smiled. 'Now that is a good question.' In a hushed whisper he outlined what he wanted the man to do, then pushed back his chair and left.

The man sat there in silence. What Paul had asked of him didn't seem too harsh and he was already doing a ten-year stretch, and wouldn't be due parole for years. If life on the inside could be made easier, then Paul knew the man would take this opportunity while he could.

Friday night was movie night and something all of the inmates looked forward to. It gave them all a chance to mingle with other inmates. No sooner had the evening meal been eaten and cleared away than they were all called to stand in line on their landings, before being instructed to form an orderly queue and go to the cinema room, as they called it.

As each whistle blew, the Jamaican man watched the steam rise from his kettle, full of boiling water and sugar. It was an old trick and used regularly, but he had been given short notice to prepare anything else. Quickly grabbing his kettle, he ran down the landing and threw the boiling water mixture at his enemy. Hearing his howls of pain as the boiling mixture burnt and melted the man's skin, the prison guards ran forward and wrestled the Jamaican man to the ground. Hearing another high-pitched scream, everyone looked on in shock as Barrow fell from the highest landing. As he landed in an odd position on the ground floor, with his neck at an odd angle, it was clear that he had fallen or been pushed from the top landing and was dead. The mad panic that ensued by the guards to get everyone back to their cells caused mayhem. Only the Jamaican man lying face down on the floor with his arms behind his back in handcuffs raised his head slightly and saw Paul on the top landing. Paul nodded his head in approval, and then walked back into his cell.

Satisfied with the outcome, Paul poured himself a well-earned whisky and shut his cell door to drown out the noise. Gulping back his drink, he laughed to himself. 'One down, one to go.'

17

SUSPICIOUS TIMES

'Now, now tiger, rein it in,' Maggie laughed as she stood at the worktop making a cup of coffee with her back to Alex. His arms had wrapped around her waist and found their way up into her vest top, while he nuzzled her neck.

'Why?' he murmured in between kisses while he massaged her breasts. 'The kids are at school, it's still early and no staff are in yet.'

Putting her hand behind her, she could feel the hardness of his manhood against her back and felt her own excitement building, as his hand slipped down her leggings and stroked her gently. Turning around to face him, she kissed him lovingly. 'I love you, Alex.'

'I love you too. So does that mean I'm in with a chance?' Alex asked, kissing her now exposed breasts.

Maggie felt her pulse racing. 'We don't have time to go back to bed.'

Slipping down her leggings, Alex steered her towards the dining table and bent her over it, while unzipping his trousers. 'We don't need a bed,' he said and within a moment they were locked in passion as he thrust himself inside her.

'Jesus Alex, where did that come from?' Maggie panted as she stood up afterwards and straightened her clothing.

'You're a very sexy woman Maggie... what can I say?'

'Well, whatever it is, keep doing it. You're like your old self again. Where has this sudden burst of energy come from your randy bugger?' She laughed and went to freshen up.

Sitting at the kitchen table to catch his breath, Alex thought about what she'd said. It was true that for a long time now he had been in a slump. Possibly even a bit of depression had crept in without him knowing it. But suddenly, since he had met Luke, he had adrenalin racing through his veins. He had money stashed away and felt more like his old self again. Life was dangerous, but it was fun and he had something to get up for in the mornings. Now he had his own things to think about and it had given him a new lease of life. Not only had he saved Luke's life, he had breathed fresh air back into his own.

True to form, Luke had acquired two mobile phones for them which made life easier. And he'd done a few more jobs for Mark over the last couple of weeks too. Mark had brushed off the woman's missing car. The woman had confirmed that Mark had picked it up and presumably delivered it and when the police had told her that her car was burnt out, she was happy to claim on her insurance.

It was the end of the month and that meant payday when everyone went out for dinner for with their kids. This meant they were busier than ever. People liked the food, the ambience and the friendliness of the staff. Sighing to himself, he waited for the call from downstairs asking for his help behind the bar.

Today, he really didn't mind. The day had started off great and so he could afford to be benevolent. Checking himself in the mirror, he admired his pink shirt and sprayed on just a touch more aftershave.

Walking behind the bar and flashing a row of perfect white teeth at everyone, he walked up to one of the regulars who seemed to have the weight of the world on his shoulders.

'What's up, Martin? It's payday, shouldn't you be smiling?' Picking up a glass, he started pouring him a pint of lager. 'Where are your friends?' Alex had nicknamed the three middle-aged married men who stood at the bar constantly moaning about their lives but doing nothing to change them, the witches' coven.

'They're on their way. I'm on a taxi shift today, but Mick's due in any minute now.' No sooner had he said it than Mick walked in laughing. 'Has he told you then?' Mick bellowed.

Puzzled, Alex looked up. 'Told me what?' he asked.

'Martin's fed up because his wife hasn't been giving him any since they stopped sleeping in the same bed. He tried his best yesterday and she totally pissed on his parade, didn't he pal?' The third member of the coven walked in and waited for his drink. Mick was about to carry on, but Alex held up his hand to stop him. 'Hang on a minute, lad. Why don't you sleep with your wife Martin?' The very thought of not sharing a bed with Maggie was alien to Alex.

'Snoring.' Martin rolled his eyes to the ceiling while his friends burst out laughing.

'What, yours or hers?' Alex laughed. Blushing at being the brunt of the joke, Martin did his best to stop Mick from carrying on.

'No way Martin, Alex has got to hear this. He's been banished to the spare room cos she's fed up of the noise. Anyway,' Mick laughed while trying to tell the story, 'he told his wife he had been cold in bed last night and thought about getting in with her. And what did she do Alex? She went out this morning and bought him an electric blanket!' Everyone burst out laughing, even the customers who were eavesdropping.

'Fuck her, she's crap in bed anyway,' mumbled Martin, trying to save face.

'She's fucked you up big time!' bellowed Mick. 'Look at Alex here, with that grin on his face. I'd say he's getting it regular. Take a tip from him.'

'You either have it or you don't.' Alex winked. And he definitely had it, he thought while casting a glance at Maggie who seemed to have an extra skip in her step today.

After a couple of hours, Alex looked at his watch. It was nearly his allotted time to speak to Luke. They always arranged a specific time to chat, that way Alex could be near his mobile. Spilling beer down his shirt purposely, he made his excuses to Maggie about changing it and headed to the bathroom. There behind an old vent he had stashed the mobile and he saw the mobile already lighting up with Luke's call. Running the shower to hide his voice, Alex answered the call.

'Alex mate, can you get out later? I want you to come to my place. You haven't met my brother Kev yet, have you?'

'No, why? I'm not sure about tonight, but what's your brother got to do with anything?'

'You need to meet him. We've had an idea and as I'm supposed to be dead, that's where you come in. And don't give me that shit about being tagged Alex. You've broken that curfew of yours more than once.'

Cursing himself, Alex realised he had fallen into his own lie, but intrigued, he couldn't help asking, 'Go on Luke, give me an idea. You can't leave me hanging.'

'Do you remember me telling you about the sideline I used to have with the prescription drugs? People would message me asking if I was working and I used to drop all kinds of stuff off for them. Well, I found an old mobile that still has hundreds of those messages on it. It's just been shoved in a drawer, but I was thinking we could contact those numbers and ask them if they need anything...'

'But Luke, people don't just want cannabis and that's all you have to offer at the moment.'

'That's why you need to meet my brother Kev. He has contacts, good ones who can get their hands on prescription drugs from real prescription pads. We could make money Alex... what do you think?' Luke paused, waiting for an answer.

'What do you need me for? It sounds like you have it all worked out. You go for it, Luke.' Alex wanted to laugh, but didn't. Luke reminded him of himself in his younger days. Anything to make the next payday come quicker.

'Fuck Alex, I thought we were partners but you can be a boring bastard at times. I'll put that down to your age.' Luke laughed. 'I've also found a good cocaine supplier too.'

'So where do I come in?' asked Alex suspiciously. 'And who is this supplier you've found.'

'Alex... I'm dead. Do I have to spell it out? We need a cover and someone with a disguised van who can park anywhere at any time is the perfect cover story. And the supplier is this woman from Scotland. I don't know much about her but it's good stuff; this woman doesn't sell shit.'

Alex grinned. 'A woman from Scotland who deals in drugs. Would her name be Diamond by any chance?' Alex knew of a woman called Diamond who ran a very good syndicate and didn't get her hands dirty.

'I don't know the details. I've never spoke to her. She's a bit far up the ranks for me.'

Frowning, Alex pondered Luke's words. The last he had heard, the Diamond woman had married a French man, if it was the same person they were talking about.

'Do you know of her then?' Luke asked.

'I thought everyone had heard of her to be honest. Let me think about it and I'll call you later.' Ending the call, Alex couldn't help feeling excited. It all sounded like another adventure, and he welcomed it. He was already champing at the bit to get out.

Hastily, he changed and ran back down to the bar. 'I wondered where you were, but then I heard the shower and realised you were making yourself look beautiful.' Giving him a peck, Maggie smiled.

'I couldn't come down here stinking of beer. I needed a shower.'

Just then, Percy waved him over.

'What can I do for you Percy?'

'A bloke was around here the other day asking about you,' Percy whispered. 'Wanted to know how long you'd been here.'

Alex frowned. 'Well, I'm sure everyone could fill them in on that news. Any idea who it was?' Alex's nonchalance didn't betray his nervousness. Had someone finally tracked them down?

'I don't know, but I've never seen him before. Definitely not local and he didn't give his name.'

'Two pints here Phyllis please.' Alex waited for his drinks and steered Percy out the back to the beer garden. 'Why do I get the feeling that you know more than you're letting on, Percy?'

Wide eyed, Percy shook his head and took a sip of his free drink. 'I just thought you might want to know. The guy had a similar accent to yours. Don't know if you know it, but your foreign accent comes out now and again. But like I said, he just wanted to know how long you'd been here and what we knew about you.'

Suspiciously, Alex spied him. 'Why would they ask you Percy? Why would any stranger come to these parts and seek you out?'

'I was just hanging around, I guess. He saw me outside the pub and asked before he left and got in his car. He'd been in the pub, so I presumed he was an old friend of yours.'

'An old friend looking for me, but who never asked my wife about me? Don't you find that strange?'

Shrugging, Percy stared at him blankly. 'I never gave it much thought Alex. Just thought I would let you know. One good turn deserves another, and all that. Anyway, thanks for this,' Percy said, taking another sip of his drink.

'Well, if you see him around again Percy mate, let me know. Some people are just born nosey,' he laughed, going back indoors.

Alex felt unnerved by the conversation. If someone was asking questions about him, it wasn't the police. It sounded like he had been found, which wasn't altogether unexpected. It had been just a matter of time.

'Alex mate, over here. I've got something that might interest you.'

Looking over, Alex saw Mark standing with his usual posse surrounding him. He was boasting about one thing or another and at that moment in time, Alex couldn't be bothered to play along. Suddenly he felt drained after the conversation with Percy and knew he should probably tell Maggie the news.

'Alex!' Mark beckoned again loudly and with sunken shoulders, Alex walked over.

'What's up?' He smiled to acknowledge the others.

'I don't suppose you want to pop out for a couple of hours on a job tonight, do you? I'm going to have a few more beers with the lads and then we're going back to mine.' Mark winked. 'Pop by for a drink later if you want.'

Amidst his own turmoil, Alex knew exactly what Mark meant. He had obviously got hold of some cocaine from his dealer. It was payday, and every businessman would open their doors knowing people had money in their pockets.

'So what's this job you need doing?'

'Oh, it's a green card two streets away. He's had a bang in his car and needs the door respraying. I think it's due its MOT as well. I've changed the bulbs and put in a new oil filter and I said I would drop it off tonight but as you can see' – Mark waved his pint glass in the air, spilling some on the carpet – 'I'm busy.'

'Green card?' Puzzled, this was one job Alex hadn't come across before.

'Yeah, she was a schoolteacher or something in Africa then she only comes back with a husband from the Gambia thirty years younger than herself. If that's not a green card I don't know what is. It must be like living with his mother!'

The others who were just as drunk as Mark laughed and carried on with their crude jokes. As Alex was facing the bar, he saw Pauline scowl and Maggie indicating with her thumb to get Mark and his friends out of there as they were disturbing the other customers. As he looked at Mark, he could see he had already sniffed one or two samples of cocaine. His pupils were wide and he was louder than usual.

'Yeah, look, you get off Mark and have a good night. I'll pop round for the address later, okay? I'll just give Maggie a hand here. I don't know where all these people have come from but it's manic tonight.'

'Yeah, yeah we're going. Later Alex, eh? Don't forget now.' Like the Pied Piper, Mark walked towards the doors with his sheep following him.

Alex, walked over to the bar and apologised to Maggie. 'He's had one too many. He had a job on tonight; I've told him I'll do it for him. I don't want him driving like that.'

'You? Since when were you a mechanic's apprentice?'

'I'm just doing a favour for a mate Maggie. He's pissed! For God's sake, do you have to reprimand me in front of everyone for just doing a favour for someone?' No sooner had he snapped at her, he could have bitten his tongue. He knew he was taking out his frustrations on Maggie.

Maggie's face dropped, and she blushed to her roots, casting sideways glances at the staff, who also looked embarrassed.

'I'm just a bit rushed off my feet, that's all. You go about your business.' As their eyes met over the bar, Alex knew he had hurt her by biting her head off like that. His nerves felt stretched like piano wires and at the moment he was juggling so many balls in the air, he was afraid he would drop one.

18

KEV'S PLACE

It was beginning to get dark, and intrigued by Luke's constant mentions of his brother Kev, Alex wanted to meet this entrepreneur with contacts everywhere. Strolling over to Mark's, he could hear the loudness of the singing coming from his house and his heart sank. And on approaching Mark's house, he could see that Mark and all his friends were as drunk as skunks and as high as kites. It was a mystery to Alex why people needed vices to have a good time. But, like all addictions, people couldn't stop, be it chocolate, alcohol or cigarettes. Personally, that wasn't him. He'd dabbled in his younger days, but he had felt awful the following mornings and had decided he needed a clear head in his business and being drugged up to the eyeballs meant you didn't have the guts to go through with your orders, and needed back-up, or you wasted your well earnt money and kept someone else rich.

Being greeted and hugged by Mark, Alex smiled and looked at this shower of misfits. No wonder Mark's business was going tits up. And then there was the issue of his wife. Olivia was clingy and hated Mark being out of her sight. She had even cancelled her driving test when she'd realised that Mark wouldn't need to pick her up any more. She constantly rang him or texted him during the day, telling him what their son George had done. And as Maggie had said on one of the evenings she had been forced to go to one of their parties, 'I don't know why she's worried Alex, I wouldn't fuck him with yours!' Even now it made him smile.

Looking up at Mark stood in his shorts and vest, singing away loudly, Alex tried imagining any part of him that wasn't hairy. His long bushy beard lay on his hairy chest. You could barely see the tattoos through the hairs on his arms, and his beer gut hung over his waistband down to hairy legs. From Maggie's point of view, he could see what she meant. Only Olivia thought he was an Adonis and her jealousy raised its ugly head on more than a few occasions if she caught some woman looking at him. She had even caused a bit of a stir in the pub when a woman had turned away from the bar to go back to her seat and had accidentally spilt a drink on Mark. Out of courtesy she had offered to buy him one in return but Olivia had seen it as her 'chatting him up' and had had to be frog-marched out of the bar by Mark. She had apologised to Maggie the next day for her outburst and Maggie had brushed it off – it wasn't worth losing their friendship over. And even now, Olivia's arm was tightly wrapped around Mark's waist to ward off any interest from other women.

'Just come for the address Mark and the keys to the van.' Seeing Mark's drunken stupor gave Alex an idea. He didn't know why he hadn't thought of it before.

After shouting towards his friends that Alex couldn't have a drink because he was working for him, he handed over the keys and address. 'Thanks for this Alex, come and have a drink when you're finished,' he whispered.

Alex nodded, having no intention of having a drink with Mark and the others, and made his way to the van before driving to Luke's.

Parking further up the road from Luke's house, Alex walked the rest of the way and knocked.

'Alex, come in!' Luke beckoned excitedly, opening the door wide. 'Let me introduce you to Mum first. She knows Jehovah's Witnesses don't turn up this late, so let's put her mind at rest.'

Donned in Mark's long waterproof coat and his balaclava, he followed Luke into the lounge. 'Mum, this is my mate Alex I was telling you about. He's come to say hello and then we're popping out for a few beers. Is that okay?'

Musing to himself, Alex didn't think Luke's mum looked blind. She was a pleasant old lady with grey hair and decently dressed, considering Luke seemed to be her only carer.

Standing up, she smiled and beckoned Alex towards her, feeling his face and pulling back his balaclava. 'You're older than his other friends Alex, I hope you set a good example for him.' She smiled and sat down again. 'It's always nice to meet Luke's friends. Off you go and have a good time boys. Luke, put the television on, I like to hear the news.'

'I'll make you a cup of tea before I go Mum and a sandwich for later.' Seeing her nod, Luke beckoned Alex to follow and they walked towards the basement. Opening the hatch, which almost blinded Alex, Luke grinned broadly and walked into the basement. 'Take a look at this Alex!' he exclaimed. 'We're sitting on a fucking gold mine.'

Once Alex had got used to the light, he looked around. All of the plants were in full bloom. It looked like a florist's shop. Pulling him by the arm of his coat, Luke steered him to the other end of the basement, pushing away odd bits of furniture and junk that were covered in cobwebs. 'These are the seedlings.'

Alex looked at the hundreds of small pots containing seedlings in amazement. There were rows and rows of them. 'Christ your gardener's good Luke. All this in only a few weeks?'

'He's a big fan of that Alan Titchmarsh gardening programme and has been using that tomato feed grower. That lot over there are ready to sell, but they'll need transporting to my mate's so that he can prepare them. That's where you come in.'

Alex burst out laughing. 'Tomato feed grower? For fuck's sake Luke I wouldn't write to Titchmarsh's programme and tell him that!'

'If we leave it raw and uncut Alex, that will mean it's good stuff and people will come back for more. People pay for good stuff.' Luke grinned. 'Of course, once they're hooked, psychology kicks in and they think it's good stuff even when we put herbs in it. We've started a herb garden out the back – all above board. But we'll give them the good stuff first and let word spread.'

Alex liked Luke. He was likeable and a good businessman. He was also honest, which was unusual. 'Whatever you say Luke, you're the CEO of the outfit, I'm just a worker bee,' Alex laughed.

'I'd better go and make Mum's tea and take her her meds. She can be a bit unsteady on her legs sometimes,' Luke explained.

'What's wrong with her? She looks okay to me.'

'Cancer. I thought I told you. I'm not putting her in some old people's home, where she can't find her way around and is stuck in a chair all day. She's okay here and I can look after her.' Casting his eyes downwards, a sad note crept into Luke's voice. 'She hasn't got that long left Alex and spends a lot of time in bed lately. Life is just shit sometimes. It's bad enough her being blind, but cancer as well. I sometimes give her cannabis to ease the pain and it really does help. If those bastards had killed me, like they were supposed to, then God knows what would have happened to Mum. Who would look after her? To cover my tracks, I've hired a carer to come in twice a day. If those Liverpudlian bastards have a gut feeling that I might still be alive, they will see someone else is looking after her and not me.'

'I see your point and that's a big responsibility. But I don't mean to be rude, but you're only young and she looks older than I would expect your mother to be.'

'Yeah, she had me and Kev late in life. She lived life to the full in the early days and what with the cancer, people think she's my grandmother. Wouldn't you look old with all of that shit chemo running through your veins? It ages you, Alex.'

'You're doing a great job mate and I am sure she appreciates it.' Admiringly, Alex looked at Luke. For a shady businessman, his heart was definitely in the right place. 'She's lucky to have you, Luke.'

Alex thought he saw tears well up in Luke's eyes and decided to change the subject. 'And what about this brother Kev of yours? Does he help?'

'Oh yeah, let's go and meet him. You want to see his place, though – it's a shithole,' Luke laughed, 'so don't say you haven't been warned! But he is definitely our man. Plus, look at this...' Going to a drawer, Luke held up an old mobile phone and switched it on. 'This used to belong to the Liverpudlians. They were the ones who gave it to me, so it's been switched off for ages, but I've been making a note of the numbers stored in it. See what I mean?'

Alex looked on as Luke scrolled through message after message – there were hundreds of them all asking for Luke to deliver drugs to various locations. The key phrase would be 'are you working tonight?' which seemed innocuous, but meant Luke was on for a deal.

'And what happens when the people mention they are being contacted by a new dealer on a different number? You're going to get caught out, Luke. Even though WhatsApp is encrypted, the mobile isn't, so they could potentially track you down from this. My advice would be to use it on the move. Catch a train to somewhere new, do your selling and then switch it off.' Alex scrolled through some of the addresses already stored on the phone and noted Mark's address and telephone number. He said nothing, but wondered if he knew Percy's Liverpudlian friends. Was he deeper in with them than he had thought?

Slapping Alex on the back, Luke burst out laughing. 'If I didn't know any better Alex, I'd say you've done this before! Come on, let's go and see Kev.'

They walked towards a tower block that Luke had pointed out once before. It was the usual estate tower block and the lift wasn't working. People were milling around outside and Luke gave a thumbs up as they approached a metal door which resembled a prison cell door with a sliding hatch. 'Come on in Alex.' Luke waved excitedly.

Coughing as he walked in, Alex found his eyes nearly watering from all of the different kinds of smoke in the air. 'My God, what the hell is that smell?'

Luke walked in, shrugging. 'It's chasing the dragon. It can be done with meth, heroin, anything pretty much.'

Peering beyond the curtain of smoke, Alex's eyes focused on a group of teenagers watching an enormous, thin man with a glass tube. Using his lighter, he lit the bottom of the tube to melt whatever was inside, and inhaled it from the top. Frowning, Alex had to admit to himself that he'd heard the saying many times, but never actually witnessed it. It looked gross and everyone was completely off their heads with it.

The walls of the flat were either vandalised or spray painted in some elaborate mural. Walking further towards the kitchen area, he saw the worktops were covered in empty cans of lager and pizza boxes. It had a microwave, even an oven and sink, but the place was a dump.

Lying on a sun lounger, a man about Luke's age was tying a band around his arm ready to shoot up heroin with his friends.

He was wearing sunglasses and Alex presumed he was Luke's brother.

'Hey Kev, not yet mate, this is Alex. I told you about him.'

Kev took off his dark glasses and gave Luke a high five. 'Just in time bro, I was on my way to heaven.' His lopsided grin resembled Luke's, Alex thought to himself. Looking around and feeling like a pig in a poke, Alex took in all the people coming and going and making their way to their designated drug spot of choice. The dress code was mainly jeans and a T-shirt, until he saw an unshaven, grey-haired man. He was obviously homeless because he had all of his possessions with him in a rucksack.

Following his eyeline, Luke shrugged. 'Think he just comes in out of the rain, but he doesn't steal anything and sometimes he earns his keep by clearing away the surfaces. Probably gets off on all the smells in here.'

'I thought we were here to talk business, Luke. Is he up to it?' Alex pointed at Kev. 'And are there any lights in here apart from dimly lit lamps for Christ's sake? Does this place ever get raided?'

'Yeah, the police come every now and again and raid it, but this is personal use. We aren't selling. Have you seen any money exchange hands? And we're all so fucking high, none of us remember who we got our gear from. The police aren't going to waste time on us.' Kev spoke up.

To be fair, Alex thought to himself, Kev might have been high, but he was coherent when it came to business. And he was right, he hadn't seen anyone with cash in their hand. No one cared as long as they didn't bother anyone. Now Alex felt stupid, because Kev had pointed out the obvious that he hadn't seen. Being firmly put in his place, Alex relaxed and smiled. 'Let's start again, Kev.'

'Sure, thing man.' Kev raised his arm and gave Alex a high five, which he returned. 'Come onto the balcony.'

Alex welcomed the fresh air as they walked on to the balcony and inhaled the night air into their lungs. He felt quite dizzy after being in that opium den. 'Scripts are all ready to be picked up tomorrow. Some of the housebound even have theirs delivered so all is good. Got some distributors for your plants, so get that lot chopped up and bagged. Already got orders and they are going to hit the nightclubs. So, when you going to deliver Alex?'

Astonished and surprised, Alex said, 'I've got the van now. Where do you want me to deliver to?'

'There's an allotment about six miles from here. Joey and Tyrone will be waiting for you, I'll give them a call, say you're on your way. You know where it is, don't you, Luke?' Seeing Luke nod, Kev carried on. 'Got the lads on the lookout for bins. We will screw those bastards who tried killing you.' He turned to Alex. 'They came around here, trashing the place and asking about him. Said I hadn't seen him for days. Thankfully, I was high so I didn't feel the beating they dished out. Looked like shit in the morning though, black eyes and a couple of broken ribs. Makes no difference, everyone knows I wear dark glasses anyway.' Kev laughed.

Frowning, Alex was puzzled. Although he didn't want to sound stupid, he had to ask. 'Excuse me lads, why are they on the lookout for bins?' He'd heard this mentioned before but hadn't quite grasped the significance. The dealers he had dealt with in the past were big time; they had meeting points, collection points and it was done on a much bigger scale. He'd seen truckloads of cocaine and whatever else disguised in false walls of trucks and barrels of cooking oil containing tightly, waterproof wrapped packages. But bins?

'Delivery and drop-off purposes, Alex mate. Take a look around when you're driving or walking; it's surprising how many people have more than one bin. They are allowed three, one of each colour. No one takes any notice, that's why it's ingenious. The drugs are usually put in the blue one because it's dry in there as it's only cardboard. That's the best place to hide drugs Alex, somewhere dry, without contamination. We leave the payment in there too. Those Liverpudlian lot use the bin scam – me and Luke know that. So, we look out for bins on people's driveways. Some of our prescription customers leave their unwanted pills in the bins for us to collect too. It's simple but it works. And if they're good enough for Royal Mail and Amazon to leave parcels in, then why not us?' He smiled. 'It's a much easier arrangement, as long as it's not bin collection day. Shit! Those bank holidays fuck you right up when they change the dates for collection.' He laughed. 'Christ, we're totally fucked then!'

Looking at them both, Alex had to smile. Seeing Luke and Kev laugh like that meant they had been caught out on bin collection day at some point and lost the lot!

While they talked, Alex made a mental note to do his own survey on the duplicate bins. It intrigued him. It was so simple and yet it worked.

Reaching inside, Kev grabbed a pack of four lagers off the windowsill. 'Not you Alex, you're driving. And you're going to have a load of plants in the back. And Luke is a lightweight. One can and he's legless. So I'll have four for all of us.' He laughed again.

Alex had to admit, his laughter was infectious. He was a genuine man, exactly the same as Luke. He could also see this young man had his head firmly screwed on, considering he seemed to be spaced out all the time.

Luke nodded to Alex. 'Right, we had better go then Alex. Time is cracking on and you have to get back.' After another high five each, Luke and Alex made their way to the door, and as they turned towards Kev to wave, they saw him sit back in his sun lounger and carry on where he had left off.

Around the back of the flats outside were rubbish skips full of bin liners. 'People from the top of the flats put their rubbish down these chutes in the corridor,' explained Luke. 'Every floor has one; it saves people having to walk down all those flight of stairs or get the lift when it's working just to put a rubbish bag in the bin. All the rubbish comes here and the council dustbin vans take away the skips and leave new ones in their place. Saves having a million dustbins outside.' It was simple enough, Alex thought.

Luke looked up. 'Watch, Alex. Watch and learn.' He grinned.

Suddenly, a couple of weighted-down envelopes and doggie bags came flying down the chute into a box nestled amongst the rubbish bags in the skip. Instantly, Luke put his hand in the well-buried black box and took them out and opened them, handing Alex one. 'Go on,' he urged. Pensively Alex opened the envelope. Inside was money. 'You see Alex, they all pay to enter and use the stuff in safety. But no one really gets it for free, we just don't handle cash.' Luke winked and standing on tiptoes, he reached into the box and took out a host of envelopes, stuffing them in his jacket.

Amazed, Alex looked on at the pile of doggy bags and envelopes containing cash. 'Don't people steal them?'

'No, these people like to come here, so they aren't going to fuck it up for themselves. Honour amongst druggies eh. They would rather steal the drugs than the money Alex. They are addicts; money is only a means to an end. And it's emptied regularly, just in case the bin men come early.' Laughing, Luke walked to the van. 'Come on, slow coach. All that inhaling has made you look spaced out!'

While dropping Luke back off at home, he was surprised at his next question. 'By the way Alex, how is your daughter? Diana, is it?'

'Deana, and she's okay. Why?' Suddenly Alex's fatherly instincts kicked in.

Casting a sideways glance at Alex, Luke carried on. 'Just wondering. She was a good mate to help me that night you found me.' Luke blushed. 'Her boyfriend is a really lucky guy.'

Frowning, Alex looked at him. 'Did she tell you she had a boyfriend?' Once he saw Luke shake his head, he carried on, 'Anyway she's fine and too young for you by all accounts.'

'I was only asking Alex; no need to jump down my throat,' Luke snapped.

'You know Luke, I wasn't always in my thirties. I was your age once. But my advice about Deana is I would steer clear; she would eat you for dinner and spit out the bones.'

Luke followed his kindly lecture by getting out of the van. Alex couldn't help laughing. Boys will be boys, he mused to himself and smiled.

It had been one hell of a night, Alex thought as he drove home, and he had bloody enjoyed it!

19

DARK ENTITIES

Mark hadn't even noticed when Alex had dropped the van keys back before making his way into the back entrance of the pub. Since Maggie knew about his absence, he didn't feel the need to hide his return.

But storming into the hallway the minute he shut the door, Maggie strode towards him. 'Where the hell have you been?' Maggie shouted. 'You've been gone nearly four hours!' Red faced and angry, Maggie's blonde hair seemed to fly around her head like a banshee's. Alex was used to thinking on his feet, and so he knew the closer to the truth, the better the lie would be. He hadn't realised how long he had been out; he had been so engrossed with Luke. Looking up, he saw Dante coming downstairs. 'Are you okay Dad? Mum was worried.'

Shamefully, he looked past Maggie towards his son. 'I'm fine, Dante.' Alex smiled although inside he felt like shit. He had made his family worried about his safety while he was running around having fun with a couple of druggies. 'It was supposed to be a half-hour job, but Mark's van broke down!' he lied. Instantly Dante burst out laughing and with that Maggie stopped shouting and burst out laughing, too.

'Well, that serves you right. I bet you looked like a real prick! But you're safe and that's all that matters.' Walking towards him, Maggie hugged him. 'Four hours with no contact is a long time, Alex. No more favours, okay?'

'Are you kidding me? That was my first and last favour. I had to stand in the rain trying to get his van fixed – I couldn't exactly ring a mobile mechanic, could I?' He grinned and hugged her back, looking up the stairs and winking at Dante, who walked back towards his bedroom. 'Come on Maggie, I'll help you clear away for the night. God knows, I need a distraction and an early night. Never again,' he muttered convincingly enough to satisfy her.

Alex realised tonight wasn't the night to discuss Percy's suspicions with her. He had totally fucked up and there was no way he could tell Maggie that they'd potentially been found given how worried she'd been about his absence.

While tidying up, he took some empty crates down to the cellar. Seeing that no one was behind him, he went to the old beer barrel that he had put the golf bag full of guns in. Quickly he searched around for two automatics and their ammunition and took them out.

If someone was going to enter his house upstairs, he needed something to hand. He knew Deana already had hers firmly stashed away somewhere. He had taught them all, including Maggie, to shoot. At first it had been a game, just messing around in the garden with an air rifle and some old tin cans. But as time had gone on their lessons had become more serious. Even when gangsters were your friends, there always someone who wanted you dead.

Now this was his insurance, he thought to himself. He couldn't always be there to protect them, but it made him feel better knowing there were guns in the house and that his wife and children knew how to use them.

He would also make some kind of booby trap to stop anyone in their tracks on entering. Alex realised he was being paranoid, but with Percy's news he knew they had to be on their guard. Maggie may have slipped into normal suburban life, with her friends and customers, but they weren't from normal suburbia. Their lives were in danger. Alex hadn't spent hours and hours in police stations, identifying photos of mafia members and their connections just to fail now.

Alex placed the guns in the back waistband of his trousers and pulled his shirt out to cover them. With the rifle in its black leather cover, he thought it looked like a walking stick or an umbrella even. He decided he would put it in the back hallway near the entrance. There were so many coats hanging there, no one would notice it. After hiding the rifle, he walked into the bar, where Maggie was still polishing glasses and putting them away. There were still some glasses to be put in the dishwasher.

'Why don't you go up Maggie? You look washed out. Go on, I'll finish up here. Go and have a soak or something. Sorry I made you worry, love. It's a shame we can't have mobile phones of our own.' They both looked at each other. Maggie presumably still had the one he had got her to speak to her mother with. As they stared at each other, the same thought passed through their minds.

'It's a shame you don't have one, and after a couple of hours I could have seen if there was a message, just letting me know you were okay.'

His brows crossed, and he lowered his voice to a hushed whisper. 'We're not allowed them, you know that. The police have even tampered with Deana's laptop, much to her annoyance. She can't even be on Instagram like her friends. Christ, people must think we're weirdos or something,' he snapped, shaking his head. He felt angry, but couldn't do anything about it. He was stuck between a rock and a hard place. And at this moment in time, he was glad that the police did their surveillance checks. God knows who was watching his kids going to school. Maggie was an easy target behind the bar, but at least she was always surrounded by people which made an attack on her less likely, he thought to himself. He didn't care about himself, but his family meant everything to him.

'Go and have your bath, Maggie. You've had a long day on your feet and your blood pressure must be through the roof because of me. Try not to worry, I'll sort something out. My family come before anything else in life.' Walking forward, he wrapped his arms around her and hugged her tight.

'I think I will have a bath and soak my feet. Thank you.' Blowing a kiss, she left.

Pouring himself a brandy, Alex looked around the empty pub, with beer-stained glasses waiting to be stacked in the dishwasher. What a night, he thought to himself. Gulping back the brandy and feeling it warm his throat, he felt better. 'Right Silva,' he said out loud, while rolling up his sleeves, 'time to earn some brownie points and clean up.'

* * *

Although investigations had gone on into Barrow's terrible fall, no one in the prison had seen anything. Of course they hadn't, and the other guards hadn't expected anyone to come forward and point the finger. The prisoner with the badly burnt face had been taken to the burn's unit at the hospital, although his plight had been over-shadowed by Barrow's death. All enquiries had led nowhere, and the police had faced a stony silence. Everyone was busy saving their own skin. Barrow's death had been signed off as a tragic accident and more strategic safety measures had been put into place.

Paul Pereira stood outside his cell on the balcony, grinning to himself. He inhaled his cigar and leaned on the railings in front of him, watching everyone milling around. So far his plan was going well, but he needed to make sure Alex's death didn't raise any questions in the same way Barrow's had. His mind was in turmoil; perhaps he could make it look like an intruder or as though someone had tried to burgle this pub of his. Secretly he wanted Alex to know he had finally caught up with him and that he was behind his murder. He smiled. It was just a damn shame he wouldn't be there in person to see it happen.

Going back into his cell, he shut the door and knelt down behind it. He had got one of his henchmen to chip out a brick from the wall. With a little force, the brick came loose to reveal Paul's mobile phone that he had smuggled in. He used the prison's public phones regularly for calls to dismiss any suspicions of him owning his own phone that he used for only his most important conversations.

'Leon, it's time to act. I need out of this hell hole. I'm an old man and I don't intend dying in here. Make it look like an accident – a bungled robbery or something. Set the bloody place on fire if you have to, but kill Alex. I want to lie on my bed and imagine his tortured screams.' Ending the call, Paul grinned. Revenge was nearly his.

All night long, Alex had tossed and turned. What if his suspicions were wrong and it was just some nosey bugger asking about him? He knew it wasn't Percy's Liverpudlian contacts because then Percy wouldn't have mentioned it to him in the first place – that he was sure of.

He didn't want to alarm his family unless he had to, but it was time he brought them all back to earth and reminded them why they were all here in the first place. During the early hours he had got up and checked the pub, making a mental note to buy some extra bolts for the back door.

Sitting at the kitchen table in darkness, Alex rehearsed how he would tell his family about his fears, and that they had to be on alert. He couldn't remember how long he had been sitting there while nursing a cup of cold coffee, but one by one, yawning and bleary eyed, his children slowly wandered into the kitchen.

'Oh my God Dad, you made me jump. How long have you been up?' Deana jumped back with a start and wrapped her thick towelling robe around her tightly. 'It's a shame you didn't put the bloody heating on, it's freezing in here!' she moaned and switched on the kettle, while turning on the radio.

Dante sat down at the table next. 'Make me some toast Deana please, I'm starving and Mum's in the shower.'

'Make your own bloody toast, you lazy twat!' Throwing the loaf of bread at him, Deana laughed and then noticed her dad seemed rooted to the spot, not saying anything as they bantered between them. 'You okay Dad?' she asked, knowing he wasn't. It was pretty clear he had something on his mind.

Before he could answer, Maggie walked in with a towel wrapped around her wet hair and her robe on. 'Blimey, didn't anyone think to make me a cup of tea?'

'Sit down,' Alex commanded. 'All of you sit down. I have something to say.'

Maggie, Deana and Dante cast furtive glances at each other, but knew by the look on Alex's face that this was no laughing matter. The air seemed tense as they all sat at the kitchen table and Maggie made a pot of tea.

'It seems someone has been asking about me. Not a regular in the pub. It could just be some nosey passerby; after all, anyone can come in here and ask questions, but I think we have been found. And so we need to be on our guard.'

Wide eyed, Maggie stared at him. 'And just how long have you known this piece of information and kept it to yourself?'

'Not long. I was going to tell you last night, but with one thing and another I left it. It was someone Percy didn't know, which surprises me, because he knows everyone, asking questions about me and about how long I have lived here.'

Downheartedly, Deana looked down at the table and put her head in her hands. 'So, what do we do now Dad? What are you saying, we pack up this morning and move on?' she asked.

Raising her voice, Maggie looked at them all. 'I'll tell you what we do Deana. We tell the people who are bloody supposed to be protecting us – the police! It's only a suspicion at this stage, isn't it Alex? How do you know we've been found for definite?'

'The only way to know for definite Maggie is when I have a bullet in the back of my head. Then, and only then, will we know for certain we've been found.'

Tears fell from Dante's eyes. 'Don't say things like that, Dad.' He sniffed.

'The truth is always the hardest pill to swallow, Dante. That's why I'm having this meeting with you all. We all need to be on our guard.' Alex pushed his hair back with his hand, which immediately fell back into place over his face. 'We've let things slide a little. And I include myself in that. I am not pointing blame.' Alex's usual cheerful voice was monotone and serious, showing no emotion. 'If we tell the police Maggie, they will move us on today for sure. Is that what you want? This place is yours and you have made it a going concern. I'm not going to take that away from you, so that choice is yours and only you can make it.'

Looking around the table, Maggie saw her children's worried faces. 'For now, we say nothing. But, I agree, we have to be more vigilant. After all Alex, how much longer will we end up staying here?'

'I take it you mean when the court case comes up? I really don't know love. I haven't looked that far ahead. Although...' He faltered. 'I do have fifty odd thousand stashed away in the cellar. If you need to get out of here quickly and I am not around, you have money. It belongs to all of us and it's only to be used in an emergency, okay?'

Maggie sat back in her chair and folded her arms. 'Well Mark really does pay good wages, doesn't he?' she snapped. 'Anything else you've kept from us?'

'Stop it!' Deana shouted. 'For God's sake, let's not argue with each other. There are people out there wanting to tear us to pieces, and we're doing their job for them. Dad, it feels like you've already given up with all your talk about dying and a bullet in your head. And Mum, you want to tell the police, but you don't want to leave here. How does that work then?' Reaching over to her brother, she stroked his hand on the table. 'We are Silvas. We don't give up that easily.' Feeling better once she had said her piece, Deana sat back and looked from Alex to Maggie.

A grin crossed Alex's face and he reached out for hers and Dante's hands. 'Well, I guess that told us. I'm proud of you two. You've had a lot to cope with and you've done it without complaint. You're right. We will see this through, but you now know that you have back-up. There is money. We keep alert and check in with each other. Believe me, whatever is going to happen, is going to happen soon. If we have been found, they are not going to wait.'

20

THE BARE FACTS

Once downstairs, Alex could hear the grumbling chef, Phil, barking orders at the other kitchen staff. Popping his head into the bar, he saw the cleaner singing away polishing the tables under Pauline's evil watch, while she was eating a bacon sandwich. 'How come she thinks she's cleaning when every day she polishes those tables with the same old dirty duster? What bloody difference does it make?' she said, nudging Alex in the ribs.

She had a point, thought Alex and looked towards Betty in her cleaning tabard. 'Why does she wear a tabard with the local council logo Phyllis?'

'She comes straight from the leisure centres and schools. Probably uses the same bloody duster. I've watched her and all she does is spray polish in the air when she hears Maggie coming downstairs.' Phyllis continued taking a bite of her sandwich and slurping on her mug of tea, which was marked with a giant P on the front. Alex thought that was pretty pointless too, especially as the other barmaid was called Pauline! They were good staff though, and he had come to like them. Phyllis seemed to collect gossip before she arrived and he had to admit, he now looked forward to it.

Seeing the pub door open, he looked up and winced. The Zumba class! It was their mission to get rid of all their extra Christmas pounds before their summer holidays. 'Aren't you doing the Zumba class any more Phyllis?'

'No, I'm bloody not. Paid every week and nearly had a heart attack while turning purple and never lost a pound.'

Biting his tongue, Alex smiled as Phyllis took another large bite of her bacon sandwich.

He shrugged. 'Personally, I think exercise is overrated. I prefer a bacon sandwich.' He needed to get out of there before they all turned up with their water bottles and specially bought tracksuit bottoms and tops. Women, he thought to himself, they were a mystery to him and always would be.

'What are you laughing at?' Maggie asked as she proceeded to come down the stairs. Her blonde hair was tied back into a ponytail, and she had her water bottle in hand.

'Nothing, just Phyllis keeping an eagle eye on Betty the cleaner. Nothing gets past her.' As he heard the music and the Zumba instructor starting her warmup, he made himself scarce. 'Deana!' he shouted upstairs and seeing her head pop around the balcony, he beckoned her down. 'Outside.'

Once they were alone, she looked at him quizzically. 'What have I done now?'

'Just checking that thing I gave you is well hidden, but accessible if you need it. Also there is something bigger stored in the hallway by the coat rack.' Giving her a knowing look, they both knew what he meant.

Deana nodded. 'All safe and sound Dad. Mum doesn't go in my room any more now I'm a grown-up and entitled to my privacy.'

'Just checking, love. By the way,' he said. 'Do you remember that young Luke we helped out?'

She nodded. 'Course I do. He looked like a car crash.'

'Well, I saw him the other day and he asked after you. Just thought I'd let you know.' He grinned teasingly. Especially when he saw the disgusted look on her face.

'I wouldn't recognise him if I passed him in the street. Don't even know what he looks like under all that bruising and blood. Why is he asking about me?'

'Just courtesy, I suppose.' Alex knew he was fishing to see if she had seen or heard from him. He found it odd that Luke had asked, but maybe he was overthinking it. He was a father and she was his little girl after all.

Deana threw her head back and rolled her eyes towards the ceiling. 'That's where you've got the money from, isn't it? I take it he has been in touch about the plants we helped him with?'

'Yes, we sold the plants and to be fair, Luke is an honest thief and paid up.'

'Fair enough. I presume he is just grateful you saved his arse.' As an afterthought, a frown crossed her brow. 'So if you get fifty k, what do I get? I helped him too,' she laughed. 'Don't I get a percentage?'

'Well, I'm not sure what he wants to give you.' Alex winked. 'But he was asking about you.'

Slapping him on the arm, Deana laughed. 'Don't be rude, he doesn't look like he's got it in him.'

'How would you know? You just said, you don't know what he looks like.' They both burst out laughing. Just then Maggie reappeared and smiled at them both. 'What are you two laughing about? And what are your plans for today Alex?' she asked.

'I'm going to get some new bolts for the back doors,' he answered. Looking up, he saw Pauline passing through the hallway. 'Those ones up there look a bit old to me,' he corrected himself.

'Old? Bloody hell Alex, I doubt they've been replaced since they built the place. I'm going for my tea break now Maggie, if that's okay.' Without waiting for an answer and making her way to the kitchen and small sitting room, Pauline shouted back to them, 'Do you want one?'

Grinning, Alex shook his head. 'This place just gets better and better. The staff are offering us our own tea and biscuits now.' Alex laughed and leaned in closer to Maggie so that only she could hear.

'I've also got to go to the police station today, Maggie. Another glorious day in their back room.' Rolling his eyes to the ceiling, he sighed. 'Just keep your eyes open while I am gone.' He was about to walk out of the door, when surprisingly Percy was stood there about to knock. 'Shit Percy, you made me jump! What is it?'

'I need a word,' Percy whispered, and looked around furtively. 'Outside.'

'Well, as I was going outside anyway, I'll come.' Alex wondered what other snippets Percy had in store.

'Some friends of mine, they are from Liverpool... they were wondering if you knew anyone called Luke?'

Taken aback, Alex tried keeping his composure, 'Luke who?' he asked nonchalantly.

'Just Luke. He's a bad lot and owes them money and stuff.'

Puzzled, Alex tried to get a bit more information from Percy. 'What's that got to do with me, Percy? A lot of people come in the pub, but I don't know all of their names. Can't be arsed asking most of the time.'

'No I don't think he comes into the pub. But they bought something the other day and they wondered if it was from this Luke bloke. He hasn't been seen for a while, but a van like Mark's was seen in the supermarket car park. They wondered if Mark might have said something to you about it?'

'Percy, I've no idea what you're talking about. If it was Mark's van then ask Mark why he was at a supermarket. Why do people go to supermarkets Percy? To bloody shop of course! I'm not sure what this has to do with me.'

Stammering and blushing slightly, Percy bowed his head. 'No, no offence Alex. It's just that you hear and see a lot in the pub, and I wondered if you had heard anything.'

'Well, I do hear a lot, but I'm not sure what it is that I am supposed to have heard.'

'You spoke to a friend of mine the other week. He was in his car – a BMW – and you spoke to him apparently. He asked who you were.'

'I didn't know you had any friends Percy.' Drumming his fingers on his chin, Alex recalled that night instantly, not that he was going to reveal this to Percy. 'It doesn't spring to mind Percy. What else did he say?' Alex snapped, although a thought did cross his mind. Maybe they hadn't been found at all. Maybe it *had* just been Percy's friend asking about him and Alex had jumped to conclusions. 'Is this the same bloke that you said asked about me the other day? Because I suggest you tell him that if he wants to know anything about me, then he should come and bloody well ask me.'

Realising he had annoyed Alex, Percy shook his head. 'Oh no Alex, it's not the same bloke, honest. No offence mate. I just thought I would ask.'

'Well now you've wasted my time with your conundrums. I'm going out and if I bump into anyone from Liverpool in a BMW on the way, I will talk to them and tell them to mind their own fucking business about me.' Alex stormed off, leaving a very sheepish Percy in his wake.

As Alex walked, his mind wandered. He knew someone would have been watching that night when he'd dropped off the plants. Thankfully, he had been dressed as Mark and in Mark's van, but that could become a problem. He needed to inform Luke that they had their suspicions about him still being alive. The fire investigators had never announced they had found the remains of a body in the house and there had been no police investigation regarding it. So they could think that Luke had escaped somehow and that he had maybe caused the explosion himself. That was, of course, after he had taken what he could of the plants and sold it back to them. Was that why Percy was asking him about Luke? Alex had given Percy the message from a 'friend' himself and they now wanted to know if this mysterious friend was Luke, back from the dead.

* * *

Alex felt stunned as he sat in the back room of the police station surrounded by specialist detectives. After going through a few more things with them, they had announced that the case was almost ready to go to court.

'It seems that one of the heads of the families has had heart problems. We want him to stand trial, which will hopefully give him a heart attack,' one detective scoffed disgustedly. 'I want him more than the others, that Spanish shit. He trafficked girls and boys abroad. Most of them were homeless and he and his gang groomed and sold them. We haven't found half of them and of the ones we have found, none of them will give evidence at the trial. Some are so hooked on drugs, you can hardly see their arms for the track marks. The guy is Pereira's cousin. Did you know him?' The detective glared at Alex. He knew full well that Alex knew him; what he really wanted to know was whether Alex had been involved in any of that.

Stern-faced, Alex looked up towards the detective. 'You know I know Diego. But no, I wasn't involved in his sex rackets. You know what I am. I'm just a hired killer.'

The police officers looked tired and drawn sat drinking coffee out of plastic cups. Spanish detectives had also been flown in and after dealing with things from their part of the world, they had also contacted the FBI. too.

Alex had always known the court case was coming, but now it all seemed very real and he felt suddenly nervous. His stomach somersaulted at the thought of sitting there in front of his old 'friends' giving evidence against them. His hands felt clammy as he reached for his coffee.

'Are you ready for this, Alex? A lot of Pereira's men have turned on him and agreed to give evidence. It seems like all we needed was one sure thing – you Alex – and all the others followed like sheep.' Slapping Alex on the shoulder, another detective gave a weak smile. 'Thanks Alex, we all appreciate it. There are a lot of civilians out there who will sleep better at night, knowing that lot are going away for a long time.'

'What happens to me and my family after the trial? That's if we live that long.'

'That is entirely up to you Alex. There is still a bounty on your head and there probably always will be. We've given our word to keep you safe. We can move you all to another country, give you new identities, whatever you want.'

'It's going to crush Maggie and the kids to leave. She has grown to love that pub and the kids love the area and their schools. But the threat of death will always hang over us. And you won't always be there to provide protection. Christ, sometimes I wish I hadn't bothered!'

Casting a furtive glance towards each other, the officers could both see the strain it was taking on Alex. 'We do understand. But you opted out of the programme and chose to go by your own name against our advice,' they stressed.

Looking up at them both, Alex felt drained. 'When I die, if I die, I want my own name on my headstone. I want any friends or family I have left to be able to find me and visit my grave. Changing my name makes no difference to those people. There are no hiding places. I am going to have to walk into that court as Joe Bloggs or Alex Silva and I choose Alex Silva. I am no coward and by walking into court with a different name, that is what I would look like.' He banged his fist on the table to get his point across. 'I'm fucking sick of hiding. My whole family are sick of hiding. If they want to kill me then let them get it over with. The only thing I ask of you is to look after Maggie and the kids. Keep them safe. Is that fair?'

'You have our word on that Alex.' The officer patted him on the shoulder. 'You're not having suicidal thoughts or anything are you?'

Alex looked up at him and shrugged. 'Are you afraid for my wellbeing or yours? No mate, my aim is to stay alive. I don't need suicidal thoughts, because someone out there is prepared to do the job for me. Fucking suicide, I ask you,' Alex scoffed.

The other detective patted him on the shoulder. 'For the record Alex, I don't think you're a coward. In fact, you're one brave bastard facing those lot in court. They want your blood and you know it. Maybe when this is all over you will consider changing your name again and moving on – maybe to another pub, in another country eh?' Weakly, he smiled at Alex and then at his colleague.

'Maybe,' Alex mumbled. 'Let's see if I live long enough to hear the verdicts first. What about me, will I do a stretch in prison? I presume it will be solitary confinement because prison would be the easiest way to find and kill me. I deserve what I get. But my family, well, they never hurt anyone.' Tears brimmed on his dark lashes and fell down his cheeks, as he wiped them away with the back of his sleeve. 'These tears are not for me or my sins. They are for my family and what happens next.'

'Look Alex, cross that bridge when it comes to it. There is no point in thinking about it now.'

Knowing they were right, Alex nodded his head. There was no point in worrying about it until it happened.

Alex needed to think. His head was in absolute turmoil. He knew Maggie was no fool and that she knew there was a court case looming. But what did she think would happen once the court case started, and it all came out about who they really were? Would she really want to stand behind that bar while customers came in knowing who she was and what her previous life had entailed? She was enjoying her freedom while she could and he could understand that. After all, who knew what the future would bring?

21

A THIEF IN THE NIGHT

A week had passed since Alex's visit with the police. He had updated his family about the court case being imminent and they had all seemed resigned to the fact that changes would have to be made and accepted it.

Maggie had reached out for his hand and squeezed it. 'We're family, Alex. It's been a nice interlude between all the upheaval, but this place is just bricks and mortar. So let's just enjoy things for now and wing it when we have to.'

And that was what they had done, although he felt like he hadn't slept in ages. Every creak on the staircase had him up in the night. Some nights when Maggie was asleep, he would sit by the bedroom window staring into space. He'd even secretly put baby monitors downstairs, so that he could see and hear any movement from upstairs.

He was exhausted, permanently treading on eggshells and looking over his shoulder. And lying back on the pillow beside Maggie tonight, he finally felt himself drifting off to sleep. Suddenly, he woke with a start and sat up in the dark bedroom.

Something had woken him, but he didn't know what. Was he dreaming? Holding his breath, he waited. He could almost hear his heart thumping in his chest, in the silent darkness of the bedroom. Pulling back the duvet, he checked the baby monitor, but he could see nothing. Another noise from downstairs startled him and confirmed his suspicions. Kneeling on the bed beside Maggie, he nudged her gently. 'Maggie, don't jump or make a sound,' he whispered.

'What's up Alex?' she mumbled, bleary eyed.

'There is a noise downstairs, I'm going to check it out.'

Maggie sat up, more alert now. The chink in the curtains cast a weak light into the bedroom and Maggie looked on as Alex opened the drawer in the dresser and took out his gun. Silently he opened the bedroom door and closed it behind him.

As Alex reached the top of the stairs, he decided not to step down each creaking stair. Instead, he cocked his leg over the banister and slowly and silently slid down it. Scanning the hallway, he saw no one, and checked the back door. It was still bolted which puzzled him. His ears were pricked for any noise, although at this time of the morning there seemed to be noises everywhere. As he adjusted his eyes to the darkness, he heard another noise coming from the bar. Slowly he crept towards it and smiled; he had his own surprise waiting for his assailant.

Then he heard a thud, as if a stool had fallen over and then the sound of a gunshot being fired into the darkness. Turning the handle of the door, he pushed it wide open. Swinging from above the bar was a life-sized stuffed dummy Alex had made. It was shoddy, but in the darkness it looked like a figure of a man and he knew it would startle anyone that came in. It had obviously done the trick, which is why his assailant had fired the first shot.

Standing behind the bar in the shadows, was a lone figure. Alex squinted to see him, and instantly on hearing him, the man turned and fired his gun towards the doorway, missing Alex by inches. Alex cocked his own gun and fired quickly twice towards the figure who cried out in pain and fell to the ground. Fumbling in the darkness, Alex knelt down beside the man. 'Who sent you?' he asked.

From behind him, Alex heard a sound and another bullet whistled past his ear. Quickly he ducked for cover.

'Everyone has a stooge Alex,' the husky Spanish voice whispered from the darkness behind Alex. 'The man you've just shot was mine and that stuffed Guy Fawkes you have made was yours. Pathetic really. Why don't you finish him off? He's nothing to me.'

Recognising the voice from his past, Alex's blood turned cold. It belonged to a man Alex had worked with many times and who he knew was a crack shot: Jacob. Still with his back to him, Alex stood. 'Well, why don't you shoot me as you have been paid to do, Jacob? What's taking you so long?' Jacob was a professional hitman, like himself, so he couldn't understand his hesitance.

'Because it's been a long time and the boss doesn't want it over with so easily. He wants to make you suffer first. So, my predicament is, do I tie you up and let you watch me murder all of your family, while you are helpless to do anything to save them? Or do I bring them all down and let them watch their beloved Alex die in front of them? What would you do?' Jacob sniggered.

Turning slowly, Alex blinked hard, and focused on his other senses which seemed to sharpen more in the darkness. He thought about firing the gun in his hand, but knew Jacob would fire too, which would mean both of them would possibly die or be wounded which would leave the other man on the floor to possibly finish the job. That was if he wasn't dead already. But Alex could still hear him moaning, which meant he still had the opportunity to murder his family.

'I would kill me outright Jacob, then your job is done. I'd also finish this guy off – no witnesses, remember? That's how we were taught in the good old days. What you do when I am dead is your business, Jacob. I have no power over that.' Raising his gun quickly, while Jacob was off guard, Alex fired. As the shot rang out he heard Jacob cry out and then stumble, smashing glasses as he fell. Instinctively, he knew he hadn't finished him off. Mentally, Alex decided enough was enough and walked towards the lights, switching them on. If he was going to die tonight, he wanted to look his murderer in the eye.

Two more shots fired instantaneously, informing Alex of what he already guessed. Jacob was not dead. Injured maybe, but not dead. Dropping to his knees at the other side of the bar, Alex put his arms over his head, covering himself from the shattered glass raining down on him. Quickly, Alex fired his gun again in Jacob's direction and ducked, but then he heard someone else in the room as they trod on the broken glass. Then he saw Deana standing with a rifle pointed directly at Jacob's head. 'Go on you bastard, fire. But remember, you're next.' Jacob's hand was covered in blood, making it slippery as he held his gun. By the looks of it, Alex's shot had gone through the other man's shoulder or arm. Standing up, Alex saw him grasp his gun with the other hand, but Alex fired three more shots, one after the other with a final lone bullet fired into Jacob's forehead as he keeled over.

Wiping his sweaty, bloody brow, Alex nodded his head towards his daughter. 'Thanks Deana. Shit, no wonder my bullet never killed him.' He pointed to the bullet-proof vest Jacob had been wearing under his coat. From nowhere, another shot fired. Alex had momentarily forgotten about the other man lying on the floor, and this time his bullet hit Alex in the shoulder blade, making him slump to his knees.

'Dad!' Deana shouted, and swiftly turned, firing her rifle and killing the other man instantly.

Sweat poured from Alex's brow as he groaned in pain and blood ran down his neck and arm. Only adrenalin was keeping him conscious. 'See if there's anyone else Deana,' he panted, while still on his knees. He ripped at his T-shirt to assess the damage. 'Has the bullet gone through?'

'You need a doctor, Dad. We need to get you to the hospital,' Deana rambled as tears rolled down her cheeks.

'No Deana. If I die, I die. Now go and see if the others are safe.'

'Me and Mum are fine. We've checked too, and the coast is clear.' Dante spoke in a calm voice, making Deana look up in surprise and relief to see him.

Maggie ran forward and knelt beside Alex and used her dressing gown and anything near to hand to try and stop his blood flow. After close inspection, Maggie nodded. 'I can see the head of the bullet. It must have chipped the bone.' Maggie looked into Alex's half-conscious eyes and saw him nod as he passed out.

'I've got some sterile lint bandage in the bathroom.' Trying to compose herself, Maggie stood up. She was soaked in blood; her face was smeared with it where she had brushed her blonde hair away from her face. She was distraught and wanted to cry, but she knew she had to be strong. Not only for Alex, but for her children. The three of them worked silently – all that mattered now was saving Alex.

'Can't we call the police and tell them we've been found and that they shot Dad?'

'What? With two dead bodies on the floor and you with a rifle?' Dante replied. 'For fuck's sake, Deana, get a grip. I know you're not thinking straight, but look around you.'

A weak smile crossed Deana's red, tear-stained face. 'Well, thank God you are, Dante.'

Maggie returned. 'Here's the bandages, and I've brought the pliers. We need to pull the head of the bullet out.'

Grimacing, Deana nodded.

Now fully composed, Maggie took charge. 'We'll use vodka to sterilise the wound, then we'll pull the bullet out.' Maggie looked for Dante who was stood on a chair, cutting down the makeshift dummy Alex had hung from the bar. 'What are you doing Dante?' she snapped. 'For Christ's sake, help us.'

'I am,' he replied. 'The lights are on and there is the shape of someone hanging and swinging around the bar. I'm cutting it down so the neighbours won't see it. We need antibiotics after this to clean any infection, and painkillers. Lots of really strong painkillers. Any ideas?'

A thought crossed Deana's mind. Antibiotics and painkillers? Luke! If anyone could get their hands on some prescription medication quickly, it would be him. Recalling where he lived, she felt it was worth a try. 'I might be able to help there, but I've got to go to the other side of town.' She averted her eyes from both of them, knowing they would be looking at each other questioningly about where she could get such items. But if she could help, what did it matter now?

Once they had moved Alex into a better position, Maggie and Deana could see the head of the bullet protruding through his chest more clearly.

'Thank God it was his right side, Mum. That could have gone through the heart if it had been the other side.'

'It could have gone through his head, but it didn't. I need to try and get these pliers around the bullet. It's so slippery with all that blood,' Maggie sighed.

Dante walked forward and while adjusting his glasses, put some vodka on the pliers to clean them and then a piece of bandage on the top to give Maggie a better grip. Maggie nodded her head and pulled with all her might, but nothing happened. 'It's not shifting Dante.'

They could see the sweat pouring down Maggie's face as she twisted and tried loosening the bullet from Alex's chest. With all her might she heaved and suddenly the bullet popped out, causing Maggie to fall backwards off her haunches. Blood poured from the wound and Maggie was panting for breath as Deana and Dante knelt beside Alex and tried to stop the flow.

'We need to get this place cleaned up before opening time. But what are we going to do with these dead bodies?' Maggie asked when the blood flow was staunched. She ran her bloody hands through her bedraggled hair.

'I've got an idea,' Dante said. 'We do what they do in all of the good gangster movies and put them in the freezer until we can dispose of them.' He grinned. 'And we, Deana, have three massive walk-in freezers. I suggest we wrap them up in cling film, and put them under the bottom shelves. If need be, we take out the plug and tell Chef the freezer is broken. That will stop him from entering. We can replace any food we lose by using some of that money Dad said he had stashed away. And as far as the blood is concerned, we have an industrial carpet washer. It might not clear it all up but this is a pub and the carpet is already full of beer and food stains. It's going to take a lot of hard work, but with the three of us we can manage.'

Frowning, Deana looked him squarely in the face. 'For fuck's sake Dante, you're scary. For a fucking wimp, you're a genius. Let's get Dad upstairs and then get the cling film out for these two.' For the first time that night, she laughed.

Maggie stood up and looked around the bar properly for the first time. Everywhere seemed to be covered in blood. Alex's chest was rising and falling, but he still wasn't conscious. 'Dante's right. Let's get rid of these two bodies and if you know where to get a prescription, I suggest you go. The sooner the better, Deana.' Picking up a bar towel, Maggie mopped her sweaty face.

Deana looked at Maggie, her brows furrowed with worry. 'Do you think he'll be okay Mum?'

'I don't know, but we've done our best. We just have to clean up and cope with the fallout now. Your dad's well out of it. Come on, let's get this place sorted.'

22

DANGEROUS GROUND

Deana remembered where Luke lived and the location of the house, but in the early-morning daylight, they all looked the same. Sighing, she looked around for inspiration. She knew the house was one of three, so she decided to use her initiative and knocked on the first one. The landing light went on and a woman popped her head out of the bedroom window. 'What do you want?'

Standing back on the path, Deana smiled up at the window. 'Sorry to bother you, but a young man called Luke called us. I'm a district nurse.' She grinned. 'I thought it was this house. Did you call a district nurse?' she asked politely.

'No, two doors down. Number twelve.' The woman thumbed in the direction of the house. 'Is his mum ill?' the woman asked, sticking her head out of the window further.

'Just need to do some bloods. Nothing serious,' Deana lied, not knowing what else to say. Why else would a district nurse be going that early in the morning? It had been the first thing that popped into her head. 'Thank you, sorry to wake you!' Wanting to end the conversation quickly, Deana waved and walked out of the gate, knowing full well that the woman from the window was still watching her.

Once she had knocked on the door of number twelve, she waited, but there was no response. In desperation she opened the letter box and shouted Luke's name and then cast a glance to see if the woman at the bedroom window was still watching her. Fortunately, Deana could see the window was shut. Suddenly it sounded like a herd of elephants were stomping down the staircase and then the door swung open. Standing in his boxer shorts and T-shirt, Luke rubbed his face. 'What's with all the bloody shouting? My mum's asleep.' Then, through his half-dazed state, he saw Deana.

'Diana, it's you. What's up?' He yawned.

'Deana, you prick. And you can call me Nurse Deana.' Deana cast her eyes to the woman's house she had just come from.

Taking her lead, Luke opened the door and let Deana in. 'Oh nurse, thanks for coming so quickly, I really appreciate it,' he said in a loud voice.

Rubbing her hands together from the cold, she followed Luke into the kitchen and welcomed the heat to warm her. 'Blimey, it's hot in here.'

'Mum feels the cold,' Luke said. It wasn't a lie, but he didn't mention the other reason for it being so warm: they were sat on top of a basement full of cannabis plants and heaters.

'It's my dad. I need some antibiotics,' Deana blurted out.

Puzzled, Luke looked at her suspiciously. 'I'm just going to check on Mum upstairs and then you can tell me everything, Nurse Deana,' he emphasised. 'Like why you haven't called a doctor for your dad for a start.'

Blushing slightly, Deana nodded and rubbed her hands together again.

Once Luke disappeared, she decided to make herself useful and put the kettle on. She needed a hot drink herself. Looking around the gaily coloured kitchen, Deana couldn't help but notice how clean and tidy it was with everything in its place. The only odd thing she noticed when searching for a mug, was that there weren't any. There were only little flowery china teacups and saucers, already prepared on a tray with a matching tea pot.

Rushing back into the kitchen, Luke startled her by saying, 'You need to come up when I take Mum her tea Deana. Your shouting has worried her, and she's a little agitated this morning.'

'Of course. Sorry,' she apologised. 'The kettle has boiled; shall I be mother?' She smiled, not knowing what else to say.

'No, I will, but you can put some bread in the toaster if you want?' Luke blushed awkwardly.

Looking at him from under her lashes, Deana saw a very different Luke to the man she'd met at Percy's. Although just out of bed and unshaven, he looked a lot different to how he had seemed on their first meeting. His hair was a chestnut brown when not smeared in blood, and matched his warm brown eyes, which seemed to have a mischievous glint in them. He was quite tall, but not beefy or muscley. Attractive though, she thought to herself as she buttered the toast.

Following Luke's lead, Deana went upstairs and into his mum's bedroom. She waited while Luke set the tray near a comfy floral chair, which his mum was already sitting in.

'This is my girlfriend, Deana, I was telling you about,' said Luke as he poured the tea. Puzzled, Deana shot him a glance. Seeing Luke nod his head, she reached out her hand to shake Luke's mum's. 'Nice to meet you. I'm sorry I woke you.'

'Kneel beside me Deana, I don't feel like standing.' She did as she was told and the woman raised her hands and stroked them around Deana's face. 'You are pretty Deana, and you have such a pretty name. But you seem flushed and worried. What's wrong?'

Blushing under the old woman's touch, Deana smiled. 'I've

been running. I thought Luke would be up by now. And I am a little worried, because I've woken you up. Sorry.'

'Tell me about yourself. Luke hasn't said much, but men don't, do they?'

Nervously, Deana looked up at Luke, who was busy passing his mum her small tray and placing it on her knee. Awkwardly, he blushed and frowned at Deana, urging her to speak.

Once Deana started speaking, she couldn't stop. She told her that her parents ran a pub, that she was at college, and that she had a brother. The old lady sipped her tea while she listened and commented in some parts. 'Well, that really has been a nice breakfast chat, Deana. You will come again, won't you? Although I feel I've kept you for far too long. I'm feeling a little tired now, Luke.'

'Come on Deana. We'll talk downstairs.'

A smile crossed the old woman's face as she patted Deana's hand. 'Off you go dear, I'm sure you have things to talk about.'

Deana followed Luke downstairs and waited until he shut the kitchen door behind them. 'So, what's going on with your dad?'

Not sure where to start or how much to say, Deana decided to blurt out a shortened version of the truth. 'Dad's been shot. We've cleaned the wound and taken the bullet out, but he'll need antibiotics. We don't want to involve a doctor, because we don't want to involve the police. I wondered if you could get any for us... for him...' Deana trailed off and looked down at the table as Luke placed her cup and saucer in front of her and sat down.

'Shot? Christ, Deana, your family don't do things by halves. I thought my life was fucked up.' Luke's eyes widened and he let out a low whistle. 'I already knew there was more to your dad than met the eye, so I'm not that surprised. And yeah,' he sighed, 'I can get you the antibiotics, but not until at least lunchtime.' Luke's brows furrowed. 'Why didn't you just use your dad's mobile to contact me? He uses it now and again if he needs to get in touch with me.'

Seeing the confused look on her face, Luke grimaced and put his head in his hands. 'Oh Christ, you didn't know about it, did you? Me and my big mouth. You can't tell him I told you.'

'I won't. But I wish he'd told me. It would have saved me one hell of a journey and you a lot of embarrassment with me turning up. Anyway, are you sure you can't get some quicker than lunchtime? I really need the meds now,' she pleaded.

'Actually…' Luke said. 'Mum had a chest infection a few weeks ago, and got given some antibiotics, but they didn't agree with her, and they prescribed some different ones. The others will still be upstairs. I can give you those to start off with. As for painkillers, I can give you some of Mum's morphine patches. The doctor always gives her more if needed, because they don't always stick on too well.'

Taking a sigh of relief, Deana smiled. 'Thank you Luke, I really appreciate you putting yourself on the line like this.'

'You put yourself on the line for me once Deana. It's payback time.' He grinned. Looking down at himself, he realised he still wasn't dressed. In all of the dashing about it had never dawned on him. Now, suddenly, he felt shy. 'I'd better get dressed and sorted. Let me get those meds for you.' Standing up, Luke reached for his wallet on the kitchen worktop. 'And here's thirty pounds. It should be enough for you to get a taxi home.'

Surprised, Deana looked at the money. 'I can't do that, Luke. I'll get the bus, but thank you.'

'Just take it Deana. Your dad clearly needs you.' Pushing the money into her hands, Luke went upstairs and came back down with the medication. 'There are some other painkillers in there as well. Naproxen is good for pain. If and when you can, let me know how he is, yeah?'

Giving him a weak smile, Deana nodded. 'I will Luke and thank you. I really appreciate it and so will Dad.' Without thinking, she reached forward and kissed him on the cheek, making him blush. Then she turned and left to catch a taxi on the high street.

As she approached the pub, Deana felt nervous. Her father could already be dead. And if things had gone differently earlier, they could have all been dead. The very thought of it made her blood run cold. Deep down, she knew whoever had sent those men would be waiting to hear news of whether the job was done. Which meant someone could come back tonight, she thought to herself. Walking into the pub, she was surprised to see that everything looked normal. It was as though last night had never happened.

Maggie was behind the bar and Deana caught her eye. Whatever Dante and her mum had done, they had cleaned this place up to perfection. Heading upstairs, Maggie was hot on her heels and once inside the bedroom, Maggie shut the door. 'Well? What happened?'

'I've got these. This is a morphine patch and here's some antibiotics. I'll be getting more later but we have to wait for now. This place looks amazing. What about all of the blood on the carpet?'

'What can I say? I've never cleaned carpets so quick in my life,' she laughed.

Deana turned towards the bed where her dad lay. 'How is he? I must confess I've feared the worst. Oh God Mum.' Deana wrapped her arms around Maggie. 'What if he had died?'

'Well, he hasn't, has he? Look. He's pale and has a temperature, but he's mumbling in his sleep. Let's put this patch on and see if it helps. I've already started to spread the word that he's ill, so if anyone asks, that's the story. Just tell them we think it's Covid. I've put an ice pack in a tea towel on his forehead to keep the temperature down. We need to get these pills inside him.' Maggie looked at the antibiotics. 'Fortunately, they are capsules, so we can take the powder out and just open his mouth and pour it in. Let's try and sit him up a little bit to get some water inside him.'

Between them they managed to get some water and the medication inside of Alex and even though he was half-conscious, he seemed co-operative before falling back to sleep. 'That's the best we can do, love. Only time will tell now.'

'Where is Dante?' Deana asked, wondering how her brother had been dealing with it all.

'Mr Cool as a Cucumber? He helped me and then went to school, keeping everything normal. Christ Deana, I don't know if we'd have managed without his idea to put the bodies in the freezer! I thought we'd have to stage a break-in and take your dad to the hospital.'

'Me too,' Deana agreed. 'What about the people who sent those gorillas? Won't they be waiting for an outcome? Surely they will want to know if the job was finished. Maybe we should have gone through their pockets to find out who they were?'

Maggie wrung her hands nervously. She wasn't sure if she should be telling Deana this but then again, what did it matter? They were all in this together now, after all. 'When your dad did a job... in the old days.' Hesitantly, she thought about her words. 'Well, the word was to keep your head down or disappear for a few days after the hit. No contact so that no one could connect you to the person who'd been killed. That old plan will still be the same I presume, so that will give us a few days' grace until we have time to think clearly. God, I'm exhausted.' Maggie sat on the edge of the bed and sighed as tears rolled down her face.

'Don't, Mum, or you will start me off. We need to carry on as normal. And I know all about Dad's past Mum, so don't worry. He told me where he had hidden the rifle I used to kill that guy,' Deana said, shaking slightly with shock.

'You were so brave, Deana love! Me and Dante looked to see if there was anyone else waiting in the shadows, but there wasn't even a car outside. They must have driven here, but I don't know where they parked their car. It will have been a stolen one, so the police will probably find it once it's reported missing.' She stood up and rubbed her hands together. 'Right, I'm going to freshen up this bedding up as best as I can. When you pick up the new medication later, will you get more bandages, too? We're going to need some.' Maggie pulled back the duvet and saw that Alex's bandage was soaked with blood and it was seeping through into the sheets and possibly the mattress.

Leaving the room, Deana let out a huge sigh. She too felt exhausted. 'What a bloody day,' she muttered to herself. But then she thought of Luke and a smile spread across her face. Maybe it hadn't been such a bad day after all, she mused to herself.

Days passed until a week had gone by. Luke had got them all the medication they needed and Alex had passed the worst. They had taken it in turns sitting with him through the night mopping his brow, but each day he had got stronger until slowly they could spoon soup into his mouth. And now he was sitting up in bed speaking coherently. Everyone had asked about him, including the police. And Luke had been better than his word and had sent a positive Covid test for them to use as proof of Alex's continued absence.

They all felt like they were treading on eggshells, permanently lying to everyone, even more than they already were. Once Deana was alone with Alex, she mentioned the mobile phone Luke had told her about and told him about the part he had played in saving his life.

'He's a good kid Deana. I saved his life and he saved mine. We're equal now. But we need to sort those bodies out,' Alex remarked. 'I've had an idea.'

'Yeah, Mum's already sorted a lot of that out. She had a couple of those suit covers in the wardrobe and after we put cling film over them, we managed to get both of them into one of those. We put them so far to the back of the freezer we nearly froze to death.' She laughed, making Alex laugh too. 'In the meantime, we have the brewery on our backs wanting to dig up half the beer garden to build a bike shed. All part of their "ditch the car, have a drink" promotion for the summer.'

'Really?' A flash of an idea passed through Alex's brain. 'They're digging up the beer garden? That means they'll have to lay cement, doesn't it?'

'Yeah, it's going to be a pain in the arse. All that noise and builders, although Mum thinks it will bring in "more custom",' Deana mimicked as Maggie entered the room.

'What are you two plotting?' she laughed.

'Deana was just telling me about the builders and the bike shed. It seems like God has sent us a winning hand – don't you think?' Alex smiled.

Following his train of thought, Maggie's eyes lit up. 'Oh my God Alex. Do you think we could get away with it? It would solve a problem. A really big problem.'

Deana looked from her dad to Maggie. 'Anyone want to let me in on the secret?'

'We're going to bury one of the bodies under the bike shed,' Alex whispered.

'Yeah, but there are two bodies, Dad, so what about the other one? More to the point, those builders are going to lay the cement in daylight. It will be set by the time they leave. How are we going to put a body underneath it?'

'Leave that to me and your mum. The second body, as you point out, well, we need him. We need to have a male body found in Kent to satisfy their boss's curiosity. It's going to be gruesome, because he can't have any DNA.'

'Oh my God!' Maggie groaned. 'I know what you're saying Alex. You're going to chop off his head and hands – no fingerprints, or dental records. Not even hair.'

'While he is frozen solid, we can transport him elsewhere and dump him. At least that way there won't be any blood trail.' Maggie and Deana could see Alex's mind working overtime. The horrendous idea made them feel sick inside.

'Well, we need to get this ball rolling. First of all, I need to tell a very twitchy Mark that his buddy is feeling much better and has now tested negative. He's been in every day asking about you. He really thinks a lot about you.' Maggie smiled. 'We'd better put a shirt on you to cover the bandage. It's much better now, but if I tell him, the whole world will know.'

Alex rubbed his shoulder. 'I need to take a look at this. Is there a big hole?'

Maggie's face lit up. 'Not any more. While you were unconscious, I got my needle out, then Dante glued it together. Quite surprisingly really, but it actually worked and it seems to be healing well.' Pleased with her and Dante's nursing skills, she smiled, although Alex winced inside.

'Thank God for that.' Alex laid his head back on his pillow. 'I need to stop taking the medication now; I think it's making me more light-headed and drugged up. I need my wits about me.'

Maggie unwrapped the bandage and waited as Alex slowly looked down at his wound. 'My God, that's amazing. In time, you will hardly notice it. Christ, I half expected you to have used pink cotton.' He grinned.

'No, Dante got some invisible thread and we used that. No wonder he's doing great in his biology classes. I have to admit Alex, he's been fantastic. You make sure you let him know that.' After putting a clean bandage on his wound, Maggie put a clean shirt on him and made him look more respectable. 'Right, I'm going down to let Mark know. I will send up some food for you.' Blowing him a kiss, Maggie left to spread the news that Alex was on the mend.

Deana waited until her mum had gone before saying, 'The phone, Dad. I want to text Luke and let him know you're okay.'

'Fair enough. It's behind the vent in the bathroom.' Just then they both heard a thumping up the stairs and looked at each other. 'Mark!' they said in unison and laughed as the door swung open.

'Alex! Christ, I thought Maggie had buried you under the patio. Great to see you mate.' Holding two bottles of beer in one hand and a plate of sandwiches in the other, Mark sat down on the end of the bed. 'Boy, have I got loads of shit to tell you.'

As Deana was about to leave the room, she cast one last look at her dad and smiled. Her mum was right, she thought to herself. Mark might be a pain in the bum, but already the colour was returning to Alex's cheeks as he listened to Mark's funny stories. He was doing him the world of good. They didn't even notice when she shut the door behind her.

* * *

Now Deana knew where the mobile phone was, she followed Alex's instructions and found it. Switching it on, she saw the only number on it was Luke's, or so she presumed. Pressing call, she waited. Finally, Luke answered the phone. 'Alex! Oh my God, it's great to hear from you, mate. I've been worried about you.'

'No,' stammered Deana. 'Erm, it's me... Deana. Dad's a lot better now, but I thought you'd like to know.' Suddenly, she felt shy. She couldn't think of anything else to say, but didn't want to end the call.

Taken aback, Luke also seemed awkward. 'Oh, Deana... He told you where to find the phone, then? Well, he must be feeling better. How's you?'

A warm feeling filled Deana, although she couldn't explain it. Maybe it was because she had found someone she didn't have to lie to, someone who would help her when times got tough. He had already proved that. 'I'm okay Luke. It's good to hear your voice. Maybe we'll talk again soon. How's your mum, by the way?'

'She's asked about you. I said you had family stuff to sort out.'

'Send my regards Luke. Maybe I will see her some time.' Deana crossed her fingers, hoping for an invite.

'Well, you know where we live Miss District Nurse,' he laughed again.

It wasn't the invitation she had hoped for, but it was better than nothing. 'Bye Luke.' Ending the call, she felt pleased she had called, but disappointed with the outcome. He hadn't seemed bothered if he saw her again or not, but at least she had passed on to him that Alex was okay.

23

MISSING PERSONS

Paul Pereira banged his fist on the table, making his plastic coffee cup wobble and slightly spilling the contents. 'You're telling me that they are still bringing the court case to trial? I thought you had come to tell me I will be out of here. I know there is a fucking court case looming! Why are you wasting my time – and my money?' His eyes widened, and his face flushed red as he glared at his lawyer. Spit dribbled from his mouth as he shouted. He was angry, bloody angry. When he had been told his lawyer was coming to visit, he had expected good news, not this!

'Mr Pereira, please calm down. I only came to tell you that they are setting a date for the trial and if there is anything you wish to go over, now is the time.'

'Go over with you! We've talked for a lifetime, now I want some action. Get me out of here. That is what you're being paid for!' Paul's anger was such that he couldn't stop shouting. He hadn't heard a word about Alex Silva's demise. He had heard nothing about Alex at all, and now this! If this court case went ahead, he would be serving a full life sentence. It had also crossed his mind that he could be deported. Knowing he had more enemies in Portugal than he did in England disturbed him.

Standing up, the lawyer started gathering his files together. 'Mr Pereira, I will be in touch when there is a definite date. I suggest you practice calming down. If you start shouting like this in court, the jury won't look upon you favourably. You will do yourself no favours, believe me.'

Throwing his hands in the air and standing up, Paul paced around the table till he was looking his lawyer directly in the eyes. 'Favours? Are you living in a bubble? They are not going to look upon me favourably anyway, given who I am. Go and fuck off out of here and don't come back until you have a freedom date for me...' He turned away from his lawyer and then, as an afterthought, Paul stopped him. 'Wait. Does Alex Silva know the case is soon? Has he been informed?'

'I can only presume that Mr Pereira, although, there have been no new statements from him over the last week and no other evidence has come to light.'

Paul looked his lawyer up and down. 'You have heard nothing about Alex for a week? I thought you had regular meetings with the police and lawyers about his accusations?' A wry grin crossed Paul's face; maybe without saying anything, his lawyer had given him the news he'd been waiting for. Not a word had been heard from Alex. Now that was good news indeed.

Picking up his briefcase, his lawyer shrugged. 'Well, he hasn't come up in any conversation I have had Mr Pereira. But he isn't the only one making accusations against you. I'll be in touch.' Walking towards the door, his lawyer knocked on it and looked through the small square glass.

Escorted back to his cell, Paul couldn't help feeling optimistic. His lawyer had heard nothing about Alex in recent days? He would call Leon later and find out what he knew. But if Alex was dead, he would have been informed by now surely?

Twitching in his cell, Paul wanted no company today. The sound of the dinner bell seemed to take forever, and that was what he was waiting for. Everyone, including the guards, would be busy during this time and then he could make his call in private. Smiling to himself, he fantasised about being free. This time next week or so, he could be drinking whisky in his own home. Oddly enough, as much as he loved his wife, being at home with her had used to annoy him. She was a good woman, mother and cook, but home matters bored him.

Now, the idea warmed him. To be sat in the comfort of his own home, being waited on hand and foot by her seemed like paradise. These grim walls were getting him down, no matter how he dressed his cell up.

Standing on the balcony, he looked around, watching everyone march in the opposite direction towards the dining room. Shutting his cell door, he removed the brick in the wall and pressed the speed dial that connected him to the outside world. Leon answered instantly. 'Boss, how you doing?'

'Stupid question Leon, I'm not doing much. Not much at all. Well, do you have news for me?'

'Not heard anything yet boss. But no news is good news, eh?'

'What the fuck does that mean?' Paul whispered, trying to control his temper.

'Boss, no one has seen or heard about Alex. Jacob never told anyone when he was going to do the job, but it's been a week. I sent one of the lads to have a drink in the pub and to ask about Alex, but they were given some cock and bull story that he's got Covid. Personally, I think the police are keeping this close to their chest. If Silva is dead they will have to use other evidence they have, we know that. A lot of rats have turned on us Paul. No bloody loyalty, considering what they have had out of you. Some of them are even killing each other; this place is like a war zone. Believe me, you're better off where you are – well out of it. I don't know anything else boss, sorry.'

Frowning, Paul was puzzled. 'What do you mean they are killing each other? No one has said anything to me about this.'

'Boss. The police are up to speed with the trafficking. People take that very seriously these days. Everyone is pointing the finger about those containers you had to transport people while they were taken out of the country to the brothels that you and Matteo owned.'

'I never got my hands dirty with that stuff Leon, that was all Matteo's doing.'

'No boss, but the word on the street is that you and the other families arranged it. Like I say, everyone is jumping ship, and your name is the forefront of everyone's tongues.'

Paul's heart sank. It seemed it was much worse than he had imagined. Surely not everyone had turned on him, had they? This was only the tip of the iceberg of what they were going to throw at him in court, which meant Alex was not the only one who was giving evidence against him. Suddenly fear gripped him. The cold light of day was looming, and God only knew what they were going to throw at him, whether Alex was dead or not. He obviously hadn't been quite kept up to speed as much as he thought he had. 'Let me know if you hear anything Leon, I will check in on you in a couple of days' time.'

* * *

Leon ended the call and looked up nervously. Swallowing hard, he took in the man before him, who sat smoking his cigar listening to the call. 'How was that John?'

John was an extremely suave and sophisticated, well-dressed, middle-aged man. His dark blue silk-like suit shone in the lamp-light of Leon's home. Each finger had a sovereign ring and his black hair was slicked back behind his ears, showing off his diamond stud earing in his left ear.

'Very convincing Leon. If we're lucky, he will shit himself and hang himself in his cell, if not... well, I will see to that. You did well and you tell a good tale. Let's hope you don't end up with a speech impediment from that sore throat of yours.'

'I don't have a sore throat. I told him what you told me to say, that's all. What about Alex Silva? No one has seen or heard of him in days.'

'Trust me Leon, you say a word about this, and you will have a sore throat and you will never speak again.' With his finger, John drew a line across his neck, indicating that he would cut Leon's throat. 'And you leave Alex to me.' John stubbed out his Cuban cigar and stood up, slapping Leon gently on the face as he did so. 'You're a good boy Leon, keep it that way. Fish will be in touch with you. You tell her if you hear anything from Paul.'

'Fish? She's working for you now?' Stopping short, he looked down at the ground, cursing himself for asking the question.

'She sure is. And Fish takes no prisoners Leon. Her only loyalty is to her bank manager and the Botox shop that gives her that name in the first place.' Straightening his tie and jacket, John walked out.

Leon took a sigh of relief and sat down. Pouring himself a large brandy, he gulped it back quickly. John didn't have a heart; in fact, he was a cold-blooded killer and drug dealer. And now he had Fish on his side. Her beauty hid the mask of the devil. She was a real psycho, and she and John had worked for the cartel for years and there were no lengths they wouldn't go to to get what they wanted. It seemed in everyone's absence John had taken the initiative and was building his own empire. As far as he was concerned it was out with the old and in with the new.

Hearing footsteps, Paul quickly squatted down and hid the mobile phone. Standing up, he rubbed off any plaster and brick work from his sleeves.

'Pereira, the governor wants to see you.' The prison guard stood at the door with his colleague, and waited for Paul to walk out of the cell.

Knocking on the prison governor's door, the guard walked straight in. 'Prisoner Pereira, sir.'

'I'll get to the point, Pereira.' The governor sat behind his desk. 'It has come to the police's attention that a bank account which can be traced back to you was putting money into guard Barrow's account. Do you want to tell me why?'

Numbly, Paul stared at him. He wasn't prepared for this. 'I'm as shocked as you sir. As you know, all of my accounts have been frozen, so how could I do that when I am locked away? All I can think is that someone is using an account in my name.' He shrugged.

'Are you taking me for a fool? Are you telling me the whole of your mafioso knew Barrow? Was he famous in your circles then? No, but he was known here by you. You're to be transferred; that is, after the police have spoken to you, and put you in solitary confinement. Which is something they should have done a long time ago as far as I am concerned. His wife has found over a million pounds, which was paid to him days before he fell to his death.'

Shocked, Paul continued to stare at him, wide eyed.

'Now Pereira your stuff is being packed into boxes as we speak. No goodbyes to your friends and the police are waiting downstairs.'

The governor waved his hand in the air. 'Get him out of here, I've had enough of his slimy, greaseball lies.'

Paul flashed a look of hatred at him. 'You will regret this, Governor. No one insults me.'

'Really? Well, I might as well be hung for a sheep as a lamb. You're an old man living off a legacy. A parasite living off vulnerable stupid people. Personally, I think hanging is too good for you. Now, get him out of here.'

The colour drained from Paul's face as the hurl of insults flew towards him. He had never been spoken to like that in here before. In fact, he'd never been spoken to like that ever! 'I hope you die a slow and painful death. People who go looking for trouble, usually find it,' he muttered to the governor. Turning, he followed the guard back to his cell, his mind in turmoil. He couldn't get to his mobile phone. He didn't know where he was going, and he hadn't had time to tell anyone he was being transferred. Anger and rage built up inside of him. He felt helpless and he hated that feeling. As he walked down the stairs they walked in silence.

Once near the yard, Paul saw the mini bus revved up and waiting to take him to God knew where. The guard's hut was in the corner, and once they checked the paperwork, two more guards walked out of the hut, each of them with baseball bats in their hands.

Paul stood rooted to the spot and looked around, the hairs on the back of his neck standing on end as two more warders approached and took off their caps. 'You know, big man Pereira, we didn't like Barrow, but he was one of us. It's a real shame you tripped down the stairs while leaving this shit hole.' Raising the bat, he hit Paul in the guts, making him double in half and fall to his knees, while screaming out in pain. He knew there was no point in trying to fight back; all he could do was try and protect himself.

Raising his arms around his head, as each of them rained blow after blow, his screams echoed around the yard.

One of them finally raised his hand to his colleagues. As each of them stared down at the bloody mess of a man curled up into a ball, whining like a child, they laughed. 'Go on, get him out of here. The governor said he's going into solitary anyway, so nobody is going to see his baby face.' Abandoning the baseball bats, they dragged his half-conscious body off the floor. One of his arms hung awkwardly, obviously broken. Two of them put his arms around their shoulders and approached the back of the waiting mini bus and pushed him inside, slamming the doors while still hearing his moans as the driver drove off.

'Not so fucking hard now, is he?' they laughed to each other, mopping their brows and replacing their caps after wiping the blood off their hands. 'Come on lads, it's the end of our shift. Let's go home after a job well done. Anyone fancy a pint?' Each of them nodded and walked out of the yard to civvy street.

24

NO MAN'S LAND

'What the hell is that noise? It sounds like World War Two,' Alex asked, turning towards Maggie lying beside him as she ran her hands through her hair. 'Oh God, it's Monday; the builders are here.'

Pulling back the duvet and getting out of bed, Maggie reached for her robe. 'I'll go down and see if they need anything.' She yawned. 'You might as well get up Alex, they will be digging the hole and laying the foundations for the bike shed. I thought that might interest you.' Pausing, she waited till he opened his eyes properly, and gave him a knowing look. For a moment they both stared at each other, and Alex nodded.

'Time to put Plan A into action, Maggie.'

As Maggie opened her bedroom door, she could already see Deana and Dante opening their bedroom doors, scratching their heads and yawning. 'What the fuck is that racket Mum?' asked Deana, going towards the landing window.

'Oy, mouth! It's the builders. I'll go and ask them if they want a drink. You two get yourselves sorted. Breakfast in ten minutes.'

Deana tightened her dressing gown around her and followed

her mum to the kitchen. 'I'll put the kettle on. Builders are always thirsty, especially before they've even done anything. Dante, you jump in the shower first.' Maggie acknowledged Deana's help as an apology. She didn't like bad language coming out of her young daughter's mouth but accepted it in certain circumstances.

Opening the back door of the pub, Maggie saw the workmen unloading their tools. They had been a few days earlier and measured up, but to be honest, even she hadn't expected them to arrive this early and on time. 'Hi boys.' She waved, trying to catch their attention as they rummaged through their trucks that were parked on the grass. One truck was full of spades and all other kinds of building materials, and the other held the thing they were hoping for – the cement mixer – and wow, she thought to herself, it was a big one. Smiling, she wandered up to them. One middle-aged man jumped out of the driver's seat. 'Mrs Silva?'

'Indeed, I am, and you and your men look like they could do with a cup of something. Am I right?' The other three workmen cheered at the suggestion. 'Does that include biscuits missus?'

'It will include a bacon sandwich when the chef gets here,' she laughed. 'So, what are you starting with?'

'Got to dig a big rectangle hole first, but we've got our diggers.' He laughed and put on his hard hat. 'We'll section all of this off and try not to make too much mess.'

'Would it be okay if some of my regulars still come out in the beer garden for a smoke now and again?'

'Yes, sure thing and that includes us.' The builder shrugged. 'Plus, we've been told to lay some new turf for you. Brewery orders.' He gave Maggie a salute and wandered off to speak to his other workmen. 'Oh, by the way, Mrs Silva, we might have to put an extension lead through your back door if that's okay,' he shouted after her, but Maggie wasn't listening, she'd already got the information she needed.

Shivering from the early-morning cold, she ran upstairs. 'Get those lot some mugs of tea and biscuits Deana, then come straight back.' Deana had already started and picking up a tray, she placed the mugs on them. 'I'll be back in a bit, Mum. I didn't know how many there were so I've made loads.'

'That doesn't matter; they'll drink them anyway. Thanks, love.'

Alex sipped his coffee while sitting at the breakfast table. It had been a couple of weeks since his skirmish and he felt much better. Life had gone on as normal, even though it had surprised him that no one else had come looking for him. Everything had gone quiet lately and for that he was grateful.

Once Deana had come back moaning and groaning about the stupid wolf whistles and remarks the young builder had made, she sat down. 'He needs a good kicking, shit shoveller.'

'You're going to smile at him, Deana until our job is done,' Alex warned. 'Those builders are going to dig their hole and lay a foundation. Then they will fill it full of cement so people can park their bikes. That is where we come in. We have had two dead bodies in the back of the freezer for two weeks; it's time they left town.'

'But Dad, it's broad daylight. Everyone will be at work soon. How do we go in the freezer, take out two frozen bodies and walk out into broad daylight and put them in cement in front of the workmen? And, I might add, whoever might be having a cigarette out there?' asked Deana, while stating the obvious.

'For the moment, and for the sake of health and safety, the place is currently off limits. They can stand out the front like they do at other pubs and clubs that don't have a beer garden. The bodies we take out now will take a while before they defrost, so we can put them in the smoking shed underneath the benches.' Seeing Deana's and Dante's faces, he held up his hand. 'Maggie, you are going to offer the workmen a nice carvery lunch, free of course, but,' he said, 'they leave their boots outside, eh? I'm going

downstairs before the kitchen staff come, I have something to do.'
Alex stood up and went downstairs.

Opening the door of the huge walk-in freezer, Alex stood back
to avoid the chilly blast of cold. Inwardly he cursed himself for only
wearing jeans and a T-shirt as it was sub-zero in there. Methodically, he moved everything aside and went to the very back of the
freezer where the bodies had been hidden. Shivering, he knew he
only had a few minutes before his own body temperature dropped.
Having to lie on his stomach, which froze him even more, he
reached out his arms and eventually felt what he was looking for.
With both hands, he pulled at the bag, until he eventually felt it
move. Bit by bit, he eased it out and finally, he stood up, panting.
He felt light-headed. Heading towards the door, he opened it and
took some breaths and wrapped himself in the chef's overalls, shivering and blowing on his hands.

Walking out of the kitchen, Alex stood near the radiator and
rubbed his hands together. Looking up at the coat rack, he saw a
body warmer and putting it on, he walked back towards the
freezer. Taking a breath, he walked back towards the body bag and
dragged it out into the kitchen. Unzipping it, he looked at the
frozen body inside before standing up and looking around the
kitchen for the chef's knives. Spying a meat cleaver, he smiled.
That was just what he needed, he thought to himself, as he picked
it up. Kneeling down, he raised the cleaver and with two blows, he
hacked the head clean off the frozen body. He was glad it was
frozen; there was no blood. Raising the cleaver again, he did the
same with the hands and feet. Standing up, he searched the
drawers for a black bin liner and put the head, hands and feet
inside. All that was left was the torso. With a huge sigh, he knew
he had to go back into the freezer and get the other body and once
he had pulled it out, he methodically, put everything back into
place.

Startled, he looked up as someone entered the kitchen, and sighed with relief as he saw that it was Maggie.

'How you doing, Alex? You look blue. Here, take this.' She handed him a large brandy, which he gulped back to warm his bones. 'You could get hypothermia in there.' Walking closer, she rubbed at Alex's arms.

'I'm okay Maggie. Christ, you buried those guys so far back, we could have left them there forever.' Alex reached forward and kissed her lips. 'Mind you, my balls are stinging from lying on that floor.'

'Maybe it woke your tadpoles, Alex. They do say the cold is good for that. Maybe another little Silva could be swimming its way to the forefront,' Maggie laughed.

Cocking his head to one side and smiling, Alex nodded. 'Now that's a novel idea. Does that mean I'm on a promise or that you're feeling broody?'

'Who knows? But mind back to business Silva and out of your trousers.'

'Right, that bin liner goes into that body bag, and that one comes with me later and don't get them mixed up,' Alex laughed.

Maggie glimpsed into the bin liner she was holding and saw the back of a man's head.

'They do say two heads are better than one, Maggie.'

'Oh God Alex, you're sick and at this moment in time, while I'm holding a bin liner with someone's head in it, you are definitely not funny.'

'Make light of it. Keep reminding yourself who those people were and what they were going to do to us all.'

'Fair point, but let's keep the kids out of it. They know enough. I don't want them having nightmares.'

He nodded, realising how pale and nervous she looked. 'Come on Maggie, love. After today, it's all over. When I've finished, the news will be that the torso of a male has been found in Kent. Pereira and the mob will hopefully presume that's me. That's all I can hope for. Maybe that will take the heat off for now.'

'Well, they are going to get one hell of a shock when you turn up in court with your head still on, Alex.'

Reaching forward, he held her tight. 'I just need you to be stronger for a bit longer, okay?'

Sighing, Maggie nodded. 'I'm just having a wobbly that's all. Come on, let's get this sorted out before the staff come.'

'The man in the bag with two heads we need to get outside. The closer it is to the building site, the easier it will be to drop it in the hole without it being seen. We will have to be quick though.'

'But how are we going to get that those bags out of the kitchen without being seen?'

Trying hard to think, a light bulb switched on in Alex's brain. 'Hang on a minute, I have an idea.' Going outside, he came back through the kitchen entrance with two wheelie bins – one blue and one black. 'Now we know who's who and it will be easier to wheel this over to the hole and dump him in.' Inwardly, Alex wanted to laugh as he thought of some drug dealers opening the blue bin and finding a frozen dead man. It would scare the shit out of them! 'Put some bin liners on top, make it look full.' Slapping his hands together, he looked at Maggie, who was still staring at him in awe and wonderment. 'Ready? Let's do this.'

After a few minutes, they were both panting. 'Christ, Alex, not only are they cold, they are stiff. This one with no head fits well, but the other one sticks up. We can't close the lid.'

'Bollocks. Just put some bags on top of it. Hopefully he will melt soon and sink lower,' he laughed. 'It only looks weird to us, because we know what's in there. No one else will take any notice.' They looked at each other for a moment with worried expressions.

No sooner had they cleared away and put the bins out, Chef

walked through the door. Alex and Maggie looked at each other with relief. For now, the bodies were safe and it was just a matter of waiting for the right opportunity.

Alex strolled over to one of the builders. 'Is it possible to have a bucket of sand? We don't want people smoking out here while you're busy, so I thought we'd put a sand bucket out the front for their cigarette ends. If that lot come trailing around the back, you'd never get anything done and they'll all be trailing their mess indoors.'

'Yes, sure thing, Mr Silva.'

'How long before you'll be pouring the cement?'

'Depending on how quick we get on with the digging, could be as soon as the end of the day, then we have to wait for the cement to set before we can build the actual bike shed,' the builder said as he handed Alex the bucket of sand he didn't really need.

The day seemed to drag slowly. Alex felt he had spent the day clockwatching and even Mark wandering over and cracking his usual jokes had no effect. Once the workmen had taken their lunch break and had their free carvery, Alex had gone out the back for an inspection. They hadn't dug as deep as he'd expected. It was going to be a shallow grave, but it was better than nothing.

'Any work on tonight, Mark? Need to stretch my legs and get out of here. I feel like I haven't been out in ages.'

'Hmm, nothing major apart from picking up an exhaust for scrap. I bought a car at auction the other day. It needs a new exhaust and tyres but once I've serviced it I can sell it on.'

'I'll pick it up for you if you want.'

'Thanks Alex, I wouldn't mind a night with the lads. No offence to your place, but I have a delivery coming later, if you know what I mean. Not something Maggie would want in the pub.' Mark winked. Alex knew exactly what he meant.

'It's strange though,' Mark whispered. 'It's my usual dealer guy, but suddenly the gear is so much better. Still, I'm not complaining and if you want to go out, then be my guest. I'll pop you the details later, but it's a scrap yard the other side of town.'

Alex was excited at the thought of going out in the van unnoticed. And to the other side of town was even better.

At nearly 5 p.m., Alex looked out of the window and spotted the workmen idly having a cigarette, wasting their time until finishing time. He had seen the cement mixer already going and even he was surprised at the amount they were pouring in. It was time to go and say goodbye to the men.

'All finished for the day?' he shouted as he walked towards them.

The supervisor walked up to him and took his hard hat off, wiping his brow. 'Sure are, Mr Silva. We've covered the cement and it should dry in no time. Is it okay if we leave the cement mixers here? If we take them back to the yard, it's going to take another half an hour.'

Alex rolled his eyes up to the heavens and thanked God. 'Absolutely mate. Then you get off and I will see you bright and early in the morning.' Alex shook their hands and watched them all pile into their trucks and leave. Looking around at the makeshift building site, he smiled to himself. There was a skip full of rubble and soil and the most wonderful sight of all: the cement mixer, with a few bags of cement nearby.

Walking over to the dustbins, Alex noted that the lid was closing on one of them, which meant the body was defrosting. It had been a warm day. Fortunately, it hadn't yet defrosted enough to leave a scent.

Seeing no one was around, Alex worked quickly. Firstly, he pulled the wheelie bin to the side of the large rectangular hole and then pulled back the tarpaulin the workmen had put over the cement to dry. Looking down, he could see that it was still wet and fresh. His heart was pounding in his chest as he opened the lid of the bin and tipping it slightly, held on to it as the body slipped into the cement. His heart was in his mouth as he waited for the black-ness of the bag to disappear. Looking around, he spotted one of the workmen's spades and prodded the body to make it sink faster. Slowly, but surely, it disappeared from sight, making him let out a big sigh of relief. He could see the cement was disturbed and so turned on the cement mixer. There was still some readymade cement inside and he threw some water in to make it sloppier again and added a little more from the bags left behind. Watching the mixer pour more cement into the hole made him feel better, until it nearly poured over the grass, meaning it was too full. He wished he had put some of the rubble in the body bag to weigh it down more, but it was too late for that, he thought to himself as he lit a cigarette. He stared blankly at the cement and saw there was nothing in sight. Carefully, he loosely put the tarpaulin back. All he could do now was wait...

After showering, he went to see Mark and got the address for the pick-up. As usual, Mark was stood in his kitchen holding court, pouring drinks and boasting about whatever came to mind. Olivia had made her usual chilli and fussed around talking to their guests and offering food.

Alex could see they were settled for the night and that suited his plan. No one was watching the clock or cared about how long he would be. Going around the back of his pub, he took hold of the other bin and dragged it to the kerbside where Mark's van was waiting with the doors open. Laying it on its side behind the van out of view, he dragged out the covered torso. This one wasn't so heavy and he pushed it into the back of the van and shut the doors.

The scrap yard wasn't too hard to find, but much further than Mark had said. Jumping out, he looked around the old scrap yard, full of broken-down cars. It was more like a car cemetery. Seeing an old man approaching, he introduced himself and told him Mark had sent him for an exhaust. Disappearing, the scrap dealer seemed to be gone for ages and a thought popped into Alex's mind. He could easily put the body into the boot of one of these deserted cars.

No, he decided to himself. This one needed to be found in order to provide him with his cover story. It had to be known that a male body had been found, decapitated and dumped. Decapitation was Pereira's trademark and so everyone who needed to know would believe that Pereira had had his revenge on Alex.

Taking the rusted exhaust off the scrap dealer, Alex threw it quickly in the back.

'Tell Mark I'll pop and see him tomorrow and collect my cash.'

Giving him the thumbs up and smiling, Alex got back into the van and drove off.

Driving further out, he looked for a secluded area, but also one where people visited.

There was a long stretch of water with what looked like some night fishermen sitting amongst the trees. The water was surrounded by grass and bushes that seemed to go on forever. This place was ideal, though what the fishermen hoped to get from there apart from water rats was beyond him. Alex parked up, away from the fishermen who were sat under their huge umbrellas and couldn't see anything. Dumping the body quickly in the water, he jumped back in the van and drove off. Relief overwhelmed him. His nerves had been taut all day and all of this creeping around was exhausting him, but at least it was over and done with. Hopefully the cement would have set by morning with no trace of what was underneath it.

25

ALL'S FAIR IN LOVE AND WAR

Alex didn't feel like going straight home. All in all, it had been a long day and he wanted to compose himself before Maggie fired her questions at him. Instead, he found himself driving towards Luke's house. He'd had numerous updates on his mobile from Luke about how his plans were working out and Luke had also messaged him about a surprise he had for Alex. Now, driving along, curiosity got the better of him. What could Luke come up with now that would surprise him? Surely there was nothing left in Luke's skeleton cupboard?

Alex knocked on the door and hoped Luke was in because he didn't want to disturb his mother. Seeing the blinds at the window move, Alex felt better. His mother wouldn't be looking out of the window now, would she?

The door opened slightly and then he heard Luke's voice. 'Good to see you Alex! Now close your eyes, you're going to love this.' Suddenly the door flew open and Luke stood there in all of his glory. 'What do you think? Do you like it?' he laughed and did a twirl for good measure. 'I knew my message would make you come.'

Wide eyed and astonished, Alex stood there and marvelled at the new Luke. He didn't know whether to laugh or cry. Before him stood the Luke he half recognised, with the lopsided grin and cheeky glint in his eye, but the bright peroxide blond shaved hair, he definitely didn't.

'What the hell!' Alex burst out laughing. After the day he'd had this was just the tonic he needed. 'Blond, shaven head, oh my God, I've just noticed your eyebrows have gone ginger. Bloody hell Luke, you tried bleaching your eyebrows?' Alex let out a belly laugh as Luke pulled him inside by his coat sleeve.

'It's my disguise, Alex. Those Liverpudlians aren't looking for a blond, are they? They will expect me, dark-haired Luke. Even if I walked up the high street, they wouldn't give me a second glance.'

Trying to compose himself and brushing a tear from his eye, Alex followed Luke into the lounge and sat down. 'It's a good disguise Luke, but I don't know what to say. It's a bit drastic, but you have a point. No one is looking for those ginger eyebrows.' Again Alex laughed and reaching forward, he rubbed his hand along Luke's shaved head, which felt more like a scrubbing brush. 'So, what's all of this for Marilyn Monroe?'

'Business is about to begin Alex. Are you in?' Luke asked hopefully.

Alex shook his head. 'No, Luke. This is your project and you've worked bloody hard. You don't need my help any more. And we are even – you saved me when I needed medication. We're quits Luke, and I wish you well.'

Looking at Luke, Alex sensed that behind the laughter and his jokey ways, Luke was actually quite lonely. He could see why; he was a young man who looked after his mum, who was nearly at the end of her days. His brother, Kev, wasn't a lot of back-up. Luke, it seemed, was the only person Luke had.

Luke carried on talking. 'No Alex. Like I keep saying, we're partners. I need your knowhow and your back-up. I need a wing man who doesn't dabble in drugs. This operation is too big for me and some of those seedlings are yours. We stole them together. Those bastards are going to come looking for me Alex, I'm not that stupid. Sooner or later, they will want to finish what they started. I want you to promise me, if that ever happens, you will look after Mum...'

Alex hadn't expected this bombshell and for a moment there was a silent pause between them. 'I have my own demons Luke and I can't promise anything. But I promise whatever the future holds me or my family will keep an eye on your mum and you, you bloody numbskull.' Alex laughed. For a moment, Alex had a feeling of déjà vu. He and Luke were more alike than he had first realised. Luke was on the run, and someone wanted to see him dead. That sounded very familiar. Luke also wanted someone to look after his family in case his enemies caught up with him. That also sounded familiar. Apart from the badly bleached hair, Alex felt like he was looking in the mirror at some parallel world.

'I know you're in some kind of shit Alex, why else would someone shoot you? I'm not asking questions; I know you will tell me when you're ready. And you're a great drop-off guy too, using your mate's disguise.' He grinned. 'You could make drops too.'

Alex looked down at his coat with Mark's logo on it. 'This is my neighbour's. If I do the drops he'll get known as the dealer. Sooner or later, someone will say something to him and although he's stupid, he's not that stupid.'

'But that van lets you go anywhere, anytime. No one is paying attention to you, Alex. If the worst comes to the worst, we could get our own van and put our own logo on it. What do you think?' Taking a breath, Luke waited.

It felt good talking to another male adult, Alex mused to himself, even someone as young as Luke. He liked Mark a lot, but he had to be careful what he said with him. With Luke he didn't and he felt more relaxed in his company. Seeing Luke had been just what he'd needed, but looking at his watch Alex saw that he needed to get back. He knew Maggie would be worried but that she would be behind the bar rushed off her feet.

Letting Luke know he would be in touch, Alex drove home. As he approached, he could see a police car in the distance outside of Mark's house with the blue light flashing away. Peering closer to the windscreen, he could see Mark's house guests were stood on the pavement and a hysterical Olivia was being comforted by Emma and Maggie. Parking the van further up the street, Alex got out, took off Mark's coat and slowly made his way towards them all. His heart was in his mouth, but he couldn't understand what had happened. Maggie, Deana and Dante all looked okay and they were comforting Olivia, so it was clearly nothing to do with the pub.

The closer he got, he could see people stood in the pub doorway looking out as another police car approached. Sidling up to Maggie, he could see the relief in her eyes when she saw him. She shook her head slightly, warning him not to say anything.

Looking towards Mark's doorway, he could see Mark talking to the police, but a trickle of blood was pouring down the side of his face and nose. He had definitely been in a fight, Alex thought to himself. Had something at his party got out of hand?

'It's awful, isn't it Alex?' Maggie blurted out, trying to bring him up to speed. 'People just running into your house with baseball bats smashing your house up and then leaving.' Giving him a knowing look, she felt she had filled him in on the details as quickly as possible.

'Mark!' Alex shouted towards him. 'You okay mate?' People were so busy looking around and gossiping they wouldn't realise how long he had been there. As for Mark, well, at least he knew Alex had been out on his mission.

An ambulance was parked further up the street, which Alex had failed to notice and two paramedics were advising Mark to go with them and get his wounds checked out.

Mark beckoned him over. 'I'm fine, Alex.' Lifting up his T-shirt, he mopped the blood from the side of his face. 'Some bastards ran in and just started smashing the place up. Of course, I fought back. You know me Alex, but I didn't stand a chance. Got a punch in though,' he boasted.

Escorted to the back of the ambulance, Mark declined going to the hospital, but let them check his wounds over and patch him up. The police were milling around asking all of Mark's friends questions, which seemed pointless because they all said the same thing. They were having something to eat and drink when the front door was kicked in and three men wearing balaclavas ran in with baseball bats. Mark had run forward to defend Olivia, but they had grabbed him, punched him and shouted they would be back for their money.

Alex had a suspicion that he knew who was behind all of this. Suddenly everything fitted into place as Alex recalled the conversation he'd had with Percy at the bar. Percy had suspected Mark had something to do with the cannabis plants and had mentioned that the Liverpudlian gangsters wanted their money back: the money they'd paid for their own plants. A twinge of guilt passed through Alex. He had brought this on his friend. Mark was being blamed for his actions and Alex knew that it was Percy who had passed this information on to those men. He was sure of it.

Looking around the crowd, Alex couldn't see Percy anywhere, which was odd, considering he was always in the thick of it like some nosey old woman. His gut instinct told him Percy was up to his neck in all of this and anger rose in him. Without thinking, he pushed past everyone standing in the pub doorway and got his gun. Screwing the silencer on, he pushed it inside his jacket pocket and went out again and made his way around the back of Percy's house. Trying the door handle, he discovered it wasn't locked and quietly opened it. True enough, Percy was sat there drinking mugs of tea with three men who, Alex was sure, had been the ones who had just ransacked Mark's house.

Hearing the door, the men stood up and picked up their baseball bats menacingly, as Alex faced them. 'After everything Mark does for you old man, you let this lot beat him up?' Percy looked down sheepishly and blushed. 'Don't bother explaining yourself to me, you low life.'

'Don't come at us with that shit. We've done our homework. You're Alex Silva, ex-hitman and now a grass in witness protection. By all accounts you're worth a lot of money. Maybe we should take you with us and let your old friends know where you are?' one of the men spat out as two of them walked towards him with their baseball bats.

The oldest member of the three shouted, 'Don't kill him, let his old friends do that. He's worth more alive than dead.'

Glancing at him, Alex recognised him as the man in the BMW he had spoken to – Mr Gold Teeth and Luke's enemy. 'I remember you Silva,' he sneered. 'I should have run you over properly when I had the chance. But at least now I am going to make a huge profit by turning you over to your enemies.' He spat in Alex's face and grinned, showing his gold front teeth as they glinted in the light.

Glaring at him, Alex wiped the spit away as it dribbled down his face. 'Good, because I remember you too and that smile of yours doesn't do you any favours.' Alex looked up at the other men. Just as they were about to raise their bats to hit him, Alex quickly felt for his gun and fired three shots in quick succession. Each shot was accurate and the three of them fell to the floor in an instant, a bullet hole in each of their foreheads. The blood was minimal, almost a trickle. Alex held up his gun. 'Are you next, Percy?'

'For fuck's sake Alex, there are two police cars outside. What am I going to do with three dead bodies in my living room?' Nervous and panicking, Percy looked down at the bodies and then back at Alex still holding his gun.

'Well, why don't you go out there and tell the police you were harbouring the very men they're looking for? Or let Mark know you have sold him down the river and his friendship means nothing to you? Go on Percy, you son of a bitch! Because your police buddies can't get you out of this one, this time!'

Angry and red faced, Alex slowly put his gun away. 'I am Alex Silva, but I am sure you have known that for some time. Like I give a fuck. I have got bigger and harder men after me than your three clowns. But you're asking me what to do? Well I suggest you call your other friends and tell them that this lot are dead. They will clean the mess up, believe me. And if your friends come looking for me for revenge, remember this Percy. I have more of these,' Alex said, tapping the gun in his jacket, 'and my family know how to use them and one bullet has got your name engraved on it.'

Percy stood there as white as a sheet and shaking with fear.

'Be fucking warned!' With that, Alex left the same way he had got in. Sweat poured down his forehead and he brushed it away with his coat sleeve. He couldn't believe what he had just done. Rubbing his face, he looked up at the moonlight. No matter how many times he tried to start afresh, he was still a cold-hearted killer. As he walked back to the pub, he decided this was one secret he would definitely keep from Maggie. This new leaf he had turned over, was just an old leaf with a new colour. Old habits die hard, Alex thought to himself.

'You feeling better now Mark mate? Come and have a drink,' he shouted above the crowd. 'And then we will help you clear the decks.' Alex noticed that the ambulance had gone in his absence and people were slowly finding their way back to their homes and the pub. Looking around for Maggie, he couldn't see her. 'Where is Maggie?' he asked.

'Back in the pub with Olivia. They are having a drink to calm Olivia's nerves.' Alex waited for Mark to join him, and they both walked towards the pub.

Much to Alex's surprise, the pub was packed to the hilt. He knew Maggie would be pleased the cash register was opening and closing as people bought more drinks, and like any good tale, the story got better and better each time it was told. Mark wasted no time in gulping back a drink, smacking his lips and letting everyone know how he had fought the intruders and got a few punches in. Alex thought back to the men he had seen at Percy's and couldn't remember any of them a nursing any wounds or black eyes. In fact, they had looked very calm and composed drinking their tea and biding their time with Percy until the police had left.

'Who called the police?' Alex asked, surprised Mark had called them considering he had been sniffing cocaine.

'I did!' Olivia cried, making her red, tear-stained face even worse. 'My Mark could have been hurt. He's a hero. A bloody hero saving me and my George from those hooligans.'

Alex cast a glance towards Maggie and they stared at each other for a moment and smiled. Both of them knew that Mark was going to dine out on this tale for a long time to come!

Excusing himself, Alex walked towards his own back door and pushed his gun deep into the umbrella stand beside the rifle under the coats and hung his own coat up. For a moment, he stood there staring at the coats and wondered what Percy was doing at this precise moment. He knew his cover was blown, but what the hell. It was all going to come out soon enough anyway. He also wondered if he had just got rid of all of Luke's enemies. He doubted it, because like all puppets, somebody was always pulling their strings. These Liverpudlians would have another boss giving out the orders.

Turning around to walk into the bar, Maggie stopped him. 'Everything okay, Alex?'

'Everything is fine, darling. Sorry I took so long. This place is so boring, and the minute I go out there's a bit of action,' he laughed. As she searched his face, he kissed her on the cheek, while whispering in her ear, 'The deed is done love – all gone.'

Nodding her head and smiling, she said, 'I've told Olivia that they can stay here tonight. We will all muck in tomorrow to help them clean up their house, love.'

As much as Alex liked Maggie playing hostess, he felt it hindered him. He wanted to see the cement first thing in the morning, preferably before the builders arrived. The last thing he wanted was Mark on his heels.

Hearing a loud banging on the pub door, Alex looked at Maggie.

'That will be for me,' shouted Mark. 'I've got a bloke coming out to secure the front door. I told them to knock here.'

Alex opened the door and true enough, the carpenter stood there. Swaying, Mark put his arm around Alex's shoulder. 'He's a mate of mine,' Mark boasted. 'Owes me a favour, which is why he has come out so late.'

Seeing his drunken state, Alex decided to take over and talk to the carpenter and offer any help, if needed. He took some chipboard out of the back of his van and Alex helped him carry it to Mark's front door. As he stood with it while the workman went about his work, Alex spotted a small transit van outside of Percy's house about to drive off.

A smile spread across his face as he watched Percy come to his front gate and close it. Quickly, they glanced at each other before Percy turned swiftly and walked back into his house.

Alex realised that Percy had followed his instructions and had called his friends to get rid of the dead bodies. All in all, a job well done. He then remembered that he had left Mark's van parked further up the street. Now was the time to bring it back.

Yawning as he parked the van up and checked the back for traces of anything he might have left behind, Alex locked it and walked back towards the pub. What a bloody day, he thought to himself. He was sick of seeing dead bodies! Now he would have a drink!

26

THE AFTERMATH

Waking with a start, Alex opened his eyes to the sound of the builders turning up. He jumped out of bed so quickly he nearly fell out. He needed to see if the cement had dried properly and if the body had definitely been covered. Pulling on his jeans, he crept downstairs and went out to them.

'Morning, how you all doing?' Staring across at the tarpaulin, he watched the two young builders' apprentices pull it away. His heart was in his mouth.

Breathing a sigh of relief, he saw that it looked like it had set.

'Morning Mr Silva, don't suppose that gorgeous wife of yours has the kettle on yet?' The foreman smiled.

'I'm sure she does,' Alex laughed nervously. 'So, I presume you will be putting up the bike shed today?' he asked nonchalantly.

'Hopefully. We have the tarmac to do first. Can't leave it just concrete for safety reasons. It dries pretty quick though, and we should be out of your hair by the end of today.'

Tarmac? Alex grinned. He'd never thought of that. That was even better!

'What happened to the house over there? It's all boarded up.'

'Break-in of some kind.' Avoiding going into detail, Alex said he would go and see about the tea and wandered back indoors.

Going upstairs, he could see Maggie was up and already filling the kettle. 'You must be a mind reader Maggie. The foreman has just asked me about his early-morning tea.' Going over to her, he wrapped his arms around her waist and nuzzled her neck. 'Are the others up yet?' The slamming of bedroom doors and the shower running answered his question. 'Never mind. I was wondering about that promise you made me now my tadpoles have surfaced.'

'Go on with you, you saucy bugger. With a house full of guests and kids. You don't stand a chance.' Turning around, she slipped her arms around his neck and kissed him. 'We'll put that on ice for now.' She winked, making him laugh at her inuendo about the freezer.

'Oy, oy, am I interrupting something?' Mark stood in the doorway, large as life. His face had strips of plaster on where the paramedics had put them to glue the cut to the side of his head. His eyes were black, but he seemed to be in his usual high spirits. 'Any paracetamol going spare once you two have finished your morning snog.'

Deana pushed past him into the kitchen. 'Christ I didn't think you could look any worse, but you definitely do in the morning, and that's without your face looking like a car crash. And don't even think of scratching your balls in those boxer shorts, you hairy monster. Why is it all men do that in the morning, Mum?' she scoffed and slumped into a chair at the breakfast table.

Smiling, Maggie shook her head in answer to her question and handed Mark some paracetamol.

'You will be glad of some bloke scratching his balls in your kitchen one day,' Mark said, doing it on purpose to make Deana squirm even more. 'It wakes everything up,' he laughed. 'Ask your dad!' He sat beside Deana, making her move her chair further away from him in disgust.

'Is Olivia coming through?' Maggie asked, ignoring Deana's contempt and Mark's comments.

'Yes, but she's having one of her nervous days. She's already making a mental list of the new stuff she wants. She's been wanting a new kitchen for ages and now she has the opportunity to go bonkers at my expense.' As an afterthought, while he sipped his coffee, Mark asked, 'Did you pick up the exhaust Alex?'

'Yes, in the back of the van. The scrap dealer said he would sort out the cash with you later today.'

Nodding with satisfaction, Mark slurped his drink. 'I'll sort it, but first I need to check Olivia isn't going to decorate the kitchen in pink flamingos. Don't know why, but she likes them. Weird if you ask me. I like stags personally.'

'And I like drinking my tea without an ape sat next to me,' Deana snapped.

Alex couldn't help but laugh. He knew Olivia would get her own way and Mark would just have to swallow it. As for Deana, well, whatever sarcastic remark she made just seemed to fly over Mark's head.

'I know you would have jumped in last night and helped me, Alex. The others just stood there like idiots and ran for cover, chicken bastards! Call themselves mates. Useless, the lot of them.'

'Too right I would Mark. It's ironic I wasn't there to help. The only night I go out and you needed my help.' Although, Alex thought to himself, he wondered what Mark would think of the three dead bodies in Percy's house. He wondered what Percy had said to explain the situation. He decided he would find out later.

Dante and George left for school, Deana got ready for college and everything returned to normal. Olivia declined to go and see her house in the state it had been left and so, once showered and dressed, Alex and Mark strolled over to have a look.

'Fuck Alex, it looks worse in daylight. Let's borrow a crow bar off your workmen and get in through the front door.'

'Did you know them, Mark? Have you argued with a lot of people lately?' Alex asked.

'I don't know, they were wearing balaclavas. Although I have had a few bad online reviews about my mechanic business. One woman sent her husband to get her money back. Even threatened to go to the small claims court, but I'm not telling the police that.'

Taking the crowbar off Alex, Mark pulled away the boards protecting the front door. As they walked in, Alex looked on with horror as Mark gave a low whistle. 'Christ, Alex, they went to town on this, didn't they? My fifty-inch television is hanging off the wall smashed to pieces.' Treading on glass underfoot, they wandered into the kitchen.

'The weird thing is, they kept asking where their money was.' Puzzled by it all, Mark looked around the dark room and opened the blinds to let in some daylight. 'That job I mentioned was only a couple of hundred quid and her car was an old banger anyway. Makes me wonder though.' Pursing his lips together, Mark looked at Alex and shrugged. 'Shit happens, what can I say? I must have been more pissed than I thought, or as high as a kite; it didn't look this bad last night.'

'Things always look worse in the cold light of day. We'll soon get this lot cleared away though. I'm sure the builders at mine will take a few quid to put your cupboard doors back on and sort the door for now until Olivia gets her interior-designer head on.' Alex laughed, trying to make light of the situation, although looking around, it looked like a warzone. 'Well, he's had his money's worth now, that's for sure Mark. I doubt they will come back now the police are on to it.'

'I'll be ready next time if they do. I know people who know people.' Alex knew it was all bravado, but he left it at that.

Other neighbours popped their heads around the door and wandered in. 'We're here to help where we can,' Emma said, raising her sweeping brush and bin liners. Mark and Alex cast a furtive glance at each other. They knew she meant well, but what the hell she was going to do with those was anyone's business! No sooner said than done an army of neighbours were clearing what they could away and the place actually looked almost liveable again. 'Thank God George was at yours last night with Dante, Alex. I wouldn't want him witnessing this. Who knows what could have happened?' Sheepishly, Mark looked at Alex. Tears were almost welling up in his eyes now the aftermath of the shock had set in.

'Well, he was, and he didn't. Be grateful for small mercies. Look around you. It doesn't look too bad now all the glass has gone. All that rubbish can go in my workmen's skip. Nip out, get a new television, even bigger than the last,' Alex said, 'and we'll leave Emma to keep hoovering the same patch over and over again.'

'Have you seen that they have been upstairs? All of the clothes have been pulled out the wardrobes. It makes you wonder if they were looking for something, doesn't it?'

Trying to get him from that train of thought, Alex said, 'No Mark. They weren't looking for anything, just trying to make a mess of your house. They were hooligans with baseball bats and were probably all on drugs anyway.' Alex watched Mark's face closely as he seemed to accept his explanation.

Eventually, Olivia mustered up enough courage to come home and tears rolled down her face when she saw the smashed photo frame containing her wedding photo. Alex couldn't comprehend that that was the only thing that bothered her! In true style, her parents turned up to console her and Mark nudged Alex in the ribs. 'We're staying with you again tonight, aren't we? I'm not going to her mum's,' he emphasised through gritted teeth. The thought of spending a night with Olivia's mum terrified him more than the men who had trashed his house!

* * *

After lunchtime, everything looked almost normal again and Olivia, Emma and Maggie decided to go shopping while the workmen set about putting their cupboards back in the kitchen. As Alex had predicted, they took the extra cash offered.

Walking up the street towards Percy's house, Alex saw him on the front path. 'Morning Percy. I saw you got a special takeaway last night. What was your explanation?'

Percy paled when he saw him. 'Told them they had argued and done the business to each other.'

Frowning, Alex cocked his head to one side. 'How did they do that, if there were three of them?'

'Told them one shot the other two in temper, then shot himself in the head.'

Astonished, Alex stared at him. 'And they believed that?'

'Dunno if they believed it or not, but that's my story and I am sticking to it.'

'Was my name mentioned at all?'

'I'm not stupid Alex; your name never came up. You weren't even around, because I never saw you.' Percy was as white as a sheet and his hand trembled as he took the roll-up cigarette from behind his ear and lit it. 'No harm done eh, Alex mate?'

'I am not your mate, Percy. Be warned. You might have friends in high places, but I have friends in low, low places.' With that, Alex discarded his own cigarette on the pavement and walked away.

27

A PROPOSITION

Whilst Mark and Olivia sorted out the house, Mark had asked Alex to help him with his mechanic business. 'Only doing easy jobs, Alex. I'll turn away the big ones and give them to my mate. Are you up for it?'

Alex couldn't believe his luck. This was perfect. It meant he could pop out, see Luke and do whatever was necessary to build his own bank balance up. The nights were getting lighter and he decided to tell the police about his new job. They didn't seem too bothered as long as they knew his whereabouts. If nothing else, they felt it kept him busy and out of mischief!

Deana had offered to go to Luke's with him on occasion, claiming it looked better if the police saw that he had his young daughter with him – they knew he wouldn't risk her safety. He'd agreed it was a good cover, although Maggie hadn't liked it, but once he had filled her in on Luke and his lifestyle she had appreciated him telling her. She knew he was trying to scrape as much money together for the family in case they needed it and had accepted the situation.

Each morning, as Alex went out for his first cigarette of the day in the beer garden, he looked across at the newly built bike shed. Strangely enough, people were using it, including Dante and George. The workmen had done a really nice job.

Things were looking up, and he had another thirty thousand stuffed away in the cellar. Luke and his brother had business booming and everyone liked the new stuff they were giving out. Luke had been right, people didn't mind paying that little extra for good stuff and eventually, they wouldn't even notice they had mixed it with herbs.

On occasion, he had noticed a spark between Luke and Deana, but decided to ignore it. He hadn't liked it, but had swallowed it. Their lives would change soon enough, so why not let her have a little fun while she could? Who knew what their future would hold? And he liked Luke, but had warned him to never offer Deana any of his drugs.

Shocked, Luke had felt insulted by the insinuation. 'I wouldn't do that to you Alex, or Deana. I'm not trash. And I know you would make me wear my balls for earrings.'

Apologetically, Alex had told Luke he didn't think he was trash, not at all. He liked him, but they drew a line under their conversation and carried on as normal.

After a long evening serving behind the bar, Phyllis and Pauline had gone. Alex told Maggie to go upstairs and chill out while he locked up and cleared away. It was midnight when he looked up at the clock and he was just about to switch the hallway light off when there was a knock at the back door. Thinking it was some customer who had left something, he opened it.

Stunned, he stood rooted to the spot and paled as he looked at the man before him. '*Boa noite* Alex.' The man wearing an expensive dark grey suit was well groomed and wore a diamond earring. 'Don't bother reaching for a gun. I come in peace and am not tooled up.' He opened his jacket. Alex could see there was no gun in the holster. Still with his jacket open, the man did a slow twirl, so Alex could see there was nothing in the back of his waist band either.

Swallowing hard, and moistening his lips, Alex spoke. 'John, what brings you here? Stupid question I know, but why you?'

'I want you to come out and see for yourself, or are you too chicken these days? I assure you I have no driver with me and there is no one in the shadows at either side waiting to blow your head off. I come in peace to talk to you.'

The two men stared at each other, and with his heart in his mouth, Alex knew these could be his last living moments on this earth. Nodding, he stepped into the street and closed his eyes, waiting for the rain of bullets to hit him, but nothing happened. Opening his eyes again, he saw John smiling.

'You haven't forgotten who you are, Alex, that's good. Now, can we talk?' he asked, raising one eyebrow.

Ushering him into the small sitting room, Alex offered John a chair at the dining table. 'How did you find me. Did Pereira send you?'

'Pour us both a whisky, and I will tell you why I am here. I am sure you're curious, I would be...' He trailed off. 'But first, Maggie, put down the gun you have pointed at my head. You haven't crept down those stairs as quietly as you might think,' he added.

Entering the room fully, Maggie still held the gun in her hand.

'Leave now John, or I will blow your head off. My kids are upstairs and I won't have them seeing their father killed in his own home.'

'It's good to see you too. And how well you look. Playing the publican obviously suits you. Now this is man talk, so go and get us both a drink and join your kids upstairs.' John looked at Alex sternly, waiting for him to tell Maggie to leave.

'It's okay Maggie, love. Do as he says and go upstairs with the kids. If he was going to kill me, he would have done it by now.'

Nervously, Maggie walked forward and put the handgun in the centre of the table between them. 'One of you is the quickest draw. I'll let you decide which.' With that, she walked into the bar, brought two glasses and put the whisky bottle on the table between them. She looked at Alex, concern and fear written all over her face. John was a killer with no conscience. He and Alex had worked together on many occasions and had been close. And now it seemed they had sent his friend to murder her husband. How ironic.

Alex waved his hand in the air, dismissing her. 'Go Maggie.' And as a measure of good faith, he held up the gun. 'And take this with you. Let's not leave temptation on the table, eh?'

Once she had left, John took a sip of his whisky. 'I have taken over from Pereira now, or rather, I am in the process of doing so.' Although Portuguese, John had perfected his English accent and spoke almost like royalty. He was suave and sophisticated, even charming, and had been like a celebrity in their circle of friends.

'Pereira is in no position to look for you any more. He was transferred and put into solitary confinement weeks ago. He is allowed no visitors. Possibly because he is being beaten up at every opportunity and no one wants to show his bruises off. I've organised that, Alex. He's an old man with old ways and it's time for fresh blood. It's time for me.' He smiled. 'Did you hear that Ramos hung himself in his cell? He was sixty-five. He couldn't hold his own behind bars without his heavies protecting him. There is always some young wannabee who wants to be in charge in those places.'

Shocked, Alex shook his head in surprise. 'I haven't been told that. So that means there are only five left, plus their families.'

'Their families are scared shitless. What I want to know Alex, is why the police have never come knocking at my door? They must have wanted you to incriminate me too, along with Pereira.'

'They showed me photos of you, and they know you're not innocent John,' Alex laughed for the first time that evening, 'but they have no real proof or know of any bodies you have hidden. I said I knew of you, of course I did, but that I didn't know that much about you. My reason is not just sentiment. We were street soldiers together and had each other's backs many a time, but you were the only one that agreed Pereira was wrong about me murdering his brother. You said he deserved it after what he had done to Maggie and there should be a line drawn underneath it and a lesson to all. Pereira ignored that, but that is why your name never came up.'

John gulped back his drink and put his glass down, waiting for Alex to pour another. 'Never let sentiment come into business, that's my philosophy. All this shit: you, him, the court case, could all be done and over with if he had seen sense and drawn a line under it. He felt he looked weak if he didn't defend his stupid brother, well, he looks weak now and his brother is still dead. Now, you are going to do one last job and help me Alex, and then I am going to help you.'

Puzzled, Alex looked at him, waiting for him to carry on. 'You're already a grass with a court case looming, looking over your shoulder with every creak of the staircase. I want you to put my competition behind bars. When you're in court, I want you to spill the beans on the lot of them and put them away. What happens after that, is my business. In return Alex, I will take the heat off you as best as I can. There is a bounty on your head, but who is going to pay it? Me? Absolutely fucking not!' John burst out laughing at such a stupid notion. 'I cannot guarantee that there won't be a lone ranger out there thinking he will ingratiate himself by killing Alex Silva. No one can. But I can promise what happens to him if he does.'

'The police already know everything John. There will be convictions, so why ask me?'

'I want certainties. More fingers pointed. I want you to look them in the eye and face them when you point them out, Alex. I want them all out of the way and then the coast is clear for me to take over. No competition. They will all come to me begging for a job and that is when I take the heat off you. No one will have my order to kill you or your family. It will be over. Like I say, there are no guarantees – you know that. But, rest assured, the threat won't be coming from me. I want things tidy. No hiccups. You're already behind bars.' John laughed at his own joke when he realised he was in a pub with a bar. 'No seriously Alex. This is not who you are. You lived the good life, wore suits like mine, had fast cars and expensive holidays. Now, you're stuck in the middle of Kent running a pub without your own name above the door? To me, that's hell. I couldn't do it.'

'Some days John, neither can I.' Alex shrugged and laughed. 'I have memories, good ones. But when your own turn on you and put a bounty on your head, what's left? Our life is short and sweet, and all I want to do is live it to the full with my family, knowing they are safe.'

'Do you take my proposition then?' John looked at Alex over the top of his glass. He could see this wasn't the life he wanted to live, but was settling for it, for the sake of his family. Humdrum suburbia, with no excitement. The very thought of it made his blood run cold.

'I know you're a man of your word John, you always have been. So yes, I take your proposition. But as you say, there are no guarantees on either side. We don't know what sentences they will get, and

I don't know if some loose cannon will come looking for me. After all, what happens when it all comes out and we have to leave here? Fuck knows, John. I am winging it by the seat of my pants every day I'm alive.'

John's voice turned softer, almost a whisper. 'Do you need cash? I can help you, for old times' sake. We're friends still, well, I'd like to think so, and if you ever need a job when all this shit is over, there is one waiting for you. I need people I can trust around me. You could work on your own and not bump into any of the old gang.'

Although Alex was tempted, he shook his head. 'Let's see what happens first, eh? Talking of gangs, do you know there are a bunch of Liverpudlians in the area selling goods and waving guns around?'

John's eyes narrowed and he frowned. 'I know of some Liverpudlians who are small-time scumbags. But I didn't know they had come this far to sell their goods. I will get Jimmy Bananas to look into it for me.'

'Jimmy Bananas!' Alex laughed and recalled the man permanently chewing on bananas. His gum disease made his whole body smell; it was disgusting.

'It's the only thing he can chew Alex.' John burst out laughing. 'He has no teeth, his mouth is so rotten. It was bad enough when they were black and he grew that moustache to hide them with. He will look into this, and I guarantee they won't be stealing my custom for long.'

John reached out his hand to shake Alex's. 'It's good to see you amigo.' Looking around the room, John smiled. 'And it's not so bad here; much better than those military barracks you were in before...' Seeing Alex's jaw drop, he grinned. 'Yes, Alex, I've known where you have been hiding for a long time. Now, it's time I left. There is a black taxi rank in the high street; I will get one of those. I could do with the walk.'

Alex showed him to the door and for one moment they looked at each other. Then John opened his arms and Alex wrapped his own around him, slapping his back.

'I'll be in touch,' he said and then left.

Watching him walk away under the streetlight, Alex felt a weight had been lifted off his shoulders. True enough, there were no guarantees in life, but at least he now had some hope that they would all be okay.

After a lot of deliberation, Deana felt it was time to put her own plan into action. Her mum and dad were busy downstairs, and she felt now was the time to speak to her brother. Knocking on Dante's bedroom door, she whispered, 'Dante, I want a word with you.'

'What is it? I'm doing my homework, Deana.'

'Just open the bloody door,' she snapped impatiently. 'I need to talk to you. It's important.'

Hearing noises from inside Dante's bedroom, Deana waited impatiently. 'Christ, what are you doing in there, moving the furniture?' Slowly, the door opened, and Dante stuck his head around it. 'Go on, what is it?'

Barging her way inside she stood with her arms folded. 'Well, are you going to close the door or not?'

Standing in his red *Avengers* pyjamas and adjusting his dark horn-rimmed glasses, he looked at her pouting face and decided to do as she asked. Closing the door, he walked over to the bed and sat on it. 'Go on, Deana, say your piece.'

Now that she had got his attention, she felt better. Over the last couple of days, her own thoughts had been in turmoil, and a million things had raced through her mind. The only person she could confide in was Dante. He was the voice of reason and would see the practical and logical side of things. 'You know Dad's got this court case coming up soon? Well, they've set a date.' For a moment, they just looked at each other in silence, and Dante nodded.

'Are you scared, Deana? Because I know I am. They try and keep a lot from us, but it's not fair. It's about us too.'

Deana ruffled Dante's dark hair; he looked almost sleepy. 'I feel the same, bro. We're not kids any more. No kids I know of have lived the way we have. Forever looking over our shoulders, and afraid to say anything to anybody. They love us deeply and try to protect us, but it's just not possible, Dante. Soon, we're going to have to deal with the fallout. Dad's photo will be all over the news. Kids from my college and your school will all know we're mafia kids and what our dad used to do for a living. We're going to have to deal with all that flak, Dante. Just you and me. We have to stick together from now on.'

Listening to her, Dante lay back on his bed, putting his arms under his head for support, and let out a huge sigh. 'So, what do you want to talk about, Deana? Let's have what's on your mind.' Sitting up, Dante sat beside her and waited.

'We're gonna need money. I mean real money. God knows what the outcome of the court case will be or if we're gonna be turned out on our ear. If Dad walks free from court, do you think he's going to be stood behind the bar come opening time, pulling a pint of lager? I don't think so, that's if we have any customers to serve! I know Dad has a plan, but he hasn't said anything to me or Mum. That money that is stashed away isn't going to buy much or last long in today's financial climate. They have both done everything to keep us both safe, and now it's our turn.'

A puzzled frown crossed Dante's brows. Taking his glasses off, he wiped the lenses clean with his pyjama top before putting them back on and waited. 'Don't pause for effect, Deana. Spit it out, it's boiling up inside you. What do you intend to do?'

'I know how Dad got that money down in the cellar. More to the point, I know who from.'

'I presume you're talking about the same person who got you the antibiotics for Dad. You never did say where you got them from.'

'Luke. That's his name. He's not an old man, nor a gangster. He's young, about twenty-ish,' mused Deana. 'Anyway, his age doesn't matter. He and Dad have got some kind of cannabis scam going on. He is looking after loads of plants. And half of them belong to Dad...'

'And you're going to do what with these plants? I presume you have a plan, Deana, or you wouldn't be rambling on like this. It feels like you're way ahead of me. Why don't you start from the beginning?'

'Okay, let me just say it, and then we'll make sense of it.' Deana realised that when she said her plan out loud, it didn't sound as good as it did in her head. 'Dad's got to be squeaky clean through this court case, and God knows how long it's going to go on for. It could be months. And after, we could be thrown out of here, and then what? We'll be left on the scrap heap with the other losers. Not me, Dante. I want more from life. In fact, I want my life back.' She stuck out her chin.

Lowering his voice to a whisper, Dante nodded. 'I know what you mean, but we're not criminal masterminds. Those guys took years to form their syndicate. What have you got in mind, Deana?'

'I'm going to contact Luke. Dad has a mobile phone with his number stashed away. We're going to sell our share of those plants and more if we can. I want that fucking money for my family. I want us to buy our own home. I've learnt the hard way, and so have you. You can't do anything without money. Well, I don't intend being a bloody barmaid for the rest of my life. Are you with me, Dante?' Turning towards Dante, she could see that he was deep in thought.

'Do you think this Luke person would let you in on the act?'

'I think Luke might go along with it, but I'm not 100 per cent sure. This has just been going around and around in my head, and to be honest, I'm not even sure it's a good idea! All I know is there is money out there, and I don't intend not getting our share.'

Dante looked over his glasses at his sister seriously. He could see she was serious in her ideas, but felt she hadn't really thought it through. 'And what happens if you get caught, Deana? Prison sentence? Is that the home you want to buy, one with bars at the windows?'

'We're too young for prison,' she said dismissively. 'So, should we have a meeting? I mean you and me, have a meeting with Luke? Personally, I think we should spill our guts and tell him the truth. The whole truth. It's gonna come out anyway, and I think he would rather hear it from us than from the news.'

'Do you trust him, Deana? It seems like a lot to ask. What if he's just a greedy dealer and wants the lot for himself – have you thought about that? What if he grasses us up? Our name will be in the tabloids, and every Tom, Dick and Harry will have a story about our family to sell. Why not him? It's quick, easy money, Deana. Let me see... "I got antibiotics for Alex Silva when he'd been in a shoot-out." The tabloids would pay him a big sum of money for that story.'

'Because I think he's on the run himself. Me and Dad saved his life, and whoever wanted him dead is still looking for him. He needs a partner. Or partners.' Seeing the quizzical look on his face, Deana took a breath and decided to start from the beginning and tell Dante all about the night she and Alex had met Luke at Percy's house. During her confession, he never interrupted or said a word.

'Well, that's me all talked out, Dante. You think about it. It's an option. Not a very good one, but an option all the same. And by the way, did you know that Uncle John came to visit Dad? I don't know what was said, but it can't have been that bad, because Dad is still alive.'

Wide eyed and taken aback by this revelation, Dante's jaw almost dropped, and he shouted louder than he knew he should have. 'John! Here, in this house?' Dante exclaimed. This was a total shock to him. He couldn't believe it. 'Well, I didn't think you could top the last tale, but you just have! We could all be dead by now. By all accounts, he's one evil bastard. Why did Dad let him in?'

'Shush,' she warned, putting her finger to her lips. 'They might hear you downstairs. I told you, I don't know all the ins and outs. But he was here, believe me.'

'Christ, Deana, you're like the oracle; you know everything.' Letting her words sink in, he thought about it as they sat in silence. Deana's eyes were almost pleading with him to agree to her crazy plan. 'There are a lot of loose ends to your plan, Deana, and we could end up making things worse. Have you thought about that?'

'What could be worse than what we've already been through? For nearly two years, we have lived like ghosts. Our every move monitored. Well, not any more, Dante. We have to think for ourselves, and there is a golden opportunity just waiting for us, if we have the guts to do it. I have, but do you? I'm not doing this without you. Apart from Mum and Dad, you're all I have. The only other person in the world that I trust with my life. I know it sounds crazy, and I don't even know if we can pull it off, but what other choice do we have?' Letting out a huge sigh, she felt exhausted from her ranting and fell backwards on the bed.

'Well,' Dante began slowly, 'let's see if we have the Silva streak in us. Firstly, you need to set up a meeting with this Luke. I need to meet him, and then, and only then, Deana, will I give you my answer. Let me think. Is that a good enough answer?'

'Definitely. I knew Mr Logical and Practical wouldn't jump on board immediately. You always see the things I miss. I'll contact Luke right away and sort out a meeting. We won't mention our intentions, just a meeting to tell him the truth about Dad. Then, we will see his true colours come out.'

'And if he doesn't agree, Deana? Have you thought of that?' he asked nonchalantly.

'I haven't thought that far ahead yet. I'm winging it here, Dante; you can see that. But, desperate times call for desperate measures. And we're fucking desperate!'

Taking everything that Deana had told him on board, Dante shook his head. 'Even if it comes to nothing, you will always know that you have tried. Now, go and do what you have to do. Me, I am going to finish my homework.'

For a moment, Deana looked at him and took stock. Smiling, she put her arms around him and hugged him. 'You know, Dante, with that calm exterior and logical thinking, you're more like Dad than I am. You're even beginning to look like him, with all that dark hair. I might have his impulsive side, but you have the killer instinct.'

Hitting her playfully on the shoulder, Dante smiled. 'Oh God, Deana, don't get sentimental on me now. I think I prefer it when you're picking on me. Go on, I've got stuff to do.' Cocking his head to one side and giving her a lopsided grin, he smiled. 'And by the sounds of it, Deana, so have you. Go!'

Grinning from ear to ear, Deana got up and opened the bedroom door. She could hear everyone downstairs laughing and talking. Turning her head from side to side, she could see there was no sign of her parents. 'Tomorrow, Dante,' she whispered. 'We'll speak tomorrow.' Seeing him nod, she walked out and closed the door behind her. Standing on her own on the landing, she punched the air and grinned. 'Yes!'

* * *

Standing in the kitchen, Alex straightened his tie and looked at the two detectives beside him. 'Ready?'

'Alex, you still have the chance to do this behind a screen with a video. Any one of them could have a gun in their hand and take a pot shot at you,' Maggie cried. Tears fell down her face. She was afraid. Today everything was coming out in the open. Everyone in the neighbourhood would know who they were and she was afraid of the fallout.

'I promise you Maggie,' said one of the detectives, 'every precaution for that has been taken into consideration. Everyone is searched. But she's right Alex, you still have the opportunity to do it via video link.'

'No. I have made my bed and now it's time to face it.' He felt sick to the stomach leaving Maggie like this, but he knew he had to. 'Give us a minute eh?' Alex asked the detectives and waited until they left the room.

Taking hold of her, their lips met, and they kissed like they had never kissed before. It was loving and full of hope and longing, in case they never saw each other again.

'Take the money and run,' Alex whispered. Letting her go, he took one last look as he left and walked out.

In the courtroom, Alex was led in first and took the stand. The court was packed to the hilt. At the back he saw John; his swift glance in Alex's direction was enough acknowledgement.

The barrister stood up to start proceedings. 'Mr Silva. Do you recognise any of the men accused in court today and can you tell us their names and who they are?'

Alex saw Pereira, who looked old and withered. He'd lost a lot of weight and there were bruises covering his face. Then he looked at the other gangland bosses. 'Yes I do, sir. They are all known crime lords and gangland bosses. The heads of the families.' Each one of them glared at Alex, their eyes full of hate and loathing.

Staring directly back at them, he wouldn't let them intimidate him. John was right, he thought to himself as he looked at them. They were old men with old ways. It was time for fresh blood!

ACKNOWLEDGEMENTS

Many thanks to my patient editor and wing woman Emily Ruston for all her hard work in turning this manuscript into a book.

Many thanks to all my loyal readers and book clubs for supporting me on my author journey.

Many thanks to my publisher Boldwood for turning my ideas into books.

ABOUT THE AUTHOR

Gillian Godden is a brilliantly reviewed writer of gangland fiction as well as a full-time NHS Key Worker in Hull. She lived in London for over thirty years, where she sets her thrillers, and during this time worked in various stripper pubs and venues which have inspired her stories.

Sign up to Gillian Godden's mailing list here for news, competitions and updates on future books.

Follow Gillian on social media:

 x.com/GGodden
 instagram.com/goddengillian
facebook.com/gilliangoddenauthor

ALSO BY GILLIAN GODDEN

Gold Digger

Fools' Gold

The Lambrianus

Dangerous Games

Nasty Business

Francesca

Dirty Dealings

Bad Boy

The Diamond Series

Diamond Geezer

Rough Diamonds

Queen of Diamonds

Forever Diamond

The Silvas

The Street

PEAKY READERS

GANG LOYALTIES. DARK SECRETS. BLOODY REVENGE.

A READER COMMUNITY FOR
GANGLAND CRIME THRILLER FANS!

DISCOVER PAGE-TURNING NOVELS
FROM YOUR FAVOURITE AUTHORS
AND MEET NEW FRIENDS.

JOIN OUR BOOK CLUB FACEBOOK GROUP

BIT.LY/PEAKYREADERSFB

SIGN UP TO OUR NEWSLETTER

BIT.LY/PEAKYREADERSNEWS

Boldwood

Boldwood Books is an award-winning fiction publishing company seeking out the best stories from around the world.

Find out more at www.boldwoodbooks.com

Join our reader community for brilliant books, competitions and offers!

Follow us
@BoldwoodBooks
@TheBoldBookClub

Sign up to our weekly
deals newsletter

https://bit.ly/BoldwoodBNewsletter

Printed in Great Britain
by Amazon